The Lion's Skin

Rafael Sabatini

The Lion's Skin

The present edition is a reproduction of previous publication of this classic work. Minor typographical errors may have been corrected without note; however, for an authentic reading experience the spelling, punctuation, and capitalization have been retained from the original text.

ISBN: 978-1-63637-516-8

CONTENTS

CHAPTER I

THE FANATIC

Mr. Caryll, lately from Rome, stood by the window, looking out over the rainswept, steaming quays to Notre Dame on the island yonder. Overhead rolled and crackled the artillery of an April thunderstorm, and Mr. Caryll, looking out upon Paris in her shroud of rain, under her pall of thundercloud, felt himself at harmony with Nature. Over his heart, too, the gloom of storm was lowering, just as in his heart it was still little more than April time.

Behind him, in that chamber furnished in dark oak and leather of a reign or two ago, sat Sir Richard Everard at a vast writing-table all a-litter with books and papers; and Sir Richard watched his adoptive son with fierce, melancholy eyes, watched him until he grew impatient of this pause.

"Well?" demanded the old baronet harshly. "Will you undertake it, Justin, now that the chance has come?" And he added: "You'll never hesitate if you are the man I have sought to make you."

Mr. Caryll turned slowly. "It is because I am the man that you—that God and you—have made me that I do hesitate."

His voice was quiet and pleasantly modulated, and he spoke English with the faintest slur—perceptible, perhaps, only to the keenest ear—of a French accent. To ears less keen it would merely seem that he articulated with a precision so singular as to verge on pedantry.

The light falling full upon his profile revealed the rather singular countenance that was his own. It was not in any remarkable beauty that its distinction lay, for by the canons of beauty that prevail it was not beautiful. The features were irregular and inclined to harshness, the nose was too abruptly arched, the chin too long and square, the complexion too pallid. Yet a certain dignity haunted that youthful face, of such a quality as to stamp it upon the memory of the merest passer-by. The mouth was difficult to read and full of contradictions; the lips were full and red, and you would declare them the lips of a sensualist but for the line of stern, almost grim, determination in which they met; and yet, somewhere behind that grimness, there appeared to lurk a haunting whimsicality; a smile seemed ever to impend, but whether sweet or bitter none could have told until it broke. The eyes were as remarkable; wide-set and slow-moving, as becomes the eyes of an observant man, they were of an almost greenish color, and so level

1

in their ordinary glance as to seem imbued with an uncanny penetration. His hair—he dared to wear his own, and clubbed it in a broad ribbon of watered silk—was almost of the hue of bronze, with here and there a glint of gold, and as luxuriant as any wig.

For the rest, he was scarcely above the middle height, of an almost frail but very graceful slenderness, and very graceful, too, in all his movements. In dress he was supremely elegant, with the elegance of France, that in England would be accounted foppishness. He wore a suit of dark blue cloth, with white satin linings that were revealed when he moved; it was heavily laced with gold, and a ramiform pattern broidered in gold thread ran up the sides of his silk stockings of a paler blue. Jewels gleamed in the Brussels at his throat, and there were diamond buckles on his lacquered, red-heeled shoes.

Sir Richard considered him with anxiety and some chagrin. "Justin!" he cried, a world of reproach in his voice. "What can you need to ponder?"

"Whatever it may be," said Mr. Caryll, "it will be better that I ponder it now than after I have pledged myself."

"But what is it? What?" demanded the baronet.

"I am marvelling, for one thing, that you should have waited thirty years."

Sir Richard's fingers stirred the papers before him in an idle, absent manner. Into his brooding eyes there leapt the glitter to be seen in the eyes of the fevered of body or of mind.

"Vengeance," said he slowly, "is a dish best relished when 'tis eaten cold." He paused an instant; then continued: "I might have crossed to England at the time, and slain him. Should that have satisfied me? What is death but peace and rest?"

"There is a hell, we are told," Mr. Caryll reminded him.

"Ay," was the answer, "we are told. But I dursn't risk its being false where Ostermore is concerned. So I preferred to wait until I could brew him such a cup of bitterness as no man ever drank ere he was glad to die." In a quieter, retrospective voice he continued: "Had we prevailed in the '15, I might have found a way to punish him that had been worthy of the crime that calls for it. We did not prevail. Moreover, I was taken, and transported.

"What think you, Justin, gave me courage to endure the rigors of the plantations, cunning and energy to escape after five such years of it as had assuredly killed a stronger man less strong of purpose? What but the task that was awaiting me? It imported that I should live and be free to call a reckoning in full with my Lord Ostermore before I go to my own account.

"Opportunity has gone lame upon this journey. But it has

arrived at last. Unless—" He paused, his voice sank from the high note of exaltation to which it had soared; it became charged with dread, as did the fierce eyes with which he raked his companion's face. "Unless you prove false to the duty that awaits you. And that I'll not believe! You are your mother's son, Justin."

"And my father's, too," answered Justin in a thick voice; "and the Earl of Ostermore is that same father."

"The more sweetly shall your mother be avenged," cried the other, and again his eyes blazed with that unhealthy, fanatical light. "What fitter than the hand of that poor lady's son to pull your father down in ruins?" He laughed short and fiercely. "It seldom chances in this world that justice is done so nicely."

"You hate him very deeply," said Mr. Caryll pensively, and the look in his eyes betrayed the trend of his thoughts; they were of pity—but of pity at the futility of such strong emotions.

"As deeply as I loved your mother, Justin." The sharp, rugged features of that seared old face seemed of a sudden transfigured and softened. The wild eyes lost some of their glitter in a look of wistfulness, as he pondered a moment the one sweet memory in a wasted life, a life wrecked over thirty years ago—wrecked wantonly by that same Ostermore of whom they spoke, who had been his friend.

A groan broke from his lips. He took his head in his hands, and, elbows on the table, he sat very still a moment, reviewing as in a flash the events of thirty and more years ago, when he and Viscount Rotherby—as Ostermore was then—had been young men at the St. Germain's Court of James II.

It was on an excursion into Normandy that they had met Mademoiselle de Maligny, the daughter of an impoverished gentleman of the chetive noblesse of that province. Both had loved her. She had preferred—as women will—the outward handsomeness of Viscount Rotherby to the sounder heart and brain that were Dick Everard's. As bold and dominant as any ruffler of them all where men and perils were concerned, young Everard was timid, bashful and without assertiveness with women. He had withdrawn from the contest ere it was well lost, leaving an easy victory to his friend.

And how had that friend used it? Most foully, as you shall learn.

Leaving Rotherby in Normandy, Everard had returned to Paris. The affairs of his king gave him cause to cross at once to Ireland. For three years he abode there, working secretly in his master's interest, to little purpose be it confessed. At the end of that time he returned to Paris. Rotherby was gone. It appeared that his father, Lord Ostermore, had prevailed upon Bentinck to use his

3

influence with William on the errant youth's behalf. Rotherby had been pardoned his loyalty to the fallen dynasty. A deserter in every sense, he had abandoned the fortunes of King James—which in Everard's eyes was bad enough—and he had abandoned the sweet lady he had fetched out of Normandy six months before his going, of whom it seemed that in his lordly way he was grown tired.

From the beginning it would appear they were ill-matched. It was her beauty had made appeal to him, even as his beauty had enamoured her. Elementals had brought about their union; and when these elementals shrank with habit, as elementals will, they found themselves without a tie of sympathy or common interest to link them each to the other. She was by nature blythe; a thing of sunshine, flowers and music, who craved a very poet for her lover; and by "a poet" I mean not your mere rhymer. He was downright stolid and stupid under his fine exterior; the worst type of Briton, without the saving grace of a Briton's honor. And so she had wearied him, who saw in her no more than a sweet loveliness that had cloyed him presently. And when the chance was offered him by Bentinck and his father, he took it and went his ways, and this sweet flower that he had plucked from its Normandy garden to adorn him for a brief summer's day was left to wilt, discarded.

The tale that greeted Everard on his return from Ireland was that, broken-hearted, she had died—crushed neath her load of shame. For it was said that there had been no marriage.

The rumor of her death had gone abroad, and it had been carried to England and my Lord Rotherby by a cousin of hers—the last living Maligny—who crossed the channel to demand of that stolid gentleman satisfaction for the dishonor put upon his house. All the satisfaction the poor fellow got was a foot or so of steel through the lungs, of which he died; and there, may it have seemed to Rotherby, the matter ended.

But Everard remained—Everard, who had loved her with a great and almost sacred love; Everard, who swore black ruin for my Lord Rotherby—the rumor of which may also have been carried to his lordship and stimulated his activities in having Everard hunted down after the Braemar fiasco of 1715.

But before that came to pass Everard had discovered that the rumor of her death was false—put about, no doubt, out of fear of that same cousin who had made himself champion and avenger of her honor. Everard sought her out, and found her perishing of want in an attic in the Cour des Miracles some four months later—eight months after Rotherby's desertion.

In that sordid, wind-swept chamber of Paris' most abandoned haunt, a son had been born to Antoinette de Maligny two days

4

before Everard had come upon her. Both were dying; both had assuredly died within the week but that he came so timely to her aid. And that aid he rendered like the noble-hearted gentleman he was. He had contrived to save his fortune from the wreck of James' kingship, and this was safely invested in France, in Holland and elsewhere abroad. With a portion of it he repurchased the chateau and estates of Maligny, which on the death of Antoinette's father had been seized upon by creditors.

Thither he sent her and her child—Rotherby's child—making that noble domain a christening-gift to the boy, for whom he had stood sponsor at the font. And he did his work of love in the background. He was the god in the machine; no more. No single opportunity of thanking him did he afford her. He effaced himself that she might not see the sorrow she occasioned him, lest it should increase her own.

For two years she dwelt at Maligny in such peace as the broken-hearted may know, the little of life that was left her irradiated by Everard's noble friendship. He wrote to her from time to time, now from Italy, now from Holland. But he never came to visit her. A delicacy, which may or may not have been false, restrained him. And she, respecting what instinctively she knew to be his feelings, never bade him come to her. In their letters they never spoke of Rotherby; not once did his name pass between them; it was as if he had never lived or never crossed their lives. Meanwhile she weakened and faded day by day, despite all the care with which she was surrounded. That winter of cold and want in the Cour des Miracles had sown its seeds, and Death was sharpening his scythe against the harvest.

When the end was come she sent urgently for Everard. He came at once in answer to her summons; but he came too late. She died the evening before he arrived. But she had left a letter, written days before, against the chance of his not reaching her before the end. That letter, in her fine French hand, was before him now.

"I will not try to thank you, dearest friend," she wrote. "For the thing that you have done, what payment is there in poor thanks? Oh, Everard, Everard! Had it but pleased God to have helped me to a wiser choice when it was mine to choose!" she cried to him from that letter, and poor Everard deemed that the thin ray of joy her words sent through his anguished soul was payment more than enough for the little that he had done. "God's will be done!" she continued. "It is His will. He knows why it is best so, though we discern it not. But there is the boy; there is Justin. I bequeath him to you who already have done so much for him. Love him a little for my sake; cherish and rear him as your own, and make of him such a

5

gentleman as are you. His father does not so much as know of his existence. That, too, is best so, for I would not have him claim my boy. Never let him learn that Justin exists, unless it be to punish him by the knowledge for his cruel desertion of me."

Choking, the writing blurred by tears that he accounted no disgrace to his young manhood, Everard had sworn in that hour that Justin should be as a son to him. He would do her will, and he set upon it a more definite meaning than she intended. Rotherby should remain in ignorance of his son's existence until such season as should make the knowledge a very anguish to him. He would rear Justin in bitter hatred of the foul villain who had been his father; and with the boy's help, when the time should be ripe, he would lay my Lord Rotherby in ruins. Thus should my lord's sin come to find him out.

This Everard had sworn, and this he had done. He had told Justin the story almost as soon as Justin was of an age to understand it. He had repeated it at very frequent intervals, and as the lad grew, Everard watched in him—fostering it by every means in his power—the growth of his execration for the author of his days, and of his reverence for the sweet, departed saint that had been his mother.

For the rest, he had lavished Justin nobly for his mother's sake. The repurchased estates of Maligny, with their handsome rent roll, remained Justin's own, administered by Sir Richard during the lad's minority and vastly enriched by the care of that administration. He had sent the lad to Oxford, and afterwards—the more thoroughly to complete his education—on a two years' tour of Europe; and on his return, a grown and cultured man, he had attached him to the court in Rome of the Pretender, whose agent he was himself in Paris.

He had done his duty by the boy as he understood his duty, always with that grim purpose of revenge for his horizon. And the result had been a stranger compound than even Everard knew, for all that he knew the lad exceedingly well. For he had scarcely reckoned sufficiently upon Justin's mixed nationality and the circumstance that in soul and mind he was entirely his mother's child, with nothing—or an imperceptible little—of his father. As his mother's nature had been, so was Justin's—joyous. But Everard's training of him had suppressed all inborn vivacity. The mirth and diablerie that were his birthright had been overlaid with British phlegm, until in their stead, and through the blend, a certain sardonic humor had developed, an ironical attitude toward all things whether sacred or profane. This had been helped on by culture, and—in a still greater measure—by the odd training in

6

worldliness which he had from Everard. His illusions were shattered ere he had cut his wisdom teeth, thanks to the tutelage of Sir Richard, who in giving him the ugly story of his own existence, taught him the misanthropical lesson that all men are knaves, all women fools. He developed, as a consequence, that sardonic outlook upon the world. He sought to take vos non vobis for his motto, affected to a spectator in the theatre of Life, with the obvious result that he became the greatest actor of them all.

So we find him even now, his main emotion pity for Sir Richard, who sat silent for some moments, reviewing that thirty-year dead past, until the tears scalded his old eyes. The baronet made a queer noise in his throat, something between a snarl and a sob, and he flung himself suddenly back in his chair.

Justin sat down, a becoming gravity in his countenance. "Tell me all," he begged his adoptive father. "Tell me how matters stand precisely—how you propose to act."

"With all my heart," the baronet assented. "Lord Ostermore, having turned his coat once for profit, is ready now to turn it again for the same end. From the information that reaches me from England, it would appear that in the rage of speculation that has been toward in London, his lordship has suffered heavily. How heavily I am not prepared to say. But heavily enough, I dare swear, to have caused this offer to return to his king; for he looks, no doubt, to sell his services at a price that will help him mend the wreckage of his fortunes. A week ago a gentleman who goes between his majesty's court at Rome and his friends here in Paris brought me word from his majesty that Ostermore had signified to him his willingness to rejoin the Stuart cause.

"Together with that information, this messenger brought me letters from his majesty to several of his friends, which I was to send to England by a safe hand at the first opportunity. Now, amongst these letters—delivered to me unsealed—is one to my Lord Ostermore, making him certain advantageous proposals which he is sure to accept if his circumstances be as crippled as I am given to understand. Atterbury and his friends, it seems, have already tampered with my lord's loyalty to Dutch George to some purpose, and there is little doubt but that this letter"—and he tapped a document before him—"will do what else is to be done.

"But, since these letters were left with me, come you with his majesty's fresh injunctions that I am to suppress them and cross to England at once myself, to prevail upon Atterbury and his associates to abandon the undertaking."

Mr. Caryll nodded. "Because, as I have told you," said he, "King James in Rome has received positive information that in

London the plot is already suspected, little though Atterbury may dream it. But what has this to do with my Lord Ostermore?"

"This," said Everard slowly, leaning across toward Justin, and laying a hand upon his sleeve. "I am to counsel the Bishop to stay his hand against a more favorable opportunity. There is no reason why you should not do the very opposite with Ostermore."

Mr. Caryll knit his brows, his eyes intent upon the other's face; but he said no word.

"It is," urged Everard, "an opportunity such as there may never be another. We destroy Ostermore. By a turn of the hand we bring him to the gallows." He chuckled over the word with a joy almost diabolical.

"But how—how do we destroy him?" quoth Justin, who suspected yet dared not encourage his suspicions.

"How? Do you ask how? Is't not plain?" snapped Sir Richard, and what he avoided putting into words, his eloquent glance made clear to his companion.

Mr. Caryll rose a thought quickly, a faint flush stirring in his cheeks, and he threw off Everard's grasp with a gesture that was almost of repugnance. "You mean that I am to enmesh him...."

Sir Richard smiled grimly. "As his majesty's accredited agent," he explained. "I will equip you with papers. Word shall go ahead of you to Ostermore by a safe hand to bid him look for the coming of a messenger bearing his own family name. No more than that; nothing that can betray us; yet enough to whet his lordship's appetite. You shall be the ambassador to bear him the tempting offers from the king. You will obtain his answers—accepting. Those you will deliver to me, and I shall do the trifle that may still be needed to set the rope about his neck."

A little while there was silence. Outside, the rain, driven by gusts, smote the window as with a scourge. The thunder was grumbling in the distance now. Mr. Caryll resumed his chair. He sat very thoughtful, but with no emotion showing in his face. British stolidity was in the ascendant with him then. He felt that he had the need of it.

"It is... ugly," he said at last slowly.

"It is God's own will," was the hot answer, and Sir Richard smote the table.

"Has God taken you into His confidence?" wondered Mr. Caryll.

"I know that God is justice."

"Yet is it not written that 'vengeance is His own'?"

"Aye, but He needs human instruments to execute it. Such instruments are we. Can you—Oh, can you hesitate?"

8

Mr. Caryll clenched his hands hard. "Do it," he answered through set teeth. "Do it! I shall approve it when 'tis done. But find other hands for the work, Sir Richard. He is my father."

Sir Richard remained cool. "That is the argument I employ for insisting upon the task being yours," he replied. Then, in a blaze of passion, he—who had schooled his adoptive son so ably in self-control—marshalled once more his arguments. "It is your duty to your mother to forget that he is your father. Think of him only as the man who wronged your mother; the man to whom her ruined life, her early death are due—her murderer and worse. Consider that. Your father, you say!" He mocked almost. "Your father! In what is he your father? You have never seen him; he does not know that you exist, that you ever existed. Is that to be a father? Father, you say! A word, a name—no more than that; a name that gives rise to a sentiment, and a sentiment is to stand between you and your clear duty; a sentiment is to set a protecting shield over the man who killed your mother!

"I think I shall despise you, Justin, if you fail me in this. I have lived for it," he ran on tempestuously. "I have reared you for it, and you shall not fail me!"

Then his voice dropped again, and in quieter tones

"You hate the very name of John Caryll, Earl of Ostermore," said he, "as must every decent man who knows the truth of what the life of that satyr holds. If I have suffered you to bear his name, it is to the end that it should remind you daily that you have no right to it, that you have no right to any name."

When he said that he thrust his finger consciously into a raw wound. He saw Justin wince, and with pitiless cunning he continued to prod that tender place until he had aggravated the smart of it into a very agony.

"That is what you owe your father; that is the full extent of what lies between you—that you are of those at whom the world is given to sneer and point scorn's ready finger."

"None has ever dared," said Mr. Caryll.

"Because none has ever known. We have kept the secret well. You display no coat of arms that no bar sinister may be displayed. But the time may come when the secret must out. You might, for instance, think of marrying a lady of quality, a lady of your own supposed station. What shall you tell her of yourself? That you have no name to offer her; that the name you bear is yours by assumption only? Ah! That brings home your own wrongs to you, Justin! Consider them; have them ever present in your mind, together with your mother's blighted life, that you may not shrink when the hour strikes to punish the evildoer."

9

He flung himself back in his chair again, and watched the younger man with brooding eye. Mr. Caryll was plainly moved. He had paled a little, and he sat now with brows contracted and set teeth.

Sir Richard pushed back his chair and rose, recapitulating. "He is your mother's destroyer," he said, with a sad sternness. "Is the ruin of that fair life to go unpunished? Is it, Justin?"

Mr. Caryll's Gallic spirit burst abruptly through its British glaze. He crushed fist into palm, and swore: "No, by God! It shall not, Sir Richard!"

Sir Richard held out his hands, and there was a fierce joy in his gloomy eyes at last. "You'll cross to England with me, Justin?"

But Mr. Caryll's soul fell once more into travail. "Wait!" he cried. "Ah, wait!" His level glance met Sir Richard's in earnestness and entreaty. "Answer me the truth upon your soul and conscience: Do you in your heart believe that it is what my mother would have had me do?"

There was an instant's pause. Then Everard, the fanatic of vengeance, the man whose mind upon that one subject was become unsound with excess of brooding, answered with conviction: "As I have a soul to be saved, Justin, I do believe it. More—I know it. Here!" Trembling hands took up the old letter from the table and proffered it to Justin. "Here is her own message to you. Read it again."

And what time the young man's eyes rested upon that fine, pointed writing, Sir Richard recited aloud the words he knew by heart, the words that had been ringing in his ears since that day when he had seen her lowered to rest: "'Never let him learn that Justin exists unless it be to punish him by the knowledge for his cruel desertion of me.' It is your mother's voice speaking to you from the grave," the fanatic pursued, and so infected Justin at last with something of his fanaticism.

The green eyes flashed uncannily, the white young face grew cruelly sardonic. "You believe it?" he asked, and the eagerness that now invested his voice showed how it really was with him.

"As I have a soul to be saved," Sir Richard repeated.

"Then gladly will I set my hand to it." Fire stirred through Justin now, a fire of righteous passion. "An idea—no more than an idea—daunted me. You have shown me that. I cross to England with you, Sir Richard, and let my Lord Ostermore look to himself, for my name—I who have no right to any name—my name is judgment!"

The exaltation fell from him as suddenly as it had mounted. He dropped into a chair, thoughtful again and slightly ashamed of his sudden outburst.

10

Sir Richard Everard watched with an eye of gloomy joy the man whom he had been at such pains to school in self-control.

Overhead there was a sudden crackle of thunder, sharp and staccato as a peal of demoniac laughter.

CHAPTER II

AT THE "ADAM AND EVE"

Mr. Caryll, alighted from his traveling chaise in the yard of the "Adam and Eve," at Maidstone, on a sunny afternoon in May. Landed at Dover the night before, he had parted company with Sir Richard Everard that morning. His adoptive father had turned aside toward Rochester, to discharge his king's business with plotting Bishop Atterbury, what time Justin was to push on toward town as King James' ambassador to the Earl of Ostermore, who, advised of his coming, was expecting him.

Here at Maidstone it was Mr. Caryll's intent to dine, resuming his journey in the cool of the evening, when he hoped to get at least as far as Farnborough ere he slept.

Landlady, chamberlain, ostler and a posse of underlings hastened to give welcome to so fine a gentleman, and a private room above-stairs was placed at his disposal. Before ascending, however, Mr. Caryll sauntered into the bar for a whetting glass to give him an appetite, and further for the purpose of bespeaking in detail his dinner with the hostess. It was one of his traits that he gave the greatest attention to detail, and held that the man who left the ordering of his edibles to his servants was no better than an animal who saw no more than nourishment in food. Nor was the matter one to be settled summarily; it asked thought and time. So he sipped his Hock, listening to the landlady's proposals, and amending them where necessary with suggestions of his own, and what time he was so engaged, there ambled into the inn yard a sturdy cob bearing a sturdy little man in snuff-colored clothes that had seen some wear.

The newcomer threw his reins to the stable-boy—a person of all the importance necessary to receive so indifferent a guest. He got down nimbly from his horse, produced an enormous handkerchief of many colors, and removed his three-cornered hat that he might the better mop his brow and youthful, almost cherubic face. What time he did so, a pair of bright little blue eyes were very busy with Mr. Caryll's carriage, from which Leduc, Mr. Caryll's valet, was in the act of removing a portmantle. His mobile mouth fell into lines of satisfaction.

Still mopping himself, he entered the inn, and, guided by the drone of voices, sauntered into the bar. At sight of Mr. Caryll leaning there, his little eyes beamed an instant, as do the eyes of one who espies a friend, or—apter figure—the eyes of the hunter when they sight the quarry.

He advanced to the bar, bowing to Mr. Caryll with an air almost apologetic, and to the landlady with an air scarcely less so, as he asked for a nipperkin of ale to wash the dust of the road from his throat. The hostess called a drawer to serve him, and departed herself upon the momentous business of Mr. Caryll's dinner.

"A warm day, sir," said the chubby man.

Mr. Caryll agreed with him politely, and finished his glass, the other sipping meanwhile at his ale.

"A fine brew, sir," said he. "A prodigious fine brew! With all respect, sir, your honor should try a whet of our English ale."

Mr. Caryll, setting down his glass, looked languidly at the man. "Why do you exclude me, sir, from the nation of this beverage?" he inquired.

The chubby man's face expressed astonishment. "Ye're English, sir! Ecod! I had thought ye French!"

"It is an honor, sir, that you should have thought me anything."

The other abased himself. "'Twas an unwarrantable presumption, Codso! which I hope your honor'll pardon." Then he smiled again, his little eyes twinkling humorously. "An ye would try the ale, I dare swear your honor would forgive me. I know ale, ecod! I am a brewer myself. Green is my name, sir—Tom Green—your very obedient servant, sir." And he drank as if pledging that same service he professed.

Mr. Caryll observed him calmly and a thought indifferently. "Ye're determined to honor me," said he. "I am your debtor for your reflections upon whetting glasses; but ale, sir, is a beverage I don't affect, nor shall while there are vines in France."

"Ah!" sighed Mr. Green rapturously. "'Tis a great country, France; is it not, sir?"

"'Tis not the general opinion here at present. But I make no doubt that it deserves your praise."

"And Paris, now," persisted Mr. Green. "They tell me 'tis a great city; a marvel o' th' ages. There be those, ecod! that say London's but a kennel to't."

"Be there so?" quoth Mr. Caryll indifferently.

"Ye don't agree with them, belike?" asked Mr. Green, with eagerness.

"Pooh! Men will say anything," Mr. Caryll replied, and added pointedly: "Men will talk, ye see."

13

"Not always," was the retort in a sly tone. "I've known men to be prodigious short when they had aught to hide."

"Have ye so? Ye seem to have had a wide experience." And Mr. Caryll sauntered out, humming a French air through closed lips.

Mr. Green looked after him with hardened eyes. He turned to the drawer who stood by. "He's mighty close," said he. "Mighty close!"

"Ye're not perhaps quite the company he cares for," the drawer suggested candidly.

Mr. Green looked at him. "Very like," he snapped. "How long does he stay here?"

"Ye lost a rare chance of finding out when ye let him go without inquiring," said the drawer.

Mr. Green's face lost some of its chubbiness. "When d'ye look to marry the landlady?" was his next question.

The man stared. "Cod!" said he. "Marry the—Are ye daft?"

Mr. Green affected surprise. "I'm mistook, it seems. Ye misled me by your pertness. Get me another nipperkin."

Meanwhile Mr. Caryll had taken his way above stairs to the room set apart for him. He dined to his satisfaction, and thereafter, his shapely, silk-clad legs thrown over a second chair, his waistcoat all unbuttoned, for the day was of an almost midsummer warmth— he sat mightily at his ease, a decanter of sherry at his elbow, a pipe in one hand and a book of Mr. Gay's poems in the other. But the ease went no further than the body, as witnessed the circumstances that his pipe was cold, the decanter tolerably full, and Mr. Gay's pleasant rhymes and quaint conceits of fancy all unheeded. The light, mercurial spirit which he had from nature and his unfortunate mother, and which he had retained in spite of the stern training he had received at his adoptive father's hands, was heavy-fettered now.

The mild fatigue of his journey through the heat of the day had led him to look forward to a voluptuous hour of indolence following upon dinner, with pipe and book and glass. The hour was come, the elements were there, but since he could not abandon himself to their dominion the voluptuousness was wanting. The task before him haunted him with anticipatory remorse. It hung upon his spirit like a sick man's dream. It obtruded itself upon his constant thought, and the more he pondered it the more did he sicken at what lay before him.

Wrought upon by Everard's fanaticism that day in Paris some three weeks ago, infected for the time being by something of his adoptive father's fever, he had set his hands to the task in a glow of passionate exaltation. But with the hour, the exaltation went, and reaction started in his soul. And yet draw back he dared not; too

14

long and sedulously had Everard trained his spirit to look upon the avenging of his mother as a duty. Believing that it was his duty, he thirsted on the one hand to fulfill it, whilst, on the other, he recoiled in horror at the thought that the man upon whom he was to wreak that vengeance was his father—albeit a father whom he did not know, who had never seen him, who was not so much as aware of his existence.

He sought forgetfulness in Mr. Gay. He had the delicate-minded man's inherent taste for verse, a quick ear for the melody of words, the aesthete's love of beauty in phrase as of beauty in all else; and culture had quickened his perceptions, developed his capacity for appreciation. For the tenth time he called Leduc to light his pipe; and, that done, he set his eye to the page once more. But it was like harnessing a bullock to a cart; unmindful of the way it went and over what it travelled, his eye ambled heavily along the lines, and when he came to turn the page he realized with a start that he had no impression of what he had read upon it.

In sheer disgust he tossed the book aside, and kicking away the second chair, rose lythely. He crossed to the window, and stood there gazing out at nothing, nor conscious of the incense that came to him from garden, from orchard, and from meadow.

It needed a clatter of hoofs and a cloud of dust approaching from the north to draw his mind from its obsessing thoughts. He watched the yellow body of the coach as it came furiously onward, its four horses stretched to the gallop, postillion lusty of lungs and whip, and the great trail of dust left behind it spreading to right and left over the flowering hedge-rows to lose itself above the gold-flecked meadowland. On it came, to draw up there, at the very entrance to Maidstone, at the sign of the "Adam and Eve."

Mr. Caryll, leaning on the sill of his window, looked down with interest to see what manner of travellers were these that went at so red-hot a pace. From the rumble a lackey swung himself to the rough cobbles of the yard. From within the inn came again landlady and chamberlain, and from the stable ostler and boy, obsequious all and of no interest to Mr. Caryll.

Then the door of the coach was opened, the steps were let down, and there emerged—his hand upon the shoulder of the servant—a very ferret of a man in black, with a parson's bands and neckcloth, a coal-black full-bottomed wig, and under this a white face, rather drawn and haggard, and thin lips perpetually agrin to flaunt two rows of yellow teeth disproportionately large. After him, and the more remarkable by contrast, came a tall, black-faced fellow, very brave in buff-colored cloth, with a fortune in lace at wrist and throat, and a heavily powdered tie-wig.

15

Lackey, chamberlain and parson attended his alighting, and then he joined their ranks to attend in his turn—hat under arm—the last of these odd travellers.

The interest grew. Mr. Caryll felt that the climax was about to be presented, and he leaned farther forward that he might obtain a better view of the awaited personage. In the silence he caught a rustle of silk. A flowered petticoat appeared—as much of it as may be seen from the knee downwards—and from beneath this the daintiest foot conceivable was seen to grope an instant for the step. Another second and the rest of her emerged.

Mr. Caryll observed—and be it known that he had the very shrewdest eye for a woman, as became one of the race from which on his mother's side he sprang—that she was middling tall, chastely slender, having, as he judged from her high waist, a fine, clean length of limb. All this he observed and approved, and prayed for a glimpse of the face which her silken hood obscured and screened from his desiring gaze. She raised it at that moment—raised it in a timid, frightened fashion, as one who looks fearfully about to see that she is not remarked—and Mr. Caryll had a glimpse of an oval face, pale with a warm pallor—like the pallor of the peach, he thought, and touched, like the peach, with a faint hint of pink in either cheek. A pair of eyes, large, brown, and gentle as a saint's, met his, and Mr. Caryll realized that she was beautiful and that it might be good to look into those eyes at closer quarters.

Seeing him, a faint exclamation escaped her, and she turned away in sudden haste to enter the inn. The fine gentleman looked up and scowled; the parson looked up and trembled; the ostler and his boy looked up and grinned. Then all swept forward and were screened by the porch from the wondering eyes of Mr. Caryll.

He turned from the window with a sigh, and stepped back to the table for the tinder-box, that for the eleventh time he might relight his pipe. He sat down, blew a cloud of smoke to the ceiling, and considered. His nature triumphed now over his recent preoccupation; the matter of the moment, which concerned him not at all, engrossed him beyond any other matter of his life. He was intrigued to know in what relation one to the other stood the three so oddly assorted travellers he had seen arrive. He bethought him that, after all, the odd assortment arose from the presence of the parson; and he wondered what the plague should any Christian—and seemingly a gentleman at that—be doing travelling with a parson. Then there was the wild speed at which they had come.

The matter absorbed and vexed him. I fear he was inquisitive by nature. There came a moment when he went so far as to consider making his way below to pursue his investigations in situ. It would have been at great cost to his dignity, and this he was destined to be spared.

A knock fell upon his door, and the landlady came in. She was genial, buxom and apple-faced, as becomes a landlady.

"There is a gentleman below—" she was beginning, when Mr. Caryll interrupted her.

"I would rather that you told me of the lady," said

"La, sir!" she cried, displaying ivory teeth, her eyes cast upwards, hands upraised in gentle, mirthful protest. "La, sir! But I come from the lady, too."

He looked at her. "A good ambassador," said he, "should begin with the best news; not add it as an afterthought. But proceed, I beg. You give me hope, mistress."

"They send their compliments, and would be prodigiously obliged if you was to give yourself the trouble of stepping below."

"Of stepping below?" he inquired, head on one side, solemn eyes upon the hostess. "Would it be impertinent to inquire what they may want with me?"

"I think they want you for a witness, sir."

"For a witness? Am I to testify to the lady's perfection of face and shape, to the heaven that sits in her eyes, to the miracle she calls her ankle? Are these and other things besides of the same kind what I am required to witness? If so, they could not have sent for one more qualified. I am an expert, ma'am."

"Oh, sir, nay!" she laughed. "'Tis a marriage they need you for."

Mr. Caryll opened his queer eyes a little wider. "Soho!" said he. "The parson is explained." Then he fell thoughtful, his tone lost its note of flippancy. "This gentleman who sends his compliments, does he send his name?"

"He does not, sir; but I overheard it."

"Confide in me," Mr. Caryll invited her.

"He is a great gentleman," she prepared him.

"No matter. I love great gentlemen."

"They call him Lord Rotherby."

At that sudden and utterly unexpected mention of his half-brother's name—his unknown half-brother—Mr. Caryll came to his feet with an alacrity which a more shrewd observer would have set down to some cause other than mere respect for a viscount. The hostess was shrewd, but not shrewd enough, and if Mr. Caryll's expression changed for an instant, it resumed its habitual half-scornful calm so swiftly that it would have needed eyes of an exceptional quickness to have read it.

"Enough!" he said. "Who could deny his lordship?"

17

"Shall I tell them you are coming?" she inquired, her hand already upon the door.

"A moment," he begged, detaining her. "'Tis a runaway marriage this, eh?"

Her full-hearted smile beamed on him again; she was a very woman, with a taste for the romantic, loving love. "What else, sir?" she laughed.

"And why, mistress," he inquired, eying her, his fingers plucking at his nether lip, "do they desire my testimony?"

"His lordship's own man will stand witness, for one; but they'll need another," she explained, her voice reflecting astonishment at his question.

"True. But why do they need me?" he pressed her. "Heard you no reason given why they should prefer me to your chamberlain, your ostler or your drawer?"

She knit her brows and shrugged impatient shoulders. Here was a deal of pother about a trifling affair. "His lordship saw you as he entered, sir, and inquired of me who you might be."

"His lordship flatters me by this interest. My looks pleased him, let us hope. And you answered him—what?"

"That your honor is a gentleman newly crossed from France."

"You are well-informed, mistress," said Mr. Caryll, a thought tartly, for if his speech was tainted with a French accent it was in so slight a degree as surely to be imperceptible to the vulgar.

"Your clothes, sir," the landlady explained, and he bethought him, then, that the greater elegance and refinement of his French apparel must indeed proclaim his origin to one who had so many occasions of seeing travelers from Gaul. That might even account for Mr. Green's attempts to talk to him of France. His mind returned to the matter of the bridal pair below.

"You told him that, eh?" said he. "And what said his lordship then?"

"He turned to the parson. 'The very man for us, Jenkins,' says he."

"And the parson—this Jenkins—what answer did he make?"

"'Excellently thought,' he says, grinning."

"Hum! And you yourself, mistress, what inference did you draw?"

"Inference, sir?"

"Aye, inference, ma'am. Did you not gather that this was not only a runaway match, but a clandestine one? My lord can depend upon the discretion of his servant, no doubt; for other witness he would prefer some passer-by, some stranger who will go his ways to-morrow, and not be like to be heard of again."

18

"Lard, sir!" cried the landlady, her eyes wide with astonishment.

Mr. Caryll smiled enigmatically. "'Tis so, I assure ye, ma'am. My Lord Rotherby is of a family singularly cautious in the unions it contracts. In entering matrimony he prefers, no doubt, to leave a back door open for quiet retreat should he repent him later."

"Your honor has his lordship's acquaintance, then?" quoth the landlady.

"It is a misfortune from which Heaven has hitherto preserved me, but which the devil, it seems, now thrusts upon me. It will, nevertheless, interest me to see him at close quarters. Come, ma'am."

As they were going out, Mr. Caryll checked suddenly. "Why, what's o'clock?" said he.

She stared, so abruptly came the question. "Past four, sir," she answered.

He uttered a short laugh. "Decidedly," said he, "his lordship must be viewed at closer quarters." And he led the way downstairs.

In the passage he waited for her to come up with him. "You had best announce me by name," he suggested. "It is Caryll."

She nodded, and, going forward, threw open a door, inviting him to enter.

"Mr. Caryll," she announced, obedient to his injunction, and as he went in she closed the door behind him.

From the group of three that had been sitting about the polished walnut table, the tall gentleman in buff and silver rose swiftly, and advanced to the newcomer; what time Mr. Caryll made a rapid observation of this brother whom he was meeting under circumstances so odd and by a chance so peculiar.

He beheld a man of twenty-five, or perhaps a little more, tall and well made, if already inclining to heaviness, with a swarthy face, full-lipped, big-nosed, black-eyed, an obstinate chin, and a deplorable brow. At sight, by instinct, he disliked his brother. He wondered vaguely was Lord Rotherby in appearance at all like their common father; but beyond that he gave little thought to the tie that bound them. Indeed, he has placed it upon record that, saving in such moments of high stress as followed in their later connection, he never could remember that they were the sons of the same parent.

"I thought," was Rotherby's greeting, a note almost of irritation in his voice, "that the woman said you were from France."

It was an odd welcome, but its oddness at the moment went unheeded. His swift scrutiny of his brother over, Mr. Caryll's glance passed on to become riveted upon the face of the lady at the table's

19

head. In addition to the beauties which from above he had descried, he now perceived that her mouth was sensitive and kindly, her whole expression one of gentle wistfulness, exceeding sweet to contemplate. What did she in this galley, he wondered; and he has confessed that just as at sight he had disliked his brother, so from that hour—from the very instant of his eyes' alighting on her there—he loved the lady whom his brother was to wed, felt a surpassing need of her, conceived that in the meeting of their eyes their very souls had met, so that it was to him as if he had known her since he had known anything. Meanwhile there was his lordship's question to be answered. He answered it mechanically, his eyes upon the lady, and she returning the gaze of those queer, greenish eyes with a sweetness that gave place to no confusion.

"I am from France, sir."

"But not French?" his lordship continued.

Mr. Caryll fetched his eyes from the lady's to meet Lord Rotherby's. "More than half French," he replied, the French taint in his accent growing slightly more pronounced. "It was but an accident that my father was an Englishman."

Rotherby laughed softly, a thought contemptuously. Foreigners were things which in his untraveled, unlettered ignorance he despised. The difference between a Frenchman and a South Sea Islander was a thing never quite appreciated by his lordship. Some subtle difference he had no doubt existed; but for him it was enough to know that both were foreigners; therefore, it logically followed, both were kin.

"Your words, sir, might be oddly interpreted. 'Pon honor, they might!" said he, and laughed softly again with singular insolence.

"If they have amused your lordship I am happy," said Mr. Caryll in such a tone that Rotherby looked to see whether he was being roasted. "You wanted me, I think. I beg that you'll not thank me for having descended. It was an honor."

It occurred to Rotherby that this was a veiled reproof for the ill manners of the omission. Again he looked sharply at this man who was scanning him with such interest, but he detected in the calm, high-bred face nothing to suggest that any mockery was intended. Belatedly he fell to doing the very thing that Mr. Caryll had begged him to leave undone: he fell to thanking him. As for Mr. Caryll himself, not even the queer position into which he had been thrust could repress his characteristics. What time his lordship thanked him, he looked about him at the other occupants of the room, and found that, besides the parson, sitting pale and wide-eyed at the table, there was present in the background his lordship's man—a quiet fellow, quietly garbed in gray, with a shrewd face and shrewd, shifty eyes. Mr. Caryll saw, and registered, for future use, the reflection that eyes that are overshrewd are seldom wont to look out of honest heads.

"You are desired," his lordship informed him, "to be witness to a marriage."

"So much the landlady had made known to me."

"It is not, I trust, a task that will occasion you any scruples."

"None. On the contrary, it is the absence of the marriage might do that." The smooth, easy tone so masked the inner meaning of the answer that his lordship scarce attended to the words.

"Then we had best get on. We are in haste."

"'Tis the characteristic rashness of folk about to enter wedlock," said Mr. Caryll, as he approached the table with his lordship, his eyes as he spoke turning full upon the bride.

My lord laughed, musically enough, but overloud for a man of brains or breeding. "Marry in haste, eh?" quoth he.

"You are penetration itself," Mr. Caryll praised him.

"'Twill take a shrewd rogue to better me," his lordship agreed.

"Yet an honest man might worst you. One never knows. But the lady's patience is being taxed."

It was as well he added that, for his lordship had turned with intent to ask him what he meant.

"Aye! Come, Jenkins. Get on with your patter. Gaskell," he called to his man, "stand forward here." Then he took his place beside the lady, who had risen, and stood pale, with eyes cast down and—as Mr. Caryll alone saw—the faintest quiver at the corners of her lips. This served to increase Mr. Caryll's already considerable cogitations.

The parson faced them, fumbling at his book, Mr. Caryll's eyes watching him with that cold, level glance of theirs. The parson looked up, met that uncanny gaze, displayed his teeth in a grin of terror, fell to trembling, and dropped the book in his confusion. Mr. Caryll, smiling sardonically, stooped to restore it him.

There followed a fresh pause. Mr. Jenkins, having lost his place, seemed at some pains to find it again—amazing, indeed, in one whose profession should have rendered him so familiar with its pages.

Mr. Caryll continued to watch him, in silence, and—as an observer might have thought, as, indeed, Gaskell did think, though he said nothing at the time—with wicked relish.

CHAPTER III

THE WITNESS

At last the page was found again by Mr. Jenkins. Having found it, he hesitated still a moment, then cleared his throat, and in the manner of one hurling himself forward upon a desperate venture, he began to read.

"Dearly beloved, we are gathered here in the sight of God," he read, and on in a nasal, whining voice, which not only was the very voice you would have expected from such a man, but in accordance, too, with sound clerical convention. The bridal pair stood before him, the groom with a slight flush on his cheeks and a bright glitter in his black eyes, which were not nice to see; the bride with bowed head and bosom heaving as in response to inward tumult.

The cleric came to the end of his exordium, paused a moment, and whether because he gathered confidence, whether because he realized the impressive character of the fresh matter upon which he entered, he proceeded now in a firmer, more sonorous voice: "I require and charge you both as ye will answer on the dreadful day of judgment."

"Ye've forgot something," Mr. Caryll interrupted blandly.

His lordship swung round with an impatient gesture and an impatient snort; the lady, too, looked up suddenly, whilst Mr. Jenkins seemed to fall into an utter panic.

"Wha—what?" he stammered. "What have I forgot?"

"To read the directions, I think."

His lordship scowled darkly upon Mr. Caryll, who heeded him not at all, but watched the lady sideways.

Mr. Jenkins turned first scarlet, then paler than he had been before, and bent his eyes to the book to read in a slightly puzzled voice the italicized words above the period he had embarked upon. "And also speaking unto the persons that shall be married, he shall say:" he read, and looked up inquiry, his faintly-colored, prominent eyes endeavoring to sustain Mr. Caryll's steady glance, but failing miserably.

"'Tis farther back," Mr. Caryll informed him in answer to that mute question; and as the fellow moistened his thumb to turn back the pages, Mr. Caryll saved him the trouble. "It says, I think, that the man should be on your right hand and the woman on your left. Ye seem to have reversed matters, Mr. Jenkins. But perhaps ye're left-handed."

"Stab me!" was Mr. Jenkins' most uncanonical comment. "I vow I am over-flustered. Your lordship is so impatient with me. This gentleman is right. But that I was so flustered. Will you not change places with his lordship, ma'am?"

They changed places, after the viscount had thanked Mr. Caryll shortly and cursed the parson with circumstance and fervor. It was well done on his lordship's part, but the lady did not seem convinced by it. Her face looked whiter, and her eyes had an alarmed, half-suspicious expression.

"We must begin again," said Mr. Jenkins. And he began again.

Mr. Caryll listened and watched, and he began to enjoy himself exceedingly. He had not reckoned upon so rich an entertainment when he had consented to come down to witness this odd ceremony. His sense of humor conquered every other consideration, and the circumstance that Lord Rotherby was his brother, if remembered at all, served but to add a spice to the situation.

Out of sheer deviltry he waited until Mr. Jenkins had labored for a second time through the opening periods. Again he allowed him to get as far as "I charge and require you both-," before again he interrupted him.

"There is something else ye've forgot," said he in that sweet, quiet voice of his.

This was too much for Rotherby. "Damn you!" he swore, turning a livid face upon Mr. Caryll, and failed to observe that at the sound of that harsh oath and at the sight of his furious face, the lady recoiled from him, the suspicion lately in her face turning first to conviction and then to absolute horror.

"I do not think you are civil," said Mr. Caryll critically. "It was in your interests that I spoke."

"Then I'll thank you, in my interests, to hold your tongue!" his lordship stormed.

"In that case," said Mr. Caryll, "I must still speak in the interests of the lady. Since you've desired me to be a witness, I'll do my duty by you both and see you properly wed."

"Now, what the devil may you mean by that?" demanded his lordship, betraying himself more and more at every word.

Mr. Jenkins, in a spasm of terror, sought to pour oil upon these waters. "My lord," he bleated, teeth and eyeballs protruding from his pallid face. "My lord! Perhaps the gentleman is right. Perhaps—Perhaps—" He gulped, and turned to Mr. Caryll. "What is't ye think we have forgot now?" he asked.

"The time of day," Mr. Caryll replied, and watched the puzzled look that came into both their faces.

23

"Do ye deal in riddles with us?" quoth his lordship. "What have we to do with the time of day?"

"Best ask the parson," suggested Mr. Caryll.

Rotherby swung round again to Jenkins. Jenkins spread his hands in mute bewilderment and distress. Mr. Caryll laughed silently.

"I'll not be married! I'll not be married!"

It was the lady who spoke, and those odd words were the first that Mr. Caryll heard from her lips. They made an excellent impression upon him, bearing witness to her good sense and judgment—although belatedly aroused—and informing him, although the pitch was strained just now; that the rich contralto of her voice was full of music. He was a judge of voices, as of much else besides.

"Hoity-toity!" quoth his lordship, between petulance and simulated amusement. "What's all the pother? Hortensia, dear—"

"I'll not be married!" she repeated firmly, her wide brown eyes meeting his in absolute defiance, head thrown back, face pale but fearless.

"I don't believe," ventured Mr. Caryll, "that you could be if you desired it. Leastways not here and now and by this." And he jerked a contemptuous thumb sideways at Mr. Jenkins, toward whom he had turned his shoulder. "Perhaps you have realized it for yourself."

A shudder ran through her; color flooded into her face and out again, leaving it paler than before; yet she maintained a brave front that moved Mr. Caryll profoundly to an even greater admiration of her.

Rotherby, his great jaw set, his hands clenched and eyes blazing, stood irresolute between her and Mr. Caryll. Jenkins, in sheer terror, now sank limply to a chair, whilst Gaskell looked on—a perfect servant—as immovable outwardly and unconcerned as if he had been a piece of furniture. Then his lordship turned again to Caryll.

"You take a deal upon yourself, sir," said he menacingly.

"A deal of what?" wondered Mr. Caryll blandly.

The question nonplussed Rotherby. He swore ferociously. "By God!" he fumed, "I'll have you make good your insinuations. You shall disabuse this lady's mind. You shall—damn you!—or I'll compel you!"

Mr. Caryll smiled very engagingly. The matter was speeding excellently—a comedy the like of which he did not remember to have played a part in since his student days at Oxford, ten years and more ago.

"I had thought," said he, "that the woman who summoned me

to be a witness of this—this—ah wedding"—there was a whole volume of criticism in his utterance of the word—"was the landlady of the 'Adam and Eve.' I begin to think that she was this lady's good angel; Fate, clothed, for once, matronly and benign." Then he dropped the easy, bantering manner with a suddenness that was startling. Gallic fire blazed up through British training. "Let us speak plainly, my Lord Rotherby. This marriage is no marriage. It is a mockery and a villainy. And that scoundrel—worthy servant of his master—is no parson; no, not so much as a hedge-parson is he. Madame," he proceeded, turning now to the frightened lady, "you have been grossly abused by these villains."

"Sir!" blazed Rotherby at last, breaking in upon his denunciation, hand clapped to sword. "Do ye dare use such words to me?"

Mr. Jenkins got to his feet, in a slow, foolish fashion. He put out a hand to stay his lordship. The lady, in the background, looked on with wide eyes, very breathless, one hand to her bosom as if to control its heave.

Mr. Caryll proceeded, undismayed, to make good his accusation. He had dropped back into his slightly listless air of thinly veiled persiflage, and he appeared to address the lady, to explain the situation to her, rather than to justify the charge he had made.

"A blind man could have perceived, from the rustling of his prayer book when he fumbled at it, that the contents were strange to him. And observe the volume," he continued, picking it up and flaunting it aloft. "Fire-new; not a thumbmark anywhere; purchased expressly for this foul venture. Is there aught else so clean and fresh about the scurvy thief?"

"You shall moderate your tones, sir—" began his lordship in a snarl.

"He sets you each on the wrong side of him," continued Mr. Caryll, all imperturbable, "lacking even the sense to read the directions which the book contains, and he has no thought for the circumstance that the time of day is uncanonical. Is more needed, madame?"

"So much was not needed," said she, "though I am your debtor, sir."

Her voice was marvelously steady, ice-cold with scorn, a royal anger increasing the glory of her eyes.

Rotherby's hand fell away from his sword. He realized that bluster was not the most convenient weapon here. He addressed Mr. Caryll very haughtily. "You are from France, sir, and something may be excused you. But not quite all. You have used expressions that are not to be offered to a person of my quality. I fear you scarcely apprehend it."

"As well, no doubt, as those who avoid you, sir," answered Mr. Caryll, with cool contempt, his dislike of the man and of the business in which he had found him engaged mounting above every other consideration.

His lordship frowned inquiry. "And who may those be?"

"Most decent folk, I should conceive, if this be an example of your ways."

"By God, sir! You are a thought too pert. We'll mend that presently. I will first convince you of your error, and you, Hortensia."

"It will be interesting," said Mr. Caryll, and meant it.

Rotherby turned from him, keeping a tight rein upon his anger; and so much restraint in so tempestuous a man was little short of wonderful. "Hortensia," he said, "this is fool's talk. What object could I seek to serve?" She drew back another step, contempt and loathing in her face. "This man," he continued, flinging a hand toward Jenkins, and checked upon the word. He swung round upon the fellow. "Have you fooled me, knave?" he bawled. "Is it true what this man says of you—that ye're no parson at all?"

Jenkins quailed and shriveled. Here was a move for which he was all unprepared, and knew not how to play to it. On the bridegroom's part it was excellently acted; yet it came too late to be convincing.

"You'll have the license in your pocket, no doubt, my lord," put in Mr. Caryll. "It will help to convince the lady of the honesty of your intentions. It will show her that ye were abused by this thief for the sake of the guinea ye were to pay him."

That was checkmate, and Lord Rotherby realized it. There remained him nothing but violence, and in violence he was exceedingly at home—being a member of the Hell Fire Club and having served in the Bold Bucks under his Grace of Wharton.

"You damned, infernal marplot! You blasted meddler!" he swore, and some other things besides, froth on his lips, the veins of his brow congested. "What affair was this of yours?"

"I thought you desired me for a witness," Mr. Caryll reminded him.

"I did, let me perish!" said Rotherby. "And I wish to the devil I had bit my tongue out first."

"The loss to eloquence had been irreparable," sighed Mr. Caryll, his eyes upon a beam of the ceiling.

Rotherby stared and choked. "Is there no sense in you, you gibbering parrot?" he inquired. "What are you—an actor or a fool?"

"A gentleman, I hope," said Mr. Caryll urbanely. "What are you?"

"I'll learn you," said his lordship, and plucked at his sword.

"I see," said Mr. Caryll in the same quiet voice that thinly veiled his inward laughter—"a bully!"

With more oaths, my lord heaved himself forward. Mr. Caryll was without weapons. He had left his sword above-stairs, not deeming that he would be needing it at a wedding. He never moved hand or foot as Rotherby bore down upon him, but his greenish eyes grew keen and very watchful. He began to wonder had he indulged his amusement overlong, and imperceptibly he adjusted his balance for a spring.

Rotherby stretched out to lunge, murder in his inflamed eyes. "I'll silence you, you—"

There was a swift rustle behind him. His hand—drawn back to thrust—was suddenly caught, and ere he realized it the sword was wrenched from fingers that held it lightly, unprepared for this.

"You dog!" said the lady's voice, strident now with anger and disdain. She had his sword.

He faced about with a horrible oath. Mr. Caryll conceived that he was becoming a thought disgusting.

Hoofs and wheels ground on the cobbles of the yard and came to a halt outside, but went unheeded in the excitement of the moment. Rotherby stood facing her, she facing him, the sword in her hand and a look in her eyes that promised she would use it upon him did he urge her.

A moment thus—of utter, breathless silence. Then, as if her passion mounted and swept all aside, she raised the sword, and using it as a whip, she lashed him with it until at the third blow it rebounded to the table and was snapped. Instinctively his lordship had put up his hands to save his face, and across one of them a red line grew and grew and oozed forth blood which spread to envelop it.

Gaskell advanced with a sharp cry of concern. But Rotherby waved him back, and the gesture shook blood from his hand like raindrops. His face was livid; his eyes were upon the woman he had gone so near betraying with a look that none might read. Jenkins swayed, sickly, against the table, whilst Mr. Caryll observed all with a critical eye and came to the conclusion that she must have loved this villain.

The hilt and stump of sword clattered in the fireplace, whither she hurled it. A moment she caught her face in her hands, and a sob shook her almost fiercely. Then she came past his lordship, across the room to Mr. Caryll, Rotherby making no shift to detain her.

"Take me away, sir! Take me away," she begged him.

Mr. Caryll's gloomy face lightened suddenly. "Your servant, ma'am," said he, and made her a bow. "I think you are very well advised," he added cheerfully and offered her his arm. She took it, and moved a step or two toward the door. It opened at that moment, and a burly, elderly man came in heavily.

The lady halted, a cry escaped her—a cry of pain almost—and she fell to weeping there and then. Mr. Caryll was very mystified.

The newcomer paused at the sight that met him, considered it with a dull blue eye, and, for all that he looked stupid, it seemed he had wit enough to take in the situation.

"So!" said he, with heavy mockery. "I might have spared myself the trouble of coming after you. For it seems that she has found you out in time, you villain!"

Rotherby turned sharply at that voice. He fell back a step, his brow seeming to grow blacker than it had been. "Father!" he exclaimed; but there was little that was filial in the accent.

Mr. Caryll staggered and recovered himself. It had been indeed a staggering shock; for here, of course, was his own father, too.

CHAPTER IV

Mr. GREEN

There was a quick patter of feet, the rustle of a hooped petticoat, and the lady was in the arms of my Lord Ostermore.

"Forgive me, my lord!" she was crying. "Oh, forgive me! I was a little fool, and I have been punished enough already!"

To Mr. Caryll this was a surprising development. The earl, whose arms seemed to have opened readily enough to receive her, was patting her soothingly upon the shoulder. "Pish! What's this? What's this?" he grumbled; yet his voice, Mr. Caryll noticed, was if anything kindly; but it must be confessed that it was a dull, gruff voice, seldom indicating any shade of emotion, unless—as sometimes happened—it was raised in anger. He was frowning now upon his son over the girl's head, his bushy, grizzled brows contracted.

Mr. Caryll observed—and with what interest you should well imagine—that Lord Ostermore was still in a general way a handsome man. Of a good height, but slightly excessive bulk, he had a face that still retained a fair shape. Short-necked, florid and plethoric, he had the air of the man who seldom makes a long illness at the end. His eyes were very blue, and the lids were puffed and heavy, whilst the mouth, Mr. Caryll remarked in a critical, detached spirit, was stupid rather than sensuous. He made his survey swiftly, and the result left him wondering.

Meanwhile the earl was addressing his son, whose hand was being bandaged by Gaskell. There was little variety in his invective. "You villain!" he bawled at him. "You damned villain!" Then he patted the girl's head. "You found the scoundrel out before you married him," said he. "I am glad on't; glad on't!"

"'Tis such a reversing of the usual order of things that it calls for wonder," said Mr. Caryll.

"Eh?" quoth his lordship. "Who the devil are you? One of his friends?"

"Your lordship overwhelms me," said Mr. Caryll gravely, making a bow. He observed the bewilderment in Ostermore's eyes, and began to realize at that early stage of their acquaintance that to speak ironically to the Earl of Ostermore was not to speak at all.

It was Hortensia—a very tearful Hortensia now who explained. "This gentleman saved me, my lord," she said.

"Saved you?" quoth he dully. "How did he come to save you?"

"He discovered the parson," she explained.

The earl looked more and more bewildered. "Just so," said Mr. Caryll. "It was my privilege to discover that the parson is no parson."

"The parson is no parson?" echoed his lordship, scowling more and more. "Then what the devil is the parson?"

Hortensia freed herself from his protecting arms. "He is a villain," she said, "who was hired by my Lord Rotherby to come here and pretend to be a parson." Her eyes flamed, her cheeks were scarlet. "God help me for a fool, my lord, to have put my faith in that man! Oh!" she choked. "The shame—the burning shame of it! I would I had a brother to punish him!"

Lord Ostermore was crimson, too, with indignation. Mr. Caryll was relieved to see that he was capable of so much emotion. "Did I not warn you against him, Hortensia?" said he. "Could you not have trusted that I knew him—I, his father, to my everlasting shame?" Then he swung upon Rotherby. "You dog!" he began, and there—being a man of little invention—words failed him, and wrath alone remained, very intense, but entirely inarticulate.

Rotherby moved forward till he reached the table, then stood leaning upon it, scowling at the company from under his black brows. "'Tis your lordship alone is to blame for this," he informed his father, with a vain pretence at composure.

"I am to blame!" gurgled his lordship, veins swelling at his brow. "I am to blame that you should have carried her off thus? And—by God!—had you meant to marry her honestly and fittingly, I might find it in my heart to forgive you. But to practice such villainy! To attempt to put this foul trick upon the child!"

Mr. Caryll thought for an instant of another child whose child he was, and a passion of angry mockery at the forgetfulness of age welled up from the bitter soul of him. Outwardly he remained a very mirror for placidity.

"Your lordship had threatened to disinherit me if I married her," said Rotherby.

"'Twas to save her from you," Ostermore explained, entirely unnecessarily. "And you thought to—to—By God! sir, I marvel you have the courage to confront me. I marvel!"

"Take me away, my lord," Hortensia begged him, touching his arm.

"Aye, we were best away," said the earl, drawing her to him. Then he flung a hand out at Rotherby in a gesture of repudiation, of anathema. "But 'tis not the end on't for you, you knave! What I threatened, I will perform. I'll disinherit you. Not a penny of mine shall come to you. Ye shall starve for aught I care; starve, and—

30

and—the world be well rid of a villain. I—I disown you. Ye're no son of mine. I'll take oath ye're no son of mine!"

Mr. Caryll thought that, on the contrary, Rotherby was very much his father's son, and he added to his observations upon human nature the reflection that sinners are oddly blessed with short memories. He was entirely dispassionate again by now.

As for Rotherby, he received his father's anger with a scornful smile and a curling lip. "You'll disinherit me?" quoth he in mockery. "And of what, pray? If report speaks true, you'll be needing to inherit something yourself to bear you through your present straitness." He shrugged and produced his snuff-box with an offensive simulation of nonchalance. "Ye cannot cut the entail," he reminded his almost apoplectic sire, and took snuff delicately, sauntering windowwards.

"Cut the entail? The entail?" cried the earl, and laughed in a manner that seemed to bode no good. "Have you ever troubled to ascertain what it amounts to? You fool, it wouldn't keep you in—in—in snuff!"

Lord Rotherby halted in his stride, half-turned and looked at his father over his shoulder. The sneering mask was wiped from his face, which became blank. "My lord—" he began.

The earl waved a silencing hand, and turned with dignity to Hortensia.

"Come, child," said he. Then he remembered something. "Gad!" he exclaimed. "I had forgot the parson. I'll have him gaoled! I'll have him hanged if the law will help me. Come forth, man!"

Ignoring the invitation, Mr. Jenkins scuttled, ratlike, across the room, mounted the window-seat, and was gone in a flash through the open window. He dropped plump upon Mr. Green, who was crouching underneath. The pair rolled over together in the mould of a flowerbed; then Mr. Green clutched Mr. Jenkins, and Mr. Jenkins squealed like a trapped rabbit. Mr. Green thrust his fist carefully into the mockparson's mouth.

"Sh! You blubbering fool!" he snapped in his ear. "My business is not with you. Lie still!"

Within the room all stood at gaze, following the sudden flight of Mr. Jenkins. Then Lord Ostermore made as if to approach the winnow, but Hortensia restrained him.

"Let the wretch go," she said. "The blame is not his. What is he but my lord's tool?" And her eyes scorched Rotherby with such a glance of scorn as must have killed any but a shameless man. Then turning to the demurely observant gentleman who had done her such good service, "Mr. Caryll" she said, "I want to thank you. I want my lord, here, to thank you."

31

Mr. Caryll bowed to her. "I beg that you will not think of it," said he. "It is I who will remain in your debt."

"Is your name Caryll, sir?" quoth the earl. He had a trick of fastening upon the inconsequent, though that was scarcely the case now.

"That, my lord, is my name. I believe I have the honor of sharing it with your lordship."

"Ye'll belong to some younger branch of the family," the earl supposed.

"Like enough—some outlying branch," answered the imperturbable Caryll—a jest which only himself could appreciate, and that bitterly.

"And how came you into this?"

Rotherby sneered audibly—in self-mockery, no doubt, as he came to reflect that it was he, himself, had had him fetched.

"They needed another witness," said Mr. Caryll, "and hearing there was at the inn a gentleman newly crossed from France, his lordship no doubt opined that a traveller, here to-day and gone for good tomorrow, would be just the witness that he needed for the business he proposed. That circumstance aroused my suspicions, and—"

But the earl, as usual, seemed to have fastened upon the minor point, although again it was not so. "You are newly crossed from France?" said he. "Ay, and your name is the same as mine. 'Twas what I was advised."

Mr. Caryll flashed a sidelong glance at Rotherby, who had turned to stare at his father, and in his heart he cursed the stupidity of my Lord Ostermore. If this proposed to be a member of a conspiracy, Heaven help that same conspiracy!

"Were you, by any chance, going to seek me in town, Mr. Caryll?"

Mr. Caryll suppressed a desire to laugh. Here was a way to deal with State secrets. "I, my lord?" he inquired, with an assumed air of surprise.

The earl looked at him, and from him to Rotherby, bethought himself, and started so overtly that Rotherby's eyes grew narrow, the lines of his mouth tightened. "Nay, of course not; of course not," he blustered clumsily.

But Rotherby laughed aloud. "Now what a plague is all this mystery?" he inquired.

"Mystery?" quoth my lord. "What mystery should there be?"

"'Tis what I would fain be informed," he answered in a voice that showed he meant to gain the information. He sauntered forward towards Caryll, his eye playing mockingly over this gentleman from France. "Now, sir," said he, "whose messenger may you be, eh? What's all this—"

"Rotherby!" the earl interrupted in a voice intended to be compelling. "Come away, Mr. Caryll," he added quickly. "I'll not have any gentleman who has shown himself a friend to my ward, here, affronted by that rascal. Come away, sir!"

"Not so fast! Not so fast, ecod!"

It was another voice that broke in upon them. Rotherby started round. Gaskell, in the shadows of the cowled fireplace jumped in sheer alarm. All stared at the window whence the voice proceeded.

They beheld a plump, chubby-faced little man, astride the sill, a pistol displayed with ostentation in his hand.

Mr. Caryll was the only one with the presence of mind to welcome him. "Ha!" said he, smiling engagingly. "My little friend, the brewer of ale."

"Let no one leave this room," said Mr. Green with a great dignity. Then, with rather less dignity, he whistled shrilly through his fingers, and got down lightly into the room.

"Sir," blustered the earl, "this is an intrusion; an impertinence. What do you want?"

"The papers this gentleman carries," said Mr. Green, indicating Caryll with the hand that held the pistol. The earl looked alarmed, which was foolish in him, thought Mr. Caryll. Rotherby covered his mouth with his hand, after the fashion of one who masks a smile.

"Ye're rightly served for meddling," said he with relish.

"Out with them," the chubby man demanded. "Ye'll gain nothing by resistance. So don't be obstinate, now."

"I could be nothing so discourteous," said Mr. Caryll. "Would it be prying on my part to inquire what may be your interest in my papers?"

His serenity lessened the earl's anxieties, but bewildered him; and it took the edge off the malicious pleasure which Rotherby was beginning to experience.

"I am obeying the orders of my Lord Carteret, the Secretary of State," said Mr. Green. "I was to watch for a gentleman from France with letters for my Lord Ostermore. He had a messenger a week ago to tell him to look for such a visitor. He took the messenger, if you must know, and—well, we induced him to tell us what was the message he had carried. There is so much mystery in all this that my Lord Carteret desires more knowledge on the subject. I think you are the gentleman I am looking for."

33

Mr. Caryll looked him over with an amused eye, and laughed. "It distresses me," said he, "to see so much good thought wasted."

Mr. Green was abashed a moment. But he recovered quickly; no doubt he had met the cool type before. "Come, come!" said he. "No blustering. Out with your papers, my fine fellow."

The door opened, and a couple of men came in; over their shoulders, ere the door closed again, Mr. Caryll had a glimpse of the landlady's rosy face, alarm in her glance. The newcomers were dirty rogues; tipstaves, recognizable at a glance. One of them wore a ragged bob-wig—the cast-off, no doubt, of some gentleman's gentleman, fished out of the sixpenny tub in Rosemary Lane; it was ill-fitting, and wisps of the fellow's own unkempt hair hung out in places. The other wore no wig at all; his yellow thatch fell in streaks from under his shabby hat, which he had the ill-manners to retain until Lord Ostermore knocked it from his head with a blow of his cane. Both were fierily bottle-nosed, and neither appeared to have shaved for a week or so.

"Now," quoth Mr. Green, "will you hand them over of your own accord, or must I have you searched?" And a wave of the hand towards the advancing myrmidons indicated the searchers.

"You go too far, sir," blustered the earl.

"Ay, surely," put in Mr. Caryll. "You are mad to think a gentleman is to submit to being searched by any knave that comes to him with a cock-and-bull tale about the Secretary of State."

Mr. Green leered again, and produced a paper. "There," said he, "is my Lord Carteret's warrant, signed and sealed."

Mr. Caryll glanced over it with a disdainful eye. "It is in blank," said he.

"Just so," agreed Mr. Green. "Carte blanche, as you say over the water. If you insist," he offered obligingly, "I'll fill in your name before we proceed."

Mr. Caryll shrugged his shoulders. "It might be well," said he, "if you are to search me at all."

Mr. Green advanced to the table. The writing implements provided for the wedding were still there. He took up a pen, scrawled a name across the blank, dusted it with sand, and presented it again to Mr. Caryll. The latter nodded.

"I'll not trouble you to search me," said he. "I would as soon not have these noblemen of yours for my valets." He thrust his hands into the pockets of his fine coat, and brought forth several papers. These he proffered to Mr. Green, who took them between satisfaction and amazement. Ostermore stared, too stricken for words at this meek surrender; and well was it for Mr. Caryll that he was so stricken, for had he spoken he had assuredly betrayed himself.

Hortensia, Mr. Caryll observed, watched his cowardly yielding with an eye of stern contempt. Rotherby looked on with a dark face that betrayed nothing.

Meanwhile Mr. Green was running through the papers, and as fast as he ran through them he permitted himself certain comments that passed for humor with his followers. There could be no doubt that in his own social stratum Mr. Green must have been accounted something of a wag.

"Ha! What's this? A bill! A bill for snuff! My Lord Carteret'll snuff you, sir. He'll tobacco you, ecod! He'll smoke you first, and snuff you afterwards." He flung the bill aside. "Phew!" he whistled. "Verses! 'To Theocritus upon sailing for Albion.' That's mighty choice! D'ye write verses, sir?"

"Heyday! 'Tis an occupation to which I have succumbed in moments of weakness. I crave your indulgence, Mr. Green."

Mr. Green perceived that here was a weak attempt at irony, and went on with his investigations. He came to the last of the papers Mr. Caryll had handed him, glanced at it, swore coarsely, and dropped it.

"D'ye think ye can bubble me?'" he cried, red in the face.

Lord Ostermore heaved a sigh of relief; the hard look had faded from Hortensia's eyes.

"What is't ye mean, giving me this rubbish?"

"I offer you my excuses for the contents of my pockets," said Mr. Caryll. "Ye see, I did not expect to be honored by your inquisition. Had I but known—"

Mr. Green struck an attitude. "Now attend to me, sir! I am a servant of His Majesty's Government."

"His Majesty's Government cannot be sufficiently congratulated," said Mr. Caryll, the irrepressible.

Mr. Green banged the table. "Are ye rallying me, ecod!"

"You have upset the ink," Mr. Caryll pointed out to him.

"Damn the ink!" swore the spy. "And damn you for a Tom o' Bedlam! I ask you again—what d'ye mean, giving me this rubbish?"

"You asked me to turn out my pockets."

"I asked you for the letter ye have brought Lord Ostermore."

"I am sorry," said Mr. Caryll, and eyed the other sympathetically. "I am sorry to disappoint you. But, then, you assumed too much when you assumed that I had such a letter. I have obliged you to the fullest extent in my power. I do not think you show a becoming gratitude."

Mr. Green eyed him blankly a moment; then exploded. "Ecod, sir! You are cool."

"It is a condition we do not appear to share."

"D'ye say ye've brought his lordship no letter from France?" thundered the spy. "What else ha' ye come to England for?"

"To study manners, sir," said Mr. Caryll, bowing.

That was the last drop in the cup of Mr. Green's endurance. He waved his men towards the gentleman from France. "Find it," he bade them shortly.

Mr. Caryll drew himself up with a great dignity, and waved the bailiffs back, his white face set, an unpleasant glimmer in his eyes. "A moment!" he cried. "You have no authority to go to such extremes. I make no objection to being searched; but every objection to being soiled, and I'll not have the fingers of these scavengers about my person."

"And you are right, egad!" cried Lord Ostermore, advancing. "Harkee, you dirty spy, this is no way to deal with gentlemen. Be off, now, and take your carrion-crows with you, or I'll have my grooms in with their whips to you."

"To me?" roared Green. "I represent the Secretary of State."

"Ye'll represent a side of raw venison if you tarry here," the earl promised him. "D'ye dare look me in the eye? D'ye dare, ye rogue? D'ye know who I am? And don't wag that pistol, my fine fellow! Be off, now! Away with you!"

Mr. Green looked his name. The rosiness was all departed from his cheeks; he quivered with suppressed wrath. "If I go—giving way to constraint—what shall you say to my Lord Carteret?" he asked.

"What concern may that be of yours, sirrah?"

"It will be some concern of yours, my lord."

Mr. Caryll interposed. "The knave is right," said he. "It were to implicate your lordship. It were to give color to his silly suspicions. Let him make his search. But be so good as to summon my valet. He shall hand you my garments that you may do your will upon them. But unless you justify yourself by finding the letter you are seeking, you shall have to reckon with the consequences of discomposing a gentleman for nothing. Now, sir! Is it a bargain?" Mr. Green looked him over, and if he was shaken by the calm assurance of Mr. Caryll's tone and manner, he concealed it very effectively. "We'll make no bargains," said he. "I have my duty to do." He signed to one of the bailiffs. "Fetch the gentleman's servant," said he.

"So be it," said Mr. Caryll. "But you take too much upon yourself, sir. Your duty, I think, would have been to arrest me and carry me to Lord Carteret's, there to be searched if his lordship considered it necessary."

"I have no cause to arrest you until I find it," Mr. Green snapped impatiently.

"Your logic is faultless."

"I am following my Lord Carteret's orders to the letter. I am to effect no arrest until I have positive evidence."

"Yet you are detaining me. What does this amount to but an arrest?"

Mr. Green disdained to answer. Leduc entered, and Mr. Caryll turned to Lord Ostermore.

"There is no reason why I should detain your lordship," said he, "and these operations—The lady—" He waved an expressive hand, bent an expressive eye upon the earl.

Lord Ostermore seemed to waver. He was not—he had never been—a man to think for others. But Hortensia cut in before he could reply.

"We will wait," she said. "Since you are travelling to town, I am sure his lordship will be glad of your company, sir."

Mr. Caryll looked deep into those great brown eyes, and bowed his thanks. "If it will not discompose your lordship—"

"No, no," said Ostermore, gruff of voice and manner. "We will wait. I shall be honored, sir, if you will journey with us afterwards."

Mr. Caryll bowed again, and went to hold the door for them, Mr. Green's eyes keenly alert for an attempt at evasion. But there was none. When his lordship and his ward had departed, Mr. Caryll turned to Rotherby, who had taken a chair, his man Gaskell behind him. He looked from the viscount to Mr. Green.

"Do we require this gentleman?" he asked the spy.

A smile broke over Rotherby's swam face. "By your leave, sir, I'll remain to see fair play. You may find me useful, Mr. Green. I have no cause to wish this marplot well," he explained.

Mr. Caryll turned his back upon him, took off his coat and waistcoat. He sat down while Mr. Green spread the garments upon the table, emptied out the pockets, turned down the cuffs, ripped up the satin linings. He did it in a consummate fashion, very thoroughly. Yet, though he parted the linings from the cloth, he did so in such a manner as to leave the garments easily repairable.

Mr. Caryll watched him with interest and appreciation, and what time he watched he was wondering might it not be better straightway to place the spy in possession of the letter, and thus destroy himself and Lord Ostermore, at the same time—and have done with the task on which he was come to England. It seemed almost an easy way out of the affair. His betrayal of the earl would be less ugly if he, himself, were to share the consequences of that betrayal.

Then he checked his thoughts. What manner of mood was this? Besides, his inclination was all to become better acquainted with this odd family upon which he had stumbled in so extraordinary a manner. Down in his heart of hearts he had a feeling that the thing he was come to do would never be done—leastways, not by him. It was in vain that he might attempt to steel himself to the task. It repelled him. It went not with a nature such as his.

He thought of Everard, afire with the idea of vengence and to such an extent that he had succeeded in infecting Justin himself with a spark of it. He thought of him with pity almost; pity that a man should obsess his life by such a phantasm as this same vengeance must have been to him. Was it worth while? Was anything worth while, he wondered.

Lord Rotherby approached the table, and took up the garments upon which Mr. Green had finished. He turned them over and supplemented Mr. Green's search.

"Ye're welcome to all that ye can find," sneered Mr. Green, and turned to Mr. Caryll. "Let us have your shoes, sir."

Mr. Caryll removed his shoes, in silence, and Mr. Green proceeded to examine them in a manner that provoked Mr. Caryll's profound admiration. He separated the lining from the Spanish leather, and probed slowly and carefully in the space between. He examined the heels very closely, going over to the window for the purpose. That done, he dropped them.

"Your breeches now," said he laconically.

Meanwhile Leduc had taken up the coat, and with a needle and thread wherewith he had equipped himself he was industriously restoring the stitches that Mr. Green had taken out.

Mr. Caryll surrendered his breeches. His fine Holland shirt went next, his stockings and what other trifles he wore, until he stood as naked as Adam before the fall. Yet all in vain.

His garments were restored to him, one by one, and one by one, with Leduc's aid, he resumed them. Mr. Green was looking crestfallen.

"Are you satisfied?" inquired Mr. Caryll pleasantly, his good temper inexhaustible.

The spy looked at him with a moody eye, plucking thoughtfully at his lip with thumb and forefinger. Then he brightened suddenly. "There's your man," said he, flashing a quick eye upon Leduc, who looked up with a quiet smile.

"True," said Mr. Caryll, "and there's my portmantle above-stairs, and my saddle on my horse in the stables. It is even possible, for aught you know, that there may be a hollow tooth or two in my head. Pray let your search be thorough."

Mr. Green considered him again. "If you had it, it would be upon your person."

"Yet consider," Mr. Caryll begged him, holding out his foot that Leduc might put on his shoe again, "I might have supposed that you would suppose that, and disposed accordingly. You had better investigate to the bitter end."

Mr. Green's small eyes continued to scrutinize Leduc at intervals. The valet was a silent, serious-faced fellow. "I'll search your servant, leastways," the spy announced.

"By all means. Leduc, I beg that you will place yourself at this interesting gentleman's disposal."

What time Mr. Caryll, unaided now, completed the resumption of his garments, Leduc, silent and expressionless, submitted to being searched.

"You will observe, Leduc," said Mr. Caryll, "that we have not come to this country in vain. We are undergoing experiences that would be interesting if they were not quite so dull, amusing if they entailed less discomfort to ourselves. Assuredly, it was worth while to cross to England to study manners. And there are sights for you that you will never see in France. You would not, for instance, had you not come hither, have had an opportunity of observing a member of the noblesse seconding and assisting a tipstaff in the discharge of his duty. And doing it just as a hog wallows in foulness—for the love of it.

"The gentlemen in your country, Leduc, are too fastidious to enjoy life as it should be enjoyed; they are too prone to adhere to the amusements of their class. You have here an opportunity of perceiving how deeply they are mistaken, what relish may lie in setting one's rank on one side, in forgetting at times that by an accident—a sheer, incredible accident, I assure you, Leduc—one may have been born to a gentleman's estate."

Rotherby had drawn himself up, his dark face crimsoning.

"D'ye talk at me, sir?" he demanded. "D'ye dare discuss me with your lackey?"

"But why not, since you search me with my tipstaff! If you can perceive a difference, you are too subtle for me, sir."

Rotherby advanced a step; then checked. He inherited mental sluggishness from his father. "You are insolent!" he charged Caryll. "You insult me."

"Indeed! Ha! I am working miracles."

Rotherby governed his anger by an effort. "There was enough between us without this," said he.

"There could not be too much between us—too much space, I mean."

The viscount looked at him furiously. "I shall discuss this further with you," said he. "The present is not the time nor place. But I shall know where to look for you."

"Leduc, I am sure, will always be pleased to see you. He, too, is studying manners."

Rotherby ignored the insult. "We shall see, then, whether you can do anything more than talk."

"I hope that your lordship, too, is master of other accomplishments. As a talker, I do not find you very gifted. But perhaps Leduc will be less exigent than I."

"Bah!" his lordship flung at him, and went out, cursing him profusely, Gaskell following at his master's heels.

CHAPTER V

MOONSHINE

My Lord Ostermore, though puzzled, entertained no tormenting anxiety on the score of the search to which Mr. Caryll was to be submitted. He assured himself from that gentleman's confident, easy manner—being a man who always drew from things the inference that was obvious—that either he carried no such letter as my lord expected, or else he had so disposed of it as to baffle search.

So, for the moment, he dismissed the subject from his mind. With Hortensia he entered the parlor across the stone-flagged passage, to which the landlady ushered them, and turned wholeheartedly to the matter of his ward's elopement with his son.

"Hortensia," said he, when they were alone. "You have been foolish; very foolish." He had a trick of repeating himself, conceiving, no doubt, that the commonplace achieves distinction by repetition.

Hortensia sat in an arm-chair by the window, and sighed, looking out over the downs. "Do I not know it?" she cried, and the eyes which were averted from his lordship were charred with tears— tears of hot anger, shame and mortification. "God help all women!" she added bitterly, after a moment, as many another woman under similar and worse circumstances has cried before and since.

A more feeling man might have conceived that this was a moment in which to leave her to herself and her own thoughts, and in that it is possible that a more feeling man had been mistaken. Ostermore, stolid and unimaginative, but not altogether without sympathy for his ward, of whom he was reasonably fond—as fond, no doubt, as it was his capacity to be for any other than himself— approached her and set a plump hand upon the back of her chair.

"What was it drove you to this?"

She turned upon him almost fiercely. "My Lady Ostermore," she answered him.

His lordship frowned, and his eyes shifted uneasily from her face. In his heart he disliked his wife excessively, disliked her because she was the one person in the world who governed him, who rode rough-shod over his feelings and desires; because, perhaps, she was the mother of his unfeeling, detestable son. She may not have been the only person living to despise Lord Ostermore; but she was certainly the only one with the courage to

41

manifest her contempt, and that in no circumscribed terms. And yet, disliking her as he did, returning with interest her contempt of him, he veiled it, and was loyal to his termagant, never suffering himself to utter a complaint of her to others, never suffering others to censure her within his hearing. This loyalty may have had its roots in pride—indeed, no other soil can be assigned to them—a pride that would allow no strangers to pry into the sore places of his being. He frowned now to hear Hortensia's angry mention of her ladyship's name; and if his blue eyes moved uneasily under his beetling brows, it was because the situation irked him. How should he stand as judge between Mistress Winthrop—towards whom, as we have seen, he had a kindness—and his wife, whom he hated, yet towards whom he would not be disloyal?

He wished the subject dropped, since, did he ask the obvious question—in what my Lady Ostermore could have been the cause of Hortensia's flight—he would provoke, he knew, a storm of censure from his wife. Therefore he fell silent.

Hortensia, however, felt that she had said too much not to say more.

"Her ladyship has never failed to make me feel my position—my—my poverty," she pursued. "There is no slight her ladyship has not put upon me, until not even your servants use me with the respect that is due to my father's daughter. And my father," she added, with a reproachful glance, "was your friend, my lord."

He shifted uncomfortably on his feet, deploring now the question with which he had fired the train of feminine complaint. "Pish, pish!" he deprecated, "'tis fancy, child—pure fancy!"

"So her Ladyship would say, did you tax her with it. Yet your lordship knows I am not fanciful in other things. Should I, then, be fanciful in this?"

"But what has her ladyship ever done, child?" he demanded, thinking thus to baffle her—since he was acquainted with the subtlety of her ladyship's methods.

"A thousand things," replied Hortensia hotly, "and yet not one upon which I may fasten. 'Tis thus she works: by words, half-words, looks, sneers, shrugs, and sometimes foul abuse entirely disproportionate to the little cause I may unwittingly have given."

"Her ladyship is a little hot," the earl admitted, "but a good heart; 'tis an excellent heart, Hortensia."

"For hating-ay, my lord."

"Nay, plague on't! That's womanish in you. 'Pon honor it is! Womanish!"

"What else would you have a woman? Mannish and raffish, like my Lady Ostermore?"

"I'll not listen to you," he said. "Ye're not just, Hortensia. Ye're heated; heated! I'll not listen to you. Besides, when all is said, what reasons be these for the folly ye've committed?"

"Reasons?" she echoed scornfully. "Reasons and to spare! Her ladyship has made my life so hard, has so shamed and crushed me, put such indignities upon me, that existence grew unbearable under your roof. It could not continue, my lord," she pursued, rising under the sway of her indignation. "It could not continue. I am not of the stuff that goes to making martyrs. I am weak, and—and—as your lordship has said—womanish."

"Indeed, you talk a deal," said his lordship peevishly. But she did not heed the sarcasm.

"Lord Rotherby," she continued, "offered me the means to escape. He urged me to elope with him. His reason was that you would never consent to our marriage; but that if we took the matter into our hands, and were married first, we might depend upon your sanction afterwards; that you had too great a kindness for me to withhold your pardon. I was weak, my lord—womanish," (she threw the word at him again) "and it happened—God help me for a fool!—that I thought I loved Lord Rotherby. And so—and so—"

She sat down again, weakly, miserably, averting her face that she might hide her tears. He was touched, and he even went so far as to show something of his sympathy. He approached her again, and laid a benign hand lightly upon her shoulder.

"But—but—in that case—Oh, the damned villain!—why this mock-parson?"

"Does your lordship not perceive? Must I die of shame? Do you not see?"

"See? No!" He was thoughtful a second; then repeated, "No!"

"I understood," she informed him, a smile—a cruelly bitter smile—lifting and steadying the corner of her lately quivering lip, "when he alluded to your lordship's straitened circumstances. He has no disinheritance to fear because he has no inheritance to look for beyond the entail, of which you cannot disinherit him. My Lord Rotherby sets a high value upon himself. He may—I do not know—he may have been in love with me—though not as I know love, which is all sacrifice, all self-denial. But by his lights he may have cared for me; he must have done, by his lights. Had I been a lady of fortune, not a doubt but he would have made me his wife; as it was, he must aim at a more profitable marriage, and meanwhile, to gratify his love for me—base as it was—he would—he would—O God! I cannot say it. You understand, my lord."

My lord swore strenuously. "There is a punishment for such a crime as this."

"Ay, my lord—and a way to avoid punishment for a gentleman in your son's position, even did I flaunt my shame in some vain endeavor to have justice—a thing he knew I never could have done."

My lord swore again. "He shall be punished," he declared emphatically.

"No doubt. God will see to that," she said, a world of faith in her quivering voice.

My lord's eyes expressed his doubt of divine intervention. He preferred to speak for himself. "I'll disown the dog. He shall not enter my house again. You shall not be reminded of what has happened here. Gad! You were shrewd to have smoked his motives so!" he cried in a burst of admiration for her insight. "Gad, child! Shouldst have been a lawyer! A lawyer!"

"If it had not been for Mr. Caryll—" she began, but to what else she said he lent no ear, being suddenly brought back to his fears at the mention of that gentleman's name.

"Mr. Caryll! Save us! What is keeping him?" he cried. "Can they—can they—"

The door opened, and Mr. Caryll walked in, ushered by the hostess. Both turned to confront him, Hortensia's eyes swollen from her weeping.

"Well?" quoth his lordship. "Did they find nothing?"

Mr. Caryll advanced with the easy, graceful carriage that was one of his main charms, his clothes so skilfully restored by Leduc that none could have guessed the severity of the examination they had undergone.

"Since I am here, and alone, your lordship may conclude such to be the case. Mr. Green is preparing for departure. He is very abject; very chap-fallen. I am almost sorry for Mr. Green. I am by nature sympathetic. I have promised to make my complaint to my Lord Carteret. And so, I trust there is an end to a tiresome matter."

"But then, sir?" quoth his lordship. "But then—are you the bearer of no letter?"

Mr. Caryll shot a swift glance over his shoulder at the door. He deliberately winked at the earl. "Did your lordship expect letters?" he inquired. "That was scarcely reason enough to suppose me a courier. There is some mistake, I imagine."

Between the wink and the words his lordship was bewildered.

Mr. Caryll turned to the lady, bowing. Then he waved a hand over the downs. "A fine view," said he airily, and she stared at him. "I shall treasure sweet memories of Maidstone." Her stare grew stonier. Did he mean the landscape or some other matter? His tone was difficult to read—a feature peculiar to his tone.

"Not so shall I, sir," she made answer. "I shall never think of it other than with burning cheeks—unless it be with gratitude to your shrewdness which saved me."

"No more, I beg. It is a matter painful to you to dwell on. Let me exhort you to forget it. I have already done so."

"That is a sweet courtesy in you."

"I am compounded of sweet courtesy," he informed her modestly.

His lordship spoke of departure, renewing his offer to carry Mr. Caryll to town in his chaise. Meanwhile, Mr. Caryll was behaving curiously. He was tiptoeing towards the door, along the wall, where he was out of line with the keyhole. He reached it suddenly, and abruptly pulled it open. There was a squeal, and Mr. Green rolled forward into the room. Mr. Caryll kicked him out again before he could rise, and called Leduc to throw him outside. And that was the last they saw of Mr. Green at Maidstone.

They set out soon afterwards, Mr. Caryll travelling in his lordship's chaise, and Leduc following in his master's.

It was an hour or so after candle-lighting time when they reached Croydon, the country lying all white under a full moon that sailed in a clear, calm sky. His lordship swore that he would go no farther that night. The travelling fatigued him; indeed, for the last few miles of the journey he had been dozing in his corner of the carriage, conversation having long since been abandoned as too great an effort on so bad a road, which shook and jolted them beyond endurance. His lordship's chaise was of an old-fashioned pattern, and the springs far from what might have been desired or expected in a nobleman's conveyance.

They alighted at the "Bells." His lordship bespoke supper, invited Mr. Caryll to join them, and, what time the meal was preparing, went into a noisy doze in the parlor's best chair.

Mistress Winthrop sauntered out into the garden. The calm and fragrance of the night invited her. Alone with her thoughts, she paced the lawn a while, until her solitude was disturbed by the advent of Mr. Caryll. He, too, had need to think, and he had come out into the peace of the night to indulge his need. Seeing her, he made as if to withdraw again; but she perceived him, and called him to her side. He went most readily. Yet when he stood before her in an attitude of courteous deference, she was at a loss what she should say to him, or, rather, what words she should employ. At last, with a half-laugh of nervousness, "I am by nature very inquisitive, sir," she prefaced.

"I had already judged you to be an exceptional woman," Mr. Caryll commented softly.

45

She mused an instant. "Are you never serious?" she asked him.

"Is it worth while?" he counter-questioned, and, whether intent or accident, he let her see something of himself. "Is it even amusing—to be serious?"

"Is there in life nothing but amusement?"

"Oh, yes—but nothing so vital. I speak with knowledge. The gift of laughter has been my salvation."

"From what, sir?"

"Ah—who shall say that? My history and my rearing have been such that had I bowed before them, I had become the most gloomy, melancholy man that steps this gloomy, melancholy world. By now I might have found existence insupportable, and so—who knows? I might have set a term to it. But I had the wisdom to prefer laughter. Humanity is a delectable spectacle if we but have the gift to observe it in a dispassionate spirit. Such a gift have I cultivated. The squirming of the human worm is interesting to observe, and the practice of observing it has this advantage, that while we observe it we forget to squirm ourselves."

"The bitterness of your words belies their purport."

He shrugged and smiled. "But proves my contention. That I might explain myself, you made me for a moment serious, set me squirming in my turn."

She moved a little, and he fell into step beside her. A little while there was silence.

Presently—"You find me, no doubt, as amusing as any other of your human worms," said she.

"God forbid!" he answered soberly.

She laughed. "You make an exception in my case, then. That is a subtle flattery!"

"Have I not said that I had judged you to be an exceptional woman?"

"Exceptionally foolish, not a doubt."

"Exceptionally beautiful; exceptionally admirable," he corrected.

"A clumsy compliment, devoid of wit!"

"When we grow truthful, it may be forgiven us if we fall short of wit."

"That were an argument in favor of avoiding truth."

"Were it necessary," said he. "For truth is seldom so intrusive as to need avoiding. But we are straying. There was a score upon which you were inquisitive, you said; from which I take it that you sought knowledge at my hands. Pray seek it; I am a well, of knowledge."

46

"I desired to know—Nay, but I have asked you already. I desired to know did you deem me a very pitiful little fool?"

They had reached the privet hedge, and turned. They paused now before resuming their walk. He paused, also, before replying. Then:

"I should judge you wise in most things," he answered slowly, critically. "But in the matter to which I owe the blessing of having served you, I do not think you wise. Did you—do you love Lord Rotherby?"

"What if so?"

"After what you have learned, I should account you still less wise."

"You are impertinent, sir," she reproved him.

"Nay, most pertinent. Did you not ask me to sit in judgment upon this matter? And unless you confess to me, how am I to absolve you?"

"I did not crave your absolution. You take too much upon yourself."

"So said Lord Rotherby. You seem to have something in common when all is said."

She bit her lip in chagrin. They paced in silence to the lawn's end, and turned again. Then: "You treat me like a fool," she reproved him.

"How is that possible, when, already I think I love you."

She started from him, and stared at him for a long moment. "You insult me!" she cried angrily, conceiving that she understood his mind. "Do you think that because I may have committed a folly I have forfeited all claim to be respected—that I am a subject for insolent speeches?"

"You are illogical," said Mr. Caryll, the imperturbable. "I have told you that I love you. Should I insult the woman I have said I love?"

"You love me?" She looked at him, her face very white in the white moonlight, her lips parted, a kindling anger in her eyes. "Are you mad?"

"I a'n't sure. There have been moments when I have almost feared it. This is not one of them."

"You wish me to think you serious?" She laughed a thought stridently in her indignation. "I have known you just four hours," said she.

"Precisely the time I think I have loved you."

"You think?" she echoed scornfully. "Oh, you make that reservation! You are not quite sure?"

"Can we be sure of anything?" he deprecated.

47

"Of some things," she answered icily. "And I am sure of one—that I am beginning to understand you."

"I envy you. Since that is so, help me—of your charity!—to understand myself."

"Then understand yourself for an impudent, fleering coxcomb," she flung at him, and turned to leave him.

"That is not explanation," said Mr. Caryll thoughtfully. "It is mere abuse."

"What else do you deserve?" she asked him over her shoulder. "That you should have dared!" she withered him.

"To love you quite so suddenly?" he inquired, and misquoted: "'Whoever loved at all, that loved not at first sight?' Hortensia!"

"You have not the right to my name, sir."

"Yet I offer you the right to mine," he answered, with humble reproach.

"You shall be punished," she promised him, and in high dudgeon left him.

"Punished? Oh, cruel! Can you then be—

> "'Unsoft to him who's smooth to thee?
> Tigers and bears, I've heard some say,
> For proffered love will love repay.'"

But she was gone. He looked up at the moon, and took it into his confidence to reproach it. "'Twas your white face beglamored me," he told it aloud. "See, how execrable a beginning I've made, and, therefore, how excellent!" And he laughed, but entirely without mirth.

He remained pacing in the moonlight, very thoughtful, and, for once, it seemed, not at all amused. His life appeared to be tangling itself beyond unravelling, and his vaunted habit of laughter scarce served at present to show him the way out.

CHAPTER VI

HORTENSIA'S RETURN

Mr. Caryll needs explaining as he walks there in the moonlight; that is, if we are at all to understand him—a matter by no means easy, considering that he has confessed he did not understand himself. Did ever man make a sincere declaration of sudden passion as flippantly as he had done, or in terms-better calculated to alienate the regard he sought to win? Did ever man choose his time with less discrimination, or his words with less discretion? Assuredly not. To suppose that Mr. Caryll was unaware of this, would be to suppose him a fool, and that he most certainly was not.

His mood was extremely complex; its analysis, I fear, may baffle us. It must have seemed to you—as it certainly seemed to Mistress Winthrop—that he made a mock of her; that in truth he was the impudent, fleering coxcomb she pronounced him, and nothing more. Not so. Mock he most certainly did; but his mockery was all aimed to strike himself on the recoil—himself and the sentiments which had sprung to being in his soul, and to which— nameless as he was, pledged as he was to a task that would most likely involve his ruin—he conceived that he had no right. He gave expression to his feelings, yet chose for them the expression best calculated to render them barren of all consequence where Mistress Winthrop was concerned. Where another would have hidden those emotions, Mr. Caryll elected to flaunt them half-derisively, that Hortensia might trample them under foot in sheer disgust.

It was, perhaps, the knowledge that did he wait, and come to her as an honest, devout lover, he must in honesty tell her all there was to know of his odd history and of his bastardy, and thus set up between them a barrier insurmountable. Better, he may have thought, to make from the outset a mockery of a passion for which there could be no hope. And so, under that mocking, impertinent exterior, I hope you catch some glimpse of the real, suffering man— the man who boasted that he had the gift of laughter.

He continued a while to pace the dewy lawn after she had left him, and a deep despondency descended upon the spirit of this man who accounted seriousness a folly. Hitherto his rancor against his father had been a theoretical rancor, a thing educated into him by Everard, and accepted by him as we accept a proposition in Euclid that is proved to us. In its way it had been a make-believe rancor, a rancor on principle, for he had been made to see that unless he was inflamed by it, he was not worthy to be his mother's son. Tonight had changed all this. No longer was his grievance sentimental, theoretical or abstract. It was suddenly become real and very bitter. It was no longer a question of the wrong done his mother thirty years ago; it became the question of a wrong done himself in casting him nameless upon the world, a thing of scorn to cruel, unjust humanity. Could Mistress Winthrop have guessed the bitter self-derision with which he had, in apparent levity, offered her his name, she might have felt some pity for him who had no pity for himself.

And so, to-night he felt—as once for a moment Everard had made him feel—that he had a very real wrong of his own to avenge upon his father; and the task before him lost much of the repugnance that it had held for him hitherto.

All this because four hours ago he had looked into the brown depths of Mistress Winthrop's eyes. He sighed, and declaimed a line of Congreve's:

"'Woman is a fair image in a pool; who leaps at it is sunk.'"

The landlord came to bid him in to supper. He excused himself. Sent his lordship word that he was over-tired, and went off to bed.

They met at breakfast, at an early hour upon the morrow, Mistress Winthrop cool and distant; his lordship grumpy and mute; Mr. Caryll airy and talkative as was his habit. They set out soon afterwards. But matters were nowise improved. His lordship dozed in a corner of the carriage, while Mistress Winthrop found more interest in the flowering hedgerows than in Mr. Caryll, ignored him when he talked, and did not answer him when he set questions; till, in the end, he, too, lapsed into silence, and as a solatium for his soreness assured himself by lengthy, wordless arguments that matters were best so.

They entered the outlying parts of London some two hours later, and it still wanted an hour or so to noon when the chaise brought up inside the railings before the earl's house in Lincoln's Inn Fields.

There came a rush of footmen, a bustle of service, amid which they alighted and entered the splendid residence that was part of the little that remained Lord Ostermore from the wreck his fortunes had suffered on the shoals of the South Sea.

Mr. Caryll paused a moment to dismiss Leduc to the address in Old Palace Yard where he had hired a lodging. That done, he followed his lordship and Hortensia within doors.

From the inner hall a footman ushered him across an ante-chamber to a room on the right, which proved to be the library, and

50

was his lordship's habitual retreat. It was a spacious, pillared chamber, very richly panelled in damask silk, and very richly furnished, having long French windows that opened on a terrace above the garden.

As they entered there came a swift rustle of petticoats at their heels, and Mr. Caryll stood aside, bowing, to give passage to a tall lady who swept by with no more regard for him than had he been one of the house's lackeys. She was, he observed, of middle-age, lean and aquiline-featured, with an exaggerated chin, that ended squarely as boot. Her sallow cheeks were raddled to a hectic color, a monstrous head-dress—like that of some horse in a lord mayor's show—coiffed her, and her dress was a mixture of extravagance and incongruity, the petticoat absurdly hooped.

She swept into the room like a battleship into action, and let fly her first broadside at Mistress Winthrop from the threshold.

"Codso!" she shrilled. "You have come back! And for what have you come back? Am I to live in the same house with you, you shameless madam—that have no more thought for your reputation than a slut in a smock-race?"

Hortensia raised indignant eyes from out of a face that was very pale. Her lips were tightly pressed—in resolution, thought Mr. Caryll, who was very observant of her—not to answer her ladyship; for Mr. Caryll had little doubt as to the identity of this dragon.

"My love—my dear—" began his lordship, advancing a step, his tone a very salve. Then, seeking to create a diversion, he waved a hand towards Mr. Caryll. "Let me present—"

"Did I speak to you?" she turned to bombard him. "Have you not done harm enough? Had you been aught but a fool—had you respected me as a husband should—you had left well alone and let her go her ways."

"There was my duty to her father, to say aught of—"

"And what of your duty to me?" she blazed, her eyes puckering most malignantly. She reminded Mr. Caryll of nothing so much as a vulture. "Had ye forgotten that? Have ye no thought for decency—no respect for your wife?"

Her strident voice was echoing through the house and drawing a little crowd of gaping servants to the hall. To spare Mistress Winthrop, Mr. Caryll took it upon himself to close the door. The countess turned at the sound.

"Who is this?" she asked, measuring the elegant figure with an evil eye. And Mr. Caryll felt it in his bones that she had done him the honor to dislike him at sight.

"It is a gentleman who—who—" His lordship thought it better, apparently, not to explain the exact circumstances under which he

51

had met the gentleman. He shifted ground. "I was about to present him, my love. It is Mr. Caryll—Mr. Justin Caryll. This, sir, is my Lady Ostermore."

Mr. Caryll made her a profound bow. Her ladyship retorted with a sniff.

"Is it a kinsman of yours, my lord?" and the contempt of the question was laden with a suggestion that smote Mr. Caryll hard. What she implied in wanton offensive mockery was no more than he alone present knew to be the exact and hideous truth.

"Some remote kinsman, I make no doubt," the earl explained. "Until yesterday I had not the honor of his acquaintance. Mr. Caryll is from France."

"Ye'll be a Jacobite, no doubt, then," were her first, uncompromising words to the guest.

Mr. Caryll made her another bow. "If I were, I should make no secret of it with your ladyship," he answered with that irritating suavity in which he clothed his most obvious sarcasms.

Her ladyship opened her eyes a little wider. Here was a tone she was unused to. "And what may your business with his lordship be?"

"His lordship's business, I think," answered Mr. Caryll in a tone of such exquisite politeness and deference that the words seemed purged of all their rudeness.

"Will you answer me so, sir?" she demanded, nevertheless, her voice quivering.

"My love!" interpolated his lordship hurriedly, his florid face aflush. "We are vastly indebted to Mr. Caryll, as you shall learn. It was he who saved Hortensia."

"Saved the drab, did he? And from what, pray?"

"Madam!" It was Hortensia who spoke. She had risen, pale with anger, and she made appeal now to her guardian. "My lord, I'll not remain to be so spoken of. Suffer me to go. That her ladyship should so speak of me to my face—and to a stranger!"

"Stranger!" crowed her ladyship. "Lard! And what d'ye suppose will happen? Are you so nice about a stranger hearing what I may have to say of you—you that will be the talk of the whole lewd town for this fine escapade? And what'll the town say of you?"

"My love!" his lordship sought again to soothe her. "Sylvia, let me implore you! A little moderation! A little charity! Hortensia has been foolish. She confesses so much, herself. Yet, when all is said, 'tis not she is to blame."

"Am I?"

"My love! Was it suggested?"

"I marvel it was not. Indeed, I marvel! Oh, Hortensia is not to blame, the sweet, pure dove! What is she, then?"

"To be pitied, ma'am," said his lordship, stirred to sudden anger, "that she should have lent an ear to your disreputable son."

"My son? My son?" cried her ladyship, her voice more and more strident, her face flushing till the rouge upon it was put to shame, revealed in all its unnatural hideousness. "And is he not your son, my lord?"

"There are moments," he answered hardily, "when I find it difficult to believe."

It was much for him to say, and to her ladyship, of all people. It was pure mutiny. She gasped for air; pumped her brain for words. Meantime, his lordship continued with an eloquence entirely unusual in him and prompted entirely by his strong feelings in the matter of his son. "He is a disgrace to his name! He always has been. When a boy, he was a liar and a thief, and had he had his deserts he had been lodged in Newgate long ago—or worse. Now that he's a man, he's an abandoned profligate, a brawler, a drunkard, a rakehell. So much I have long known him for; but to-day he has shown himself for something even worse. I had thought that my ward, at least, had been sacred from his villainy. That is the last drop. I'll not condone it. Damn me! I can't condone it. I'll disown him. He shall not set foot in house of mine again. Let him keep the company of his Grace of Wharton and his other abandoned friends of the Hell Fire Club; he keeps not mine. He keeps not mine, I say!"

Her ladyship swallowed hard. From red that she had been, she was now ashen under her rouge. "And, is this wanton baggage to keep mine? Is she to disgrace a household that has grown too nice to contain your son?"

"My lord! Oh, my lord, give me leave to go," Hortensia entreated.

"Ay, go," sneered her ladyship. "Go! You had best go—back to him. What for did ye leave him? Did ye dream there could be aught to return to?"

Hortensia turned to her guardian again appealingly. But her ladyship bore down upon her, incensed by this ignoring; she caught the girl's wrist in her claw-like hand. "Answer me, you drab! What for did you return? What is to be done with you now that y' are soiled goods? Where shall we find a husband for you?"

"I do not want a husband, madam," answered Hortensia.

"Will ye lead apes in hell, then? Bah! 'Tis not what ye want, my fine madam; 'tis what we can get you; and where shall we find you a husband now?"

Her eye fell upon Mr. Caryll, standing by one of the windows, a look of profound disgust overplaying the usually immobile face. "Perhaps the gentleman from France—the gentleman who saved you," she sneered, "will propose to take the office."

"With all my heart, ma'am," Mr. Caryll startled them and himself by answering. Then, perceiving that he had spoken too much upon impulse—given utterance to what was passing in his mind—"I but mention it to show your ladyship how mistaken are your conclusions," he added.

The countess loosed her hold of Hortensia's wrist in her amazement, and looked the gentleman from France up and down in a mighty scornful manner. "Codso!" she swore, "I may take it, then, that your saving her—as ye call it—was no accident."

"Indeed it was, ma'am—and a most fortunate accident for your son."

"For my son? As how?"

"It saved him from hanging, ma'am," Mr. Caryll informed her, and gave her something other than the baiting of Hortensia to occupy her mind.

"Hang?" she gasped. "Are you speaking of Lord Rotherby?"

"Ay, of Lord Rotherby—and not a word more than is true," put in the earl. "Do you know—but you do not—the extent of your precious son's villainy? At Maidstone, where I overtook them—at the Adam and Eve—he had a make-believe parson, and he was luring this poor child into a mock-marriage."

Her ladyship stared. "Mock-marriage?" she echoed. "Marriage? La!" And again she vented her unpleasant laugh. "Did she insist on that, the prude? Y' amaze me!"

"Surely, my love, you do not apprehend. Had Lord Rotherby's parson not been detected and unmasked by Mr. Caryll, here—"

"Would you ha' me believe she did not know the fellow was no parson?"

"Oh!" cried Hortensia. "Your ladyship has a very wicked soul. May God forgive you!"

"And who is to forgive you?" snapped the countess.

"I need no forgiveness, for I have done no wrong. A folly, I confess to. I was mad to have heeded such a villain."

Her ladyship gathered forces for a fresh assault. But Mr. Caryll anticipated it. It was no doubt a great impertinence in him; but he saw Hortensia's urgent need, and he felt, moreover, that not even Lord Ostermore would resent his crossing swords a moment with her ladyship.

"You would do well, ma'am, to remember," said he, in his singularly precise voice, "that Lord Rotherby even now—and as things have fallen out—is by no means quit of all danger."

She looked at this smooth gentleman, and his words burned themselves into her brain. She quivered with mingling fear and anger.

"Wha'—what is't ye mean?" quoth she.

"That even at this hour, if the matter were put about, his lordship might be brought to account for it, and it might fare very ill with him. The law of England deals heavily with an offense such as Lord Rotherby's, and the attempt at a mock-marriage, of which there is no lack of evidence, would so aggravate the crime of abduction, if he were informed against, that it might go very hard with him."

Her jaw fell. She caught more than an admonition in his words. It almost seemed to her that he was threatening.

"Who—who is to inform?" she asked point-blank, her tone a challenge; and yet the odd change in it from its recent aggressiveness was almost ludicrous.

"Ah—who?" said Mr. Caryll, raising his eyes and fetching a sigh. "It would appear that a messenger from the Secretary of State—on another matter—was at the Adam and Eve at the time with two of his catchpolls, and he was a witness of the whole affair. Then again," and he waved a hand doorwards, "servants are servants. I make no doubt they are listening, and your ladyship's voice has scarce been controlled. You can never say when a servant may cease to be a servant, and become an active enemy."

"Damn the servants!" she swore, dismissing them from consideration. "Who is this messenger of the secretary's? Who is he?"

"He was named Green. 'Tis all I know."

"And where may he be found?"

"I cannot say."

She turned to Lord Ostermore. "Where is Rotherby?" she inquired. She was a thought breathless.

"I do not know," said he, in a voice that signified how little he cared.

"He must be found. This fellow's silence must be bought. I'll not have my son disgraced, and gaoled, perhaps. He must be found."

Her alarm was very real now. She moved towards the door, then paused, and turned again. "Meantime, let your lordship consider what dispositions you are to make for this wretched girl who is the cause of all this garboil."

And she swept out, slamming the door violently after her.

CHAPTER VII

FATHER AND SON

Mr. Caryll stayed to dine at Stretton House. Although they had journeyed but from Croydon that morning, he would have preferred to have gone first to his lodging to have made—fastidious as he was—a suitable change in his apparel. But the urgency that his task dictated caused him to waive the point.

He had a half-hour or so to himself after the stormy scene with her ladyship, in which he had played again—though in a lesser degree—the part of savior to Mistress Winthrop, a matter for which the lady had rewarded him, ere withdrawing, with a friendly smile, which caused him to think her disposed to forgive him his yesternight's folly.

In that half-hour he gave himself again very seriously to the contemplation of his position. He had no illusions on the score of Lord Ostermore, and he rated his father no higher than he deserved. But he was just and shrewd in his judgment, and he was forced to confess that he had found this father of his vastly different from the man he had been led to expect. He had looked to find a debauched old rake, a vile creature steeped in vice and wickedness. Instead, he found a weak, easy-natured, commonplace fellow, whose worst sin seemed to be the selfishness that is usually inseparable from those other characteristics. If Ostermore was not a man of the type that inspires strong affection, neither was he of the type that provokes strong dislike. His colorless nature left one indifferent to him.

Mr. Caryll, somewhat to his dismay, found himself inclined to extend the man some sympathy; caught himself upon the verge of pitying him for being burdened with so very unfilial a son and so very cursed a wife. It was one of his cherished beliefs that the evil that men do has a trick of finding them out in this life, and here, he believed, as shrew-ridden husband and despised father, the Earl of Ostermore was being made to expiate that sin of his early years.

Another of Mr. Caryll's philosophies was that, when all is said, man is little of a free agent. His viciousness or sanctity is temperamental; and not the man, but his nature—which is not self-imbued—must bear the responsibility of a man's deeds, be they good or bad.

In the abstract such beliefs are well enough; they are excellent standards by which to judge where other sufferers than ourselves are concerned. But when we ourselves are touched, they are discounted by the measure in which a man's deeds or misdeeds may affect us. And although to an extent this might be the case now with Mr. Caryll, yet, in spite of it, he found himself excusing his father on the score of the man's weakness and stupidity, until he caught himself up with the reflection that this was a disloyalty to Everard, to his training, and to his mother. And yet—he reverted—in such a man as Ostermore, sheer stupidity, a lack of imagination, of insight into things as they really are, a lack of feeling that would disable him from appreciating the extent of any wrong he did, seemed to Mr. Caryll to be extenuating circumstances.

He conceived that he was amazingly dispassionate in his judgment, and he wondered was he right or wrong so to be. Then the thought of his task arose in his mind, and it bathed him in a sweat of horror. Over in France he had allowed himself to be persuaded, and had pledged himself to do this thing. Everard, the relentless, unforgiving fanatic of vengeance, had—as we have seen—trained him to believe that the avenging of his mother's wrongs was the only thing that could justify his own existence. Besides, it had all seemed remote then, and easy as remote things are apt to seem. But now—now that he had met in the flesh this man who was his father—his hesitation was turned to very horror. It was not that he did not conceive, in spite of his odd ideas upon temperament and its responsibilities, that his mother's' wrongs cried out for vengeance, and that the avenging of them would be a righteous, fitting deed; but it was that he conceived that his own was not the hand to do the work of the executioner upon one who—after all—was still his own father. It was hideously unnatural.

He sat in the library, awaiting his lordship and the announcement of dinner. There was a book before him; but his eyes were upon the window, the smooth lawns beyond, all drenched in summer sunshine, and his thoughts were introspective. He looked into his shuddering soul, and saw that he could not—that he would not—do the thing which he was come to do. He would await the coming of Everard, to tell him so. There would be a storm to face, he knew. But sooner that than carry this vile thing through. It was vile—most damnably vile—he now opined.

The decision taken, he rose and crossed to the window. His mind had been in travail; his soul had known the pangs of labor. But now that this strong resolve had been brought forth, an ease and peace were his that seemed to prove to him how right he was, how wrong must aught else have been.

Lord Ostermore came in. He announced that they would be dining alone together. "Her ladyship," he explained, "has gone forth in person to seek Lord Rotherby. She believes that she knows where

57

to find him—in some disreputable haunt, no doubt, whither her ladyship would have been better advised to have sent a servant. But women are wayward cattle—wayward, headstrong cattle! Have you not found them so, Mr. Caryll?"

"I have found that the opinion is common to most husbands," said Mr. Caryll, then added a question touching Mistress Winthrop, and wondered would she not be joining them at table.

"The poor child keeps her chamber," said the earl. "She is overwrought—overwrought! I am afraid her ladyship—" He broke off abruptly, and coughed. "She is overwrought," he repeated in conclusion. "So that we dine alone."

And alone they dined. Ostermore, despite the havoc suffered by his fortunes, kept an excellent table and a clever cook, and Mr. Caryll was glad to discover in his sire this one commendable trait.

The conversation was desultory throughout the repast; but when the cloth was raised and the table cleared of all but the dishes of fruit and the decanters of Oporto, Canary and Madeira, there came a moment of expansion.

Mr. Caryll was leaning back in his chair, fingering the stem of his wine-glass, watching the play of sunlight through the ruddy amber of the wine, and considering the extraordinarily odd position of a man sitting at table, by the merest chance, almost, with a father who was not aware that he had begotten him. A question from his lordship came to stir him partially from the reverie into which he was beginning to lapse.

"Do you look to make a long sojourn in England, Mr. Caryll?"

"It will depend," was the vague and half-unconscious answer, "upon the success of the matter I am come to transact."

There ensued a brief pause, during which Mr. Caryll fell again into his abstraction.

"Where do you dwell when in France, sir?" inquired my lord, as if to make polite conversation.

Mr. Caryll lulled by his musings into carelessness, answered truthfully, "At Maligny, in Normandy."

The next moment there was a tinkle of breaking glass, and Mr. Caryll realized his indiscretion and turned cold.

Lord Ostermore, who had been in the act of raising his glass, fetched it down again so suddenly that the stem broke in his fingers, and the mahogany was flooded with the liquor. A servant hastened forward, and set a fresh glass for his lordship. That done, Ostermore signed to the man to withdraw. The fellow went, closing the door, and leaving those two alone.

The pause had been sufficient to enable Mr. Caryll to recover, and for all that his pulses throbbed more quickly than their habit,

58

outwardly he maintained his lazily indifferent pose, as if entirely unconscious that what he had said had occasioned his father the least disturbance.

"You—you dwelt at Maligny?" said his lordship, the usual high color all vanished from his face. And again: "You dwelt at Maligny, and—and—your name is Caryll."

Mr. Caryll looked up quickly, as if suddenly aware that his lordship was expressing surprise. "Why, yes," said he. "What is there odd in that?"

"How does it happen that you come to live there? Are you at all connected with the family of Maligny? On your mother's side, perhaps?"

Mr. Caryll took up his wine-glass. "I take it," said he easily, "that there was some such family at some time. But it is clear it must have fallen upon evil days." He sipped at his wine. "There are none left now," he explained, as he set down his glass. "The last of them died, I believe, in England." His eyes turned full upon the earl, but their glance seemed entirely idle. "It was in consequence of that that my father was enabled to purchase the estate."

Mr. Caryll accounted it no lie that he suppressed the fact that the father to whom he referred was but his father by adoption.

Relief spread instantly upon Lord Ostermore's countenance. Clearly, he saw, here was pure coincidence, and nothing more. Indeed, what else should there have been? What was it that he had feared? He did not know. Still he accounted it an odd matter, and said so.

"What is odd?" inquired Mr. Caryll. "Does it happen that your lordship was acquainted at any time with that vanished family?"

"I was, sir—slightly acquainted—at one time with one or two of its members. 'Tis that that is odd. You see, sir, my name, too, happens to be Caryll."

"True—yet I see nothing so oddly coincident in the matter, particularly if your acquaintance with these Malignys was but slight."

"Indeed, you are right. You are right. There is no such great coincidence, when all is said. The name reminded me of a—a folly of my youth. 'Twas that that made impression."

"A folly?" quoth Mr. Caryll, his eyebrows raised.

"Ay, a folly—a folly that went near undoing me, for had it come to my father's ears, he had broke me without mercy. He was a hard man, my father; a puritan in his ideas."

"A greater than your lordship?" inquired Mr. Caryll blandly, masking the rage that seethed in him.

His lordship laughed. "Ye're a wag, Mr. Caryll—a damned

wag!" Then reverting to the matter that was uppermost in his mind. "'Tis a fact, though—'pon honor. My father would ha' broke me. Luckily she died."

"Who died?" asked Mr. Caryll, with a show of interest.

"The girl. Did I not tell you there was a girl? 'Twas she was the folly—Antoinette de Maligny. But she died—most opportunely, egad! 'Twas a very damned mercy that she did. It—cut the—the—what d'ye call it—knot?"

"The Gordian knot?" suggested Mr. Caryll.

"Ay—the Gordian knot. Had she lived and had my father smoked the affair—Gad! he would ha' broke me; he would so!" he repeated, and emptied his glass.

Mr. Caryll, white to the lips, sat very still a moment. Then he did a curious thing; did it with a curious suddenness. He took a knife from the table, and hacked off the lowest button from his coat. This he pushed across the board to his father.

"To turn to other matters," said he; "there is the letter you were expecting from abroad."

"Eh? What?" Lord Ostermore took up the button. It was of silk, interwoven with gold thread. He turned it over in his fingers, looking at it with a heavy eye, and then at his guest. "Eh? Letter?" he muttered, puzzled.

"If your lordship will cut that open, you will see what his majesty has to propose." He mentioned the king in a voice charged with suggestion, so that no doubt could linger on the score of the king he meant.

"Gad!" cried his lordship. "Gad! 'Twas thus ye bubbled Mr. Green? Shrewd, on my soul. And you are the messenger, then?"

"I am the messenger," answered Mr. Caryll coldly.

"And why did you not say so before?"

For the fraction of a second Mr. Caryll hesitated. Then: "Because I did not judge that the time was come," said he.

CHAPTER VIII

TEMPTATION

His lordship ripped away the silk covering of the button with a penknife, and disembowelled it of a small packet, which consisted of a sheet of fine and very closely-folded and tightly-compressed paper. This he spread, cast an eye over, and then looked up at his companion, who was watching him with simulated indolence.

His lordship had paled a little, and there was about the lines of his mouth a look of preternatural gravity. He looked furtively towards the door, his heavy eyebrows lowering.

"I think," he said, "that we shall be more snug in the library. Will you bear me company, Mr. Caryll?"

Mr. Caryll rose instantly. The earl folded the letter, and turned to go. His companion paused to pick up the fragments of the button and slip them into his pocket. He performed the office with a smile on his lips that was half pity, half contempt. It did not seem to him that there would be the least need to betray Lord Ostermore once his lordship was wedded to the Stuart faction. He would not fail to betray himself through some act of thoughtless stupidity such as this.

In the library—the door, and that of the ante-room beyond it, carefully closed—his lordship unlocked a secretaire of walnut, very handsomely inlaid, and, drawing up a chair, he sat down to the perusal of the king's letter. When he had read it through, he remained lost in thought a while. At length he looked up and across towards Mr. Caryll, who was standing by one of the windows.

"You are no doubt a confidential agent, sir," said he. "And you will be fully aware of the contents of this letter that you have brought me."

"Fully, my lord," answered Mr. Caryll, "and I venture to hope that his majesty's promises will overcome any hesitation that you may feel."

"His majesty's promises?" said my lord thoughtfully. "His majesty may never have a chance of fulfilling them."

"Very true, sir. But who gambles must set a stake upon the board. Your lordship has been something of a gamester already, and—or so I gather—with little profit. Here is a chance to play another game that may mend the evil fortunes of the last."

The earl scanned him in surprise. "You are excellent well informed," said he, between surprise and irony.

"My trade demands it. Knowledge is my buckler."

His lordship nodded slowly, and fell very thoughtful, the letter before him, his eyes wandering ever and anon to con again some portion of it. "It is a game in which I stake my head," he muttered presently.

"Has your lordship anything else to stake?" inquired Mr. Caryll.

The earl looked at him again with a gloomy eye, and sighed, but said nothing. Mr. Caryll resumed. "It is for your lordship to declare," he said quite coolly, "whether his majesty has covered your stake. If you think not, it is even possible that he may be induced to improve his offer. Though if you think not, for my own part I consider that you set too high a value on that same head of yours."

Touched in his vanity, Ostermore looked up at him with a sudden frown. "You take a bold tone, sir," said he, "a very bold tone!"

"Boldness is the attribute next to knowledge most essential to my calling," Mr. Caryll reminded him.

His lordship's eye fell before the other's cold glance, and again he lapsed into thoughtfulness, his cheek now upon his hand. Suddenly he looked up again. "Tell me," said he. "Who else is in this thing? Men say that Atterbury is not above suspicion. Is it—"

Mr. Caryll bent forward to tap the king's letter with a rigid forefinger. "When your lordship tells me that you are ready to concert upon embarking your fortunes in this bottom, you shall find me disposed, perhaps, to answer questions concerning others. Meanwhile, our concern is with yourself."

"Dons and the devil!" swore his lordship angrily. "Is this a way to speak to me?" He scowled at the agent. "Tell me, my fine fellow, what would happen if I were to lay this letter you have brought me before the nearest justice?"

"I cannot say for sure," answered Mr. Caryll quietly, "but it is very probable it would help your lordship to the gallows. For if you will give yourself the trouble of reading it again—and more carefully—you will see that it makes acknowledgment of the offer of services you wrote his majesty a month or so ago."

His lordship's eyes dropped to the letter again. He caught his breath in sudden fear.

"Were I your lordship, I should leave the nearest justice to enjoy his dinner in peace," said Mr. Caryll, smiling.

His lordship laughed in a sickly manner. He felt foolish—a rare condition in him, as in most fools. "Well, well," said he gruffly. "The matter needs reflection. It needs reflection."

Behind them the door opened noiselessly, and her ladyship

appeared in cloak and wimple. She paused there, unperceived by either, arrested by the words she had caught, and waiting in the hope of hearing more.

"I must sleep on't, at least," his lordship was continuing. "'Tis too grave a matter to be determined thus in haste."

A faint sound caught the keen ears of Mr. Caryll. He turned with a leisureliness that bore witness to his miraculous self-control. Perceiving the countess, he bowed, and casually put his lordship on his guard.

"Ah!" said he. "Here is her ladyship returned."

Lord Ostermore gasped audibly and swung round in an alarm than which nothing could have betrayed him more effectively. "My—my love!" he cried, stammering, and by his wild haste to conceal the letter that he held, drew her attention to it.

Mr. Caryll stepped between them, his back to his lordship, that he might act as a screen under cover of which to dispose safely of that dangerous document. But he was too late. Her ladyship's quick eyes had flashed to it, and if the distance precluded the possibility of her discovering anything that might be written upon it, she, nevertheless, could see the curious nature of the paper, which was of the flimsiest tissue of a sort extremely uncommon.

"What is't ye hide?" said she, as she came forward. "Why, we are very close, surely! What mischief is't ye hatch, my lord?"'

"Mis—mischief, my love?" He smiled propitiatingly—hating her more than ever in that moment. He had stuffed the letter into an inner pocket of his coat, and but that she had another matter to concern her at the moment she would not have allowed the question she had asked to be so put aside. But this other matter upon her mind touched her very closely.

"Devil take it, whatever it may be! Rotherby is here."

"Rotherby?" His demeanor changed; from conciliating it was of a sudden transformed to indignant. "What makes he here?" he demanded. "Did I not forbid him my house?"

"I brought him," she answered pregnantly.

But for once he was not to be put down. "Then you may take him hence again," said he. "I'll not have him under my roof—under the same roof with that poor child he used so infamously. I'll not suffer it!"

The Gorgon cannot have looked more coldly wicked than her ladyship just then. "Have a care, my lord!" she muttered threateningly. "Oh, have a care, I do beseech you. I am not so to be crossed!"

"Nor am I, ma'am," he rejoined, and then, before more could be said, Mr. Caryll stepped forward to remind them of his presence—which they seemed to stand in danger of forgetting.

"I fear that I intrude, my lord," said he, and bowed in leave-taking. "I shall wait upon your lordship later. Your most devoted. Ma'am, your very humble servant." And he bowed himself out.

In the ante-room he came upon Lord Rotherby, striding to and fro, his brow all furrowed with care. At sight of Mr. Caryll, the viscount's scowl grew blacker. "Oons and the devil!" he cried. "What make you here?"

"That," said Mr. Caryll pleasantly, "is the very question your father is asking her ladyship concerning yourself. Your servant, sir." And airy, graceful, smiling that damnable close smile of his, he was gone, leaving Rotherby very hot and angry.

Outside Mr. Caryll hailed a chair, and had himself carried to his lodging in Old Palace Yard, where Leduc awaited him. As his bearers swung briskly along, Mr. Caryll sat back and gave himself up to thought.

Lord Ostermore interested him vastly. For a moment that day the earl had aroused his anger, as you may have judged from the sudden resolve upon which he had acted when he delivered him that letter, thus embarking at the eleventh hour upon a task which he had already determined to abandon. He knew not now whether to rejoice or deplore that he had acted upon that angry impulse. He knew not, indeed, whether to pity or despise this man who was swayed by no such high motives as must have affected most of those who were faithful to the exiled James. Those motives—motives of chivalry and romanticism in most cases—Lord Ostermore would have despised if he could have understood them; for he was a man of the type that despises all things that are not essentially practical, whose results are not immediately obvious. Being all but ruined by his association with the South Sea Company, he was willing for the sake of profit to turn traitor to the king de facto, even as thirty years ago, actuated by similar motives, he had turned traitor to the king de jure.

What was one to make of such a man, wondered Mr. Caryll. If he were equipped with wit enough to apprehend the baseness of his conduct, he would be easily understood and it would be easy to despise him. But Mr. Caryll perceived that he was dealing with one who never probed into the deeps of anything—himself and his own conduct least of all—and that a deplorable lack of perception, of understanding almost, deprived his lordship of the power to feel as most men feel, to judge as most men judge. And hence was it that Mr. Caryll thought him a subject for pity rather than contempt. Even in that other thirty-year-old matter that so closely touched Mr. Caryll, the latter was sure that the same pitiful shortcomings might be urged in the man's excuse.

64

Meanwhile, behind him at Stretton House, Mr. Caryll had left a scene of strife between Lady Ostermore and her son on one side and Lord Ostermore on the other. Weak and vacillating as he was in most things, it seemed that the earl could be strong in his dislike of his son, and firm in his determination not to condone the infamy of his behavior toward Hortensia Winthrop.

"The fault is yours," Rotherby sought to excuse himself again—employing the old argument, and in an angry, contemptuous tone that was entirely unfilial. "I'd ha' married the girl in earnest, but for your threats to disinherit me."

"You fool!" his father stormed at him, "did you suppose that if I should disinherit you for marrying her, I should be likely to do less for your luring her into a mock marriage? I've done with you! Go your ways for a damned profligate—a scandal to the very name of gentleman. I've done with you!"

And to that the earl adhered in spite of all that Rotherby and his mother could urge. He stamped out of the library with a final command to his son to quit his house and never disgrace it again by his presence. Rotherby looked ruefully at his mother.

"He means it,"' said he. "He never loved me. He was never a father to me."

"Were you ever greatly a son to him?" asked her ladyship.

"As much as he would ha' me be," he answered, his black face very sullen. "Oh, 'sdeath! I am damnably used by him." He paced the chamber, storming. "All this garboil about nothing!", he complained. "Was he never young himself? And when all is said, there's no harm done. The girl's been fetched home again."

"Pshaw! Ye're a fool, Rotherby—a fool, and there's an end on't," said his mother. "I sometimes wonder which is the greater fool—you or your father. And yet he can marvel that you are his son. What do ye think would have happened if you had had your way with that bread-and-butter miss? It had been matter enough to hang you."

"Pooh!" said the viscount, dropping into a chair and staring sullenly at the carpet. Then sullenly he added: "His lordship would have been glad on't—so some one would have been pleased. As it is—"

"As it is, ye'd better find the man Green who was at Maidstone, and stop his mouth with guineas. He is aware of what passed."

"Bah! Green was there on other business." And he told her of the suspicions the messenger entertained against Mr. Caryll.

It set her ladyship thinking. "Why," she said presently, "'twill be that!"

"'Twill be what, ma'am?" asked Rotherby, looking up.

"Why, this fellow Caryll must ha' bubbled the messenger in spite of the search he may have made. I found the popinjay here with your father, the pair as thick as thieves—and your father with a paper in his hand as fine as a cobweb. 'Sdeath! I'll be sworn he's a damned Jacobite."

Rotherby was on his feet in an instant. He remembered suddenly all that he had overheard at Maidstone. "Oho!" he crowed. "What cause have ye to think that?"

"Cause? Why, what I have seen. Besides, I feel it in my bones. My every instinct tells me 'tis so."

"If you should prove right! Oh, if you should prove right! Death! I'd find a way to settle the score of that pert fellow from France, and to dictate terms to his lordship at the same time."

Her ladyship stared at him. "Ye're an unnatural hound, Rotherby. Would ye betray your own father?"

"Betray him? No! But I'll set a term to his plotting. Egad! Has he not lost enough in the South Sea Bubble, without sinking the little that is left in some wild-goose Jacobite plot?"

"How shall it matter to you, since he's sworn to disinherit you?"

"How, madam?" Rotherby laughed cunningly. "I'll prevent the one and the other—and pay off Mr. Caryll at the same time. Three birds with one stone, let me perish!" He reached for his hat. "I must find this fellow Green."

"What will you do?" she asked, a slight anxiety trembling in her voice.

"Stir up his suspicions of Caryll. He'll be ready enough to act after his discomfiture at Maidstone. I'll warrant he's smarting under it. If once we can find cause to lay Caryll by the heels, the fear of the consequences should bring his lordship to his senses. 'Twill be my turn then."

"But you'll do nothing that—that will hurt your father?" she enjoined him, her hand upon his shoulder.

"Trust me," he laughed, and added cynically: "It would hardly sort with my interests to involve him. It will serve me best to frighten him into reason and a sense of his paternal duty."

CHAPTER IX

THE CHAMPION

Mr. Caryll was well and handsomely housed, as became the man of fashion, in the lodging he had taken in Old Palace Yard. Knowing him from abroad, it was not impossible that the government—fearful of sedition since the disturbance caused by the South Sea distress, and aware of an undercurrent of Jacobitism— might for a time, at least, keep an eye upon him. It behooved him, therefore, to appear neither more nor less than a lounger, a gentleman of pleasure who had come to London in quest of diversion. To support this appearance, Mr. Caryll had sought out some friends of his in town. There were Stapleton and Collis, who had been at Oxford with him, and with whom he had ever since maintained a correspondence and a friendship. He sought them out on the very evening of his arrival—after his interview with Lord Ostermore. He had the satisfaction of being handsomely welcomed by them, and was plunged under their guidance into the gaieties that the town afforded liberally for people of quality.

Mr. Caryll was—as I hope you have gathered—an agreeable fellow, very free, moreover, with the contents of his well-equipped purse; and so you may conceive that the town showed him a very friendly, cordial countenance. He fell into the habits of the men whose company he frequented; his days were as idle as theirs, and spent at the parade, the Ring, the play, the coffeehouse and the ordinary.

But under the gay exterior he affected he carried a spirit of most vile unrest. The anger which had prompted his impulse to execute, after all, the business on which he was come, and to deliver his father the letter that was to work his ruin, was all spent. He had cooled, and cool it was idle for him to tell himself that Lord Ostermore, by his heartless allusion to the crime of his early years, had proved himself worthy of nothing but the pit Mr. Caryll had been sent to dig for him. There were moments when he sought to compel himself so to think, to steel himself against all other considerations. But it was idle. The reflection that the task before him was unnatural came ever to revolt him. To gain ease, the most that he could do—and he had the faculty of it developed in a preternatural degree—was to put the business from him for the time, endeavor to forget it. And he had another matter to consider and to plague him—the matter of Hortensia Winthrop. He thought of her a great deal more than was good for his peace of mind, for all that he pretended to a gladness that things were as they were. Each morning that he lounged at the parade in St. James's Park, each evening that he visited the Ring, it was in the hope of catching some glimpse of her among the fashionable women that went abroad to see and to be seen. And on the third morning after his arrival the thing he hoped for came to pass.

It had happened that my lady had ordered her carriage that morning, dressed herself with the habitual splendor, which but set off the shortcomings of her lean and angular person, egregiously coiffed, pulvilled and topknotted, and she had sent a message amounting to a command to Mistress Winthrop that she should drive in the park with her.

Poor Hortensia, whose one desire was to hide her face from the town's uncharitable sight just then, fearing, indeed, that Rumor's unscrupulous tongue would be as busy about her reputation as her ladyship had represented, attempted to assert herself by refusing to obey the command. It was in vain. Her ladyship dispensed with ambassadors, and went in person to convey her orders to her husband's ward, and to enforce them.

"What's this I am told?" quoth she, as she sailed into Hortensia's room. "Do my wishes count for nothing, that you send me pert answers by my woman?"

Hortensia rose. She had been sitting by the window, a book in her lap. "Not so, indeed, madam. Not pert, I trust. I am none so well, and I fear the sun."

"'Tis little wonder," laughed her ladyship; "and I'm glad on't, for it shows ye have a conscience somewhere. But 'tis no matter for that. I am tender for your reputation, mistress, and I'll not have you shunning daylight like the guilty thing ye know yourself to be."

"'Tis false, madam," said Hortensia, with indignation. "Your ladyship knows it to be false."

"Harkee, ninny, if you'd have the town believe it false, you'll show yourself—show that ye have no cause for shame, no cause to hide you from the eyes of honest folk. Come, girl; bid your woman get your hood and tippet. The carriage stays for us."

To Hortensia her ladyship's seemed, after all, a good argument. Did she hide, what must the town think but that it confirmed the talk that she made no doubt was going round already. Better to go forth and brave it, and surely it should disarm the backbiters if she showed herself in the park with Lord Rotherby's own mother.

It never occurred to her that this seeming tenderness for her reputation might be but wanton cruelty on her ladyship's part; a gratifying of her spleen against the girl by setting her in the pillory of public sight to the end that she should experience the insult of supercilious glances and lips that smile with an ostentation of furtiveness; a desire to put down her pride and break the spirit which my lady accounted insolent and stubborn.

Suspecting naught of this, she consented, and drove out with her ladyship as she was desired to do. But understanding of her ladyship's cruel motives, and repentance of her own acquiescence, were not long in following. Soon—very soon—she realized that anything would have been better than the ordeal she was forced to undergo.

It was a warm, sunny morning, and the park was crowded with fashionable loungers. Lady Ostermore left her carriage at the gates, and entered the enclosure on foot, accompanied by Hortensia and followed at a respectful distance by a footman. Her arrival proved something of a sensation. Hats were swept off to her ladyship, sly glances flashed at her companion, who went pale, but apparently serene, eyes looking straight before her; and there was an obvious concealing of smiles at first, which later grew to be all unconcealed, and, later still, became supplemented by remarks that all might hear, remarks which did not escape—as they were meant not to escape—her ladyship and Mistress Winthrop.

"Madam," murmured the girl, in her agony of shame, "we were not well-advised to come. Will not your ladyship turn back?"

Her ladyship displayed a vinegary smile, and looked at her companion over the top of her slowly moving fan. "Why? Is't not pleasant here?" quoth she. "'Twill be more agreeable under the trees yonder. The sun will not reach you there, child."

"'Tis not the sun I mind, madam," said Hortensia, but received no answer. Perforce she must pace on beside her ladyship.

Lord Rotherby came by, arm in arm with his friend, the Duke of Wharton. It was a one-sided friendship. Lord Rotherby was but one of the many of his type who furnished a court, a valetaille, to the gay, dissolute, handsome, witty duke, who might have been great had he not preferred his vices to his worthier parts.

As they went by, Lord Rotherby bared his head and bowed, as did his companion. Her ladyship smiled upon him, but Hortensia's eyes looked rigidly ahead, her face a stone. She heard his grace's insolent laugh as they passed on; she heard his voice—nowise subdued, for he was a man who loved to let the world hear what he might have to say.

"Gad! Rotherby, the wind has changed! Your Dulcinea flies with you o' Wednesday, and has ne'er a glance for you o' Saturday! I' faith! ye deserve no better. Art a clumsy gallant to have been overtaken, and the maid's in the right on't to resent your clumsiness."

Rotherby's reply was lost in a splutter of laughter from a group of sycophants who had overheard his grace's criticism and were but too ready to laugh at aught his grace might deign to utter. Her cheeks burned; it was by an effort that she suppressed the tears that anger was forcing to her eyes.

The duke, 'twas plain, had set the fashion. Emulators were not wanting. Stray words she caught; by instinct was she conscious of the oglings, the fluttering of fans from the women, the flashing of quizzing-glasses from the men. And everywhere was there a suppressed laugh, a stifled exclamation of surprise at her appearance in public—yet not so stifled but that it reached her, as it was intended that it should.

In the shadow of a great elm, around which there was a seat, a little group had gathered, of which the centre was the sometime toast of the town and queen of many Wells, the Lady Mary Deller, still beautiful and still unwed—as is so often the way of reigning toasts—but already past her pristine freshness, already leaning upon the support of art to maintain the endowments she had had from nature. She was accounted witty by the witless, and by some others.

Of the group that paid its court to her and her companions— two giggling cousins in their first season were Mr. Caryll and his friends, Sir Harry Collis and Mr. Edward Stapleton, the former of whom—he was the lady's brother-in-law—had just presented him. Mr. Caryll was dressed with even more than his ordinary magnificence. He was in dove-colored cloth, his coat very richly laced with gold, his waistcoat—of white brocade with jeweled buttons, the flower-pattern outlined in finest gold thread— descended midway to his knees, whilst the ruffles at his wrists and the Steinkirk at his throat were of the finest point. He cut a figure of supremest elegance, as he stood there, his chestnut head slightly bowed in deference as my Lady Mary spoke, his hat tucked under his arm, his right hand outstretched beside him to rest upon the gold head of his clouded-amber cane.

To the general he was a stranger still in town, and of the sort that draws the eye and provokes inquiry. Lady Mary, the only goal of whose shallow existence was the attention of the sterner sex, who loved to break hearts as a child breaks toys, for the fun of seeing how they look when broken—and who, because of that, had succeeded in breaking far fewer than she fondly imagined—looked up into his face with the "most perditiously alluring" eyes in England—so Mr. Craske, the poet, who stood at her elbow now, had described them in the dedicatory sonnet of his last book of poems.

(Wherefore, in parenthesis be it observed, she had rewarded him with twenty guineas, as he had calculated that she would.)

There was a sudden stir in the group. Mr. Craske had caught sight of Lady Ostermore and Mistress Winthrop, and he fell to giggling, a flimsy handkerchief to his painted lips. "Oh, 'Sbud!" he bleated. "Let me die! The audaciousness of the creature! And behold me the port and glance of her! Cold as a vestal, let me perish!"

Lady Mary turned with the others to look in the direction he was pointing—pointing openly, with no thought of dissembling.

Mr. Caryll's eyes fell upon Mistress Winthrop, and his glance was oddly perceptive. He observed those matters of which Mr. Craske had seemed to make sardonic comment: the erect stiffness of her carriage, the eyes that looked neither to right nor left, and the pallor of her face. He observed, too, the complacent air with which her ladyship advanced beside her husband's ward, her fan moving languidly, her head nodding to her acquaintance, as in supreme unconcern of the stir her coming had effected.

Mr. Caryll had been dull indeed, knowing what he knew, had he not understood to the full the humiliation to which Mistress Hortensia was being of purpose set submitted.

And just then Rotherby, who had turned, with Wharton and another now, came by them again. This time he halted, and his companions with him, for just a moment, to address his mother. She turned; there was an exchange of greetings, in which Mistress Hortensia standing rigid as stone—took no part. A silence fell about; quizzing-glasses went up; all eyes were focussed upon the group. Then Rotherby and his friends resumed their way.

"The dog!" said Mr. Caryll, between his teeth, but went unheard by any, for in that moment Dorothy Deller—the younger of the Lady Mary's cousins—gave expression to the generous and as yet unsullied little heart that was her own.

"Oh, 'tis shameful!" she cried. "Will you not go speak with her, Molly?"

The Lady Mary stiffened. She looked at the company about her with an apologetic smile. "I beg that ye'll not heed the child," said she. "'Tis not that she is without morals—but without knowledge. An innocent little fool; no worse."

"'Tis bad enough, I vow," laughed an old beau, who sought fame as a man of a cynical turn of humor.

"But fortunately rare," said Mr. Caryll dryly. "Like charity, almost unknown in this Babylon."

His tone was not quite nice, although perhaps the Lady Mary was the only one to perceive the note of challenge in it. But Mr. Craske, the poet, diverted attention to himself by a prolonged,

71

malicious chuckle. Rotherby was just moving away from his mother at that moment.

"They've never a word for each other to-day!" he cried. "Oh, 'Sbud! not so much as the mercy of a glance will the lady afford him." And he burst into the ballad of King Francis:

> *"Souvent femme varie,*
> *Bien, fol est qui s'y fie!"*

and laughed his prodigious delight at the aptness of his quotation.

Mr. Caryll put up his gold-rimmed quizzing-glass, and directed through that powerful weapon of offence an eye of supreme displeasure upon the singer. He could not contain his rage, yet from his languid tone none would have suspected it. "Sir," said he, "ye've a singular unpleasant voice."

Mr. Craske, thrown out of countenance by so much directness, could only stare; the same did the others, though some few tittered, for Mr. Craske, when all was said, was held in no great esteem by the discriminant.

Mr. Caryll lowered his glass. "I've heard it said by the uncharitable that ye were a lackey before ye became a plagiarist. 'Tis a rumor I shall contradict in future; 'tis plainly a lie, for your voice betrays you to have been a chairman."

"Sir—sir—" spluttered the poetaster, crimson with anger and mortification. "Is this—is this—seemly—between gentlemen?"

"Between gentlemen it would not be seemly," Mr. Caryll agreed.

Mr. Craske, quivering, yet controlling himself, bowed stiffly. "I have too much respect for myself—" he gasped.

"Ye'll be singular in that, no doubt," said Mr. Caryll, and turned his shoulder upon him.

Again Mr. Craske appeared to make an effort at self-control; again he bowed. "I know—I hope—what is due to the Lady Mary Deller, to—to answer you as—as befits. But you shall hear from me, sir. You shall hear from me."

He bowed a third time—a bow that took in the entire company—and withdrew in high dudgeon and with a great show of dignity. A pause ensued, and then the Lady Mary reproved Mr. Caryll.

"Oh, 'twas cruel in you, sir," she cried. "Poor Mr. Craske! And to dub him plagiarist! 'Twas the unkindest cut of all!"

"Truth, madam, is never kind."

"Oh, fie! You make bad worse!" she cried.

"He'll put you in the pillory of his verse for this," laughed Collis. "Ye'll be most scurvily lampooned for't."

"Poor Mr. Craske!" sighed the Lady Mary again.

"Poor, indeed; but not in the sense to deserve pity. An upstart impostor such as that to soil a lady with his criticism!"

Lady Mary's brows went up. "You use a singular severity, sir," she opined, "and I think it unwise in you to grow so hot in the defence of a reputation whose owner has so little care for it herself."

Mr. Caryll looked at her out of his level gray-green eyes; a hot answer quivered on his tongue, an answer that had crushed her venom for some time and had probably left him with a quarrel on his hands. Yet his smile, as he considered her, was very sweet, so sweet that her ladyship, guessing nothing of the bitterness it was used to cover, went as near a smirk as it was possible for one so elegant. He was, she judged, another victim ripe for immolation on the altar of her goddessship. And Mr. Caryll, who had taken her measure very thoroughly, seeing something of how her thoughts were running, bethought him of a sweeter vengeance.

"Lady Mary," he cried, a soft reproach in his voice, "I have been sore mistook in you if you are one to be guided by the rabble." And he waved a hand toward the modish throng.

She knit her fine brows, bewildered.

"Ah!" he cried, interpreting her glance to suit his ends, "perish the thought, indeed! I knew that I could not be wrong. I knew that one so peerless in all else must be peerless, too, in her opinions; judging for herself, and standing firm upon her judgment in disdain of meaner souls—mere sheep to follow their bell-wether."

She opened her mouth to speak, but said nothing, being too intrigued by this sudden and most sweet flattery. Her mere beauty had oft been praised, and in terms that glowed like fire. But what was that compared with this fine appreciation of her less obvious mental parts—and that from one who had seen the world?

Mr. Caryll was bending over her. "What a chance is here," he was murmuring, "to mark your lofty detachment—to show how utter is your indifference to what the common herd may think."

"As—as how?" she asked, blinking up at him.

The others stood at gaze, scarce yet suspecting the drift of so much talk.

"There is a poor lady yonder, of whose fair name a bubble is being blown and pricked. I dare swear there's not a woman here durst speak to her. Yet what a chance for one that dared! How fine a triumph would be hers!" He sighed. "Heigho! I almost wish I were a woman, that I might make that triumph mine and mark my superiority to these painted dolls that have neither wit nor courage."

73

The Lady Mary rose, a faint color in her cheeks, a sparkle in her fine eyes. A great joy flashed into Mr. Caryll's in quick response; a joy in her—she thought with ready vanity—and a heightening admiration.

"Will you make it yours, as it should be—as it must ever be—to lead and not to follow?" he cried, flattering incredibility trembling in his voice.

"And why not, sir?" she demanded, now thoroughly aroused.

"Why not, indeed—since you are you?" quoth he. "It is what I had hoped in you, and yet—and yet what I had almost feared to hope."

She frowned upon him now, so excellently had he done his work. "Why should you have feared that?"

"Alas! I am a man of little faith—unworthy, indeed, your good opinion since I entertained a doubt. It was a blasphemy."

She smiled again. "You acknowledge your faults with such a grace," said she, "that we must needs forgive them. And now to show you how much you need forgiveness. Come, children," she bade her cousins—for whose innocence she had made apology but a moment back. "Your arm, Harry," she begged her brother-in-law.

Sir Harry obeyed her readily, but without eagerness. In his heart he cursed his friend Caryll for having set her on to this.

Mr. Caryll himself hung upon her other side, his eyes toward Lady Ostermore and Hortensia, who, whilst being observed by all, were being approached by few; and these few confined themselves to an exchange of greetings with her ladyship, which constituted a worse offence to Mistress Winthrop than had they stayed away.

Suddenly, as if drawn by his ardent gaze, Hortensia's eyes moved at last from their forward fixity. Her glance met Mr. Caryll's across the intervening space. Instantly he swept off his hat, and bowed profoundly. The action drew attention to himself. All eyes were focussed upon him, and between many a pair there was a frown for one who should dare thus to run counter to the general attitude.

But there was more to follow. The Lady Mary accepted Mr. Caryll's salutation of Hortensia as a signal. She led the way promptly, and the little band swept forward, straight for its goal, raked by the volleys from a thousand eyes, under which the Lady Mary already began to giggle excitedly.

Thus they reached the countess, the countess standing very rigid in her amazement, to receive them.

"I hope I see your ladyship well," said Lady Mary.

"I hope your ladyship does," answered the countess tartly.

Mistress Winthrop's eyes were lowered; her cheeks were

scarlet. Her distress was plain, born of her doubt of the Lady Mary's purpose, and suspense as to what might follow.

"I have not the honor of your ward's acquaintance, Lady Ostermore," said Lady Mary, whilst the men were bowing, and her cousins curtseying to the countess and her companion collectively.

The countess gasped, recovered, and eyed the speaker without any sign of affection. "My husband's ward, ma'am," she corrected, in a voice that seemed to discourage further mention of Hortensia.

"'Tis but a distinction," put in Mr. Caryll suggestively.

"Indeed, yes. Will not your ladyship present me?" The countess' malevolent eyes turned a moment upon Mr. Caryll, smiling demurely at Lady Mary's elbow. In his face—as well as in the four words he had uttered—she saw that here was work of his, and he gained nothing in her favor by it. Meanwhile there were no grounds—other than such as must have been wantonly offensive to the Lady Mary, and so not to be dreamed of—upon which to refuse her request. The countess braced herself, and with an ill grace performed the brief ceremony of presentation.

Mistress Winthrop looked up an instant, then down again; it was a piteous, almost a pleading glance.

Lady Mary, leaving the countess to Sir Harry Stapleton, Caryll and the others, moved to Hortensia's side for a moment she was at loss what to say, and took refuge in a commonplace.

"I have long desired the pleasure of your acquaintance," said she.

"I am honored, madam," replied Hortensia, with downcast eyes. Then lifting them with almost disconcerting suddenness. "Your ladyship has chosen an odd season in which to gratify this desire with which you honor me."

Lady Mary laughed, as much at the remark as for the benefit of those whose eyes were upon her. She knew there would not be wanting many who would condemn her; but these should be far outnumbered by those who would be lost in admiration of her daring, that she could so fly in the face of public opinion; and she was grateful to Mr. Caryll for having suggested to her a course of such distinction.

"I could have chosen no better season," she replied, "to mark my scorn of evil tongues and backbiters."

Color stained Hortensia's cheek again; gratitude glowed in her eyes. "You are very noble, madam," she answered with flattering earnestness.

"La!" said the Lady Mary. "Is nobility, then, so easily achieved?" And thereafter they talked of inconsequent trifles, until

Mr. Caryll moved towards them, and Lady Mary turned aside to speak to the countess.

At Mr. Caryll's approach Hortensia's eyes had been lowered again, and she made no offer to address him as he stood before her now, hat under arm, leaning easily upon his amber cane.

"Oh, heart of stone!" said he at last. "Am I not yet forgiven?"

She misread his meaning—perhaps already the suspicion she now voiced had been in her mind. She looked up at him sharply. "Was it—was it you who fetched the Lady Mary to me?" she inquired.

"Lo!" said he. "You have a voice! Now Heaven be praised! I was fearing it was lost for me—that you had made some awful vow never again to rejoice my ears with the music of it."

"You have not answered my question," she reminded him.

"Nor you mine," said he. "I asked you am I not yet forgiven."

"Forgiven what?"

"For being born an impudent, fleering coxcomb—twas that you called me, I think."

She flushed deeply. "If you would win forgiveness, you should not remind me of the offence," she answered low.

"Nay," he rejoined, "that is to confound forgiveness with forgetfulness. I want you to forgive and yet to remember."

"That were to condone."

"What else? 'Tis nothing less will satisfy me."

"You expect too much," she answered, with a touch that was almost of sternness.

He shrugged and smiled whimsically. "It is my way," he said apologetically. "Nature has made me expectant, and life, whilst showing me the folly of it, has not yet cured me."

She looked at him, and repeated her earlier question. "Was it at your bidding that Lady Mary came to speak with me?"

"Fie!" he cried. "What insinuations do you make against her?"

"Insinuations?"

"What else? That she should do things at my bidding!"

She smiled understanding. "You have a talent, sir, for crooked answers."

"'Tis to conceal the rectitude of my behavior."

"It fails of its object, then," said she, "for it deludes no one." She paused and laughed at his look of assumed blankness. "I am deeply beholden to you," she whispered quickly, breathing at once gratitude and confusion.

"Though I don't descry the cause," said he, "'twill be something to comfort me."

More he might have added then, for the mad mood was upon

76

him, awakened by those soft brown eyes of hers. But in that moment the others of that little party crowded upon them to take their leave of Mistress Winthrop.

Mr. Caryll felt satisfied that enough had been done to curb the slander concerning Hortensia. But he was not long in learning how profound was his mistake. On every side he continued to hear her discussed, and in such terms as made his ears tingle and his hands itch to be at work in her defence; for, with smirks and sneers and innuendoes, her escapade with Lord Rotherby continued to furnish a topic for the town as her ladyship had sworn it would. Yet by what right could he espouse her cause with any one of her defamers without bringing her fair name into still more odious notoriety?

And meanwhile he knew that he was under strict surveillance from Mr. Green; knew that he was watched wherever he went; and nothing but his confidence that no evidence could be produced against him allowed him to remain, as he did, all unconcerned of this.

Leduc had more than once seen Mr. Green about Old Palace Yard, besides a couple of his underlings, one or the other of whom was never absent from the place, no doubt with intent to observe who came and went at Mr. Caryll's. Once, indeed, during the absence of master and servant, Mr. Caryll's lodging was broken into, and on Leduc's return he found a confusion which told him how thoroughly the place had been ransacked.

If Mr. Caryll had had anything to hide, this would have given him the hint to take his precautions; but as he had nothing that was in the least degree in incriminating, he went his ways in supremest unconcern of the vigilance exerted over him. He used, however, a greater discretion in the resorts he frequented. And if upon occasion he visited such Tory meeting-places as the Bell Tavern in King Street or the Cocoa-Tree in Pall Mall, he was still more often to be found at White's, that ultra-Whig resort.

It was at this latter house, one evening three or four days after his meeting with Hortensia in the park, that the chance was afforded him at last of vindicating her honor in a manner that need not add to the scandal that was already abroad, nor serve to couple his name with hers unduly. And it was Lord Rotherby himself who afforded him the opportunity.

The thing fell out in this wise: Mr. Caryll was at cards with Harry Collis and Stapleton and Major Gascoigne, in a room above-stairs. There were at least a dozen others present, some also at play, others merely lounging. Of the latter was his Grace of Wharton. He was a slender, graceful gentleman, whose face, if slightly effeminate and markedly dissipated, was nevertheless of considerable beauty.

He was very splendid in a suit of green camlett and silver lace, and he wore a flaxen periwig without powder.

He was awaiting Rotherby, with whom—as he told the company—he was for a frolic at Drury Lane, where a ridotto was following the play. He spoke, as usual, in a loud voice that all might hear, and his talk was loose and heavily salted as became the talk of a rake of his exalted rank. It was chiefly concerned with airing his bitter grievance against Mrs. Girdlebank, of the Theatre Royal, of whom he announced himself "devilishly enamoured."

He inveighed against her that she should have the gross vulgarity to love her husband, and against her husband that he should have the audacity to play the watchdog over her, and bark and growl at the duke's approach.

"A plague on all husbands, say I," ended the worthy president of the Bold Bucks.

"Nay, now, but I'm a husband myself, gad!" protested Mr. Sidney, who was quite the most delicate, mincing man of fashion about town, and one of that valetaille that hovered about his Grace of Wharton's heels.

"'Tis no matter in your case," said the duke, with that contempt he used towards his followers. "Your wife's too ugly to be looked at." And Mr. Sidney's fresh protest was drowned in the roar of laughter that went up to applaud that brutal frankness. Mr. Caryll turned to the fop, who happened to be standing at his elbow.

"Never repine, man," said he. "In the company you keep, such a wife makes for peace of mind. To have that is to have much."

Wharton resumed his railings at the Girdlebanks, and was still at them when Rotherby came in.

"At last, Charles!" the duke hailed him, rising. "Another minute, and I had gone without you."

But Rotherby scarce looked at him, and answered with unwonted shortness. His eyes had discovered Mr. Caryll. It was the first time he had run against him since that day, over a week ago, at Stretton House, and at sight of him now all Rotherby's spleen was moved. He stood and stared, his dark eyes narrowing, his cheeks flushing slightly under their tan. Wharton, who had approached him, observing his sudden halt, his sudden look of concentration, asked him shortly what might ail him.

"I have seen someone I did not expect to find in a resort of gentlemen," said Rotherby, his eyes ever on Mr. Caryll, who—engrossed in his game—was all unconscious of his lordship's advent.

Wharton followed the direction of his companion's gaze, and giving now attention himself to Mr. Caryll, he fell to appraising his genteel appearance, negligent of the insinuation in what Rotherby had said.

"'Sdeath!" swore the duke. "'Tis a man of taste—a travelled gentleman by his air. Behold me the grace of that shoulder-knot, Charles, and the set of that most admirable coat. Fifty guineas wouldn't buy his Steinkirk. Who is this beau?"

"I'll present him to your grace," said Rotherby shortly. He had pretentions at being a beau himself; but his grace—supreme arbiter in such matters—had never yet remarked it.

They moved across the room, greetings passing as they went. At their approach, Mr. Caryll looked up. Rotherby made him a leg with an excessive show of deference, arguing irony. "'Tis an unlooked-for pleasure to meet you here, sir," said he in a tone that drew the attention of all present.

"No pleasures are so sweet as the unexpected," answered Mr. Caryll, with casual amiability, and since he perceived at once the errand upon which Lord Rotherby was come to him, he went half-way to meet him. "Has your lordship been contracting any marriages of late?" he inquired.

The viscount smiled icily. "You have quick wits, sir," said he, "which is as it should be in one who lives by them."

"Let your lordship be thankful that such is not your own case," returned Mr. Caryll, with imperturbable good humor, and sent a titter round the room.

"A hit! A shrewd hit, 'pon honor!" cried Wharton, tapping his snuff-box. "I vow to Gad, Ye're undone, Charles. Ye'd better play at repartee with Gascoigne, there. Ye're more of a weight."

"Your grace," cried Rotherby, suppressing at great cost his passion, "'tis not to be borne that a fellow of this condition should sit among men of quality." And with that he swung round and addressed the company in general. "Gentlemen, do you know who this fellow is? He has the effrontery to take my name, and call himself Caryll."

Mr. Caryll looked a moment at his brother in the silence that followed. Then, as in a flash, he saw his chance of vindicating Mistress Winthrop, and he seized it.

"And do you know, gentlemen, who this fellow is?" he inquired, with an air of sly amusement. "He is—Nay, you shall judge for yourselves. You shall hear the story of how we met; it is the story of his abduction of a lady whose name need not be mentioned; the story of his dastardly attempt to cozen her into a mock-marriage."

"Mock—mock-marriage?" cried the duke and a dozen others with him, some in surprise, but most in an unbelief that was already faintly tinged with horror—which argued ill for my Lord Rotherby when the story should be told.

"You damned rogue—" began his lordship, and would have flung himself upon Caryll, but that Collis and Stapleton, and Wharton himself, put forth hands to stay him by main force.

Others, too, had risen. But Mr. Caryll sat quietly in his chair, idly fingering the cards before him, and smiling gently, between amusement and irony. He was much mistaken if he did not make Lord Rotherby bitterly regret the initiative he had taken in their quarrel.

"Gently, my lord," the duke admonished the viscount. "This—this gentleman has said that which touches your honor. He shall say more. He shall make good his words, or eat them. But the matter cannot rest thus."

"It shall not, by God!" swore Rotherby, purple now. "It shall not. I'll kill him like a dog for what he has said."

"But before I die, gentlemen," said Mr. Caryll, "it were well that you should have the full story of that sorry adventure from an eye-witness."

"An eye-witness? Were ye present?" cried two or three in a breath.

"I desire to lay before you all the story of how we met my lord there and I. It is so closely enmeshed with the story of that abduction and mock-marriage that the one is scarce to be distinguished from the other."

Rotherby writhed to shake off those who held him.

"Will ye listen to this fellow?" he roared. "He's a spy, I tell you—a Jacobite spy!" He was beside himself with anger and apprehension, and he never paused to weigh the words he uttered. It was with him a question of stopping his accuser's mouth with whatever mud came under his hands. "He has no right here. It is not to be borne. I know not by what means he has thrust himself among you, but—"

"That is a knowledge I can afford your lordship," came Stapleton's steady voice to interrupt the speaker. "Mr. Caryll is here by my invitation."

"And by mine and Gascoigne's here," added Sir Harry Collis, "and I will answer for his quality to any man who doubts it."

Rotherby glared at Mr. Caryll's sponsors, struck dumb by this sudden and unexpected refutation of the charge he had leveled.

Wharton, who had stepped aside, knit his brows and flashed his quizzing-glass—through sheer force of habit—upon Lord Rotherby. Then:

"You'll pardon me, Harry," said he, "but you'll see, I hope, that

80

the question is not impertinent; that I put it to the end that we may clearly know with whom we have to deal and what consideration to extend him, what credit to attach to the communication he is to make us touching my lord here. Under what circumstances did you become acquainted with Mr. Caryll?"

"I have known him these twelve years," answered Collis promptly; "so has Stapleton, so has Gascoigne, so have a dozen other gentlemen who could be produced, and who, like ourselves, were at Oxford with him. For myself and Stapleton, I can say that our acquaintance—indeed, I should say our friendship—with Mr. Caryll has been continuous since then, and that we have visited him on several occasions at his estate of Maligny in Normandy. That he habitually inhabits the country of his birth is the reason why Mr. Caryll has not hitherto had the advantage of your grace's acquaintance. Need I say more to efface the false statement made by my Lord Rotherby?"

"False? Do you dare give me the lie, sir?" roared Rotherby.

But the duke soothed him. Under his profligate exterior his Grace of Wharton concealed—indeed, wasted—a deal of shrewdness, ability and inherent strength. "One thing at a time, my lord," said the president of the Bold Bucks. "Let us attend to the matter of Mr. Caryll."

"Dons and the devil! Does your grace take sides with him?"

"I take no sides. But I owe it to myself—we all owe it to ourselves—that this matter should be cleared."

Rotherby leered at him, his lip trembling with anger. "Does the president of the Bold Bucks pretend to administrate a court of honor?" he sneered heavily.

"Your lordship will gain little by this," Wharton admonished him, so coldly that Rotherby belatedly came to some portion of his senses again. The duke turned to Caryll. "Mr. Caryll," said he, "Sir Harry has given you very handsome credentials, which would seem to prove you worthy the hospitality of White's. You have, however, permitted yourself certain expressions concerning his lordship here, which we cannot allow to remain where you have left them. You must retract, sir, or make them good." His gravity, and the preciseness of his diction now, sorted most oddly with his foppish airs.

Mr. Caryll closed his snuff-box with a snap. A hush fell instantly upon the company, which by now was all crowding about the little table at which sat Mr. Caryll and his three friends. A footman who entered at the moment to snuff the candles and see what the gentlemen might be requiring, was dismissed the room. When the door had closed, Mr. Caryll began to speak.

81

One more attempt was made by Rotherby to interfere, but this attempt was disposed of by Wharton, who had constituted himself entirely master of the proceedings.

"If you will not allow Mr. Caryll to speak, we shall infer that you fear what he may have to say; you will compel us to hear him in your absence, and I cannot think that you would prefer that, my lord."

My lord fell silent. He was breathing heavily, and his face was pale, his eyes angry beyond words, what time Mr. Caryll, in amiable, musical voice, with its precise and at moments slightly foreign enunciation, unfolded the shameful story of the affair at the "Adam and Eve," at Maidstone. He told a plain, straightforward tale, making little attempt to reproduce any of its color, giving his audience purely and simply the facts that had taken place. He told how he himself had been chosen as a witness when my lord had heard that there was a traveller from France in the house, and showed how that slight circumstance had first awakened his suspicions of foul play. He provoked some amusement when he dealt with his detection and exposure of the sham parson. But in the main he was heard with a stern and ominous attention—ominous for Lord Rotherby.

Rakes these men admittedly were with but few exceptions. No ordinary tale of gallantry could have shocked them, or provoked them to aught but a contemptuous mirth at the expense of the victim, male or female. They would have thought little the worse of a man for running off with the wife, say, of one of his acquaintance; they would have thought nothing of his running off with a sister or a daughter—so long as it was not of their own. All these were fair game, and if the husband, father or brother could not protect the wife, sister or daughter that was his, the more shame to him. But though they might be fair game, the game had its rules—anomalous as it may seem. These rules Lord Rotherby—if the tale Mr. Caryll told was true—had violated. He had practiced a cheat, the more dastardly because the poor lady who had so narrowly escaped being his victim had nether father nor brother to avenge her. And in every eye that was upon him Lord Rotherby might have read, had he had the wit to do so, the very sternest condemnation.

"A pretty story, as I've a soul!" was his grace's comment, when Mr. Caryll had done. "A pretty story, my Lord Rotherby. I have a stomach for strong meat myself. But—odds my life!—this is too nauseous!"

Rotherby glared at him. "'Slife! your grace is grown very nice on a sudden!" he sneered. "The president of the Bold Bucks, the master of the Hell Fire Club, is most oddly squeamish where the diversions of another are concerned."

"Diversions?" said his grace, his eyebrows raised until they all but vanished under the golden curls of his peruke. "Diversions? Ha! I observe that you make no attempt to deny the story. You admit it, then?"

There was a stir in the group, a drawing back from his lordship. He observed it, trembling between chagrin and rage. "What's here?" he cried, and laughed contemptuously. "Oh, ah! You'll follow where his grace leads you! Ye've followed him so long in lewdness that now yell follow him in conversion! But as for you, sir," and he swung fiercely upon Caryll, "you and your precious story—will you maintain it sword in hand?"

"I can do better," answered Mr. Caryll, "if any doubts my word."

"As how?"

"I can prove it categorically, by witnesses."

"Well said, Caryll," Stapleton approved him.

"And if I say that you lie—you and your witnesses?"

"'T is you will be liar," said Mr. Caryll.

"Besides, it is a little late for that," cut in the duke.

"Your grace," cried Rotherby, "is this affair yours?"

"No, I thank Heaven!" said his grace, and sat down.

Rotherby scowled at the man who until ten minutes ago had been his friend and boon companion, and there was more of contempt than anger in his eyes. He turned again to Mr. Caryll, who was watching him with a gleam of amusement—that infernally irritating amusement of his—in his gray-green eyes.

"Well?" he demanded foolishly, "have you naught to say?"

"I had thought," returned Mr. Caryll, "that I had said enough." And the duke laughed aloud.

Rotherby's lip was curled. "Ha! You don't think, now, that you may have said too much?"

Mr. Caryll stifled a yawn. "Do you?" he inquired blandly.

"Ay, by God! Too much for a gentleman to leave unpunished."

"Possibly. But what gentleman is concerned in this?"

"I am!" thundered Rotherby.

"I see. And how do you conceive that you answer the description?"

Rotherby swore at him with great choice and variety. "You shall learn," he promised him. "My friends shall wait on you to-night."

"I wonder who will carry his message?" ventured Collis to the ceiling. Rotherby turned on him, fierce as a rat. "It is a matter you may discover to your cost, Sir Harry," he snarled.

"I think," put in his grace very languidly, "that you are troubling the harmony that is wont to reign here."

His lordship stood still a moment. Then, quite suddenly, he snatched up a candlestick to hurl at Mr. Caryll. But he had it wrenched from his hands ere he could launch it.

He stood a moment, discomfited, glowering upon his brother. "My friends shall wait on you to-night," he repeated.

"You said so before," Mr. Caryll replied wearily. "I shall endeavor to make them welcome."

His lordship nodded stupidly, and strode to the door. His departure was observed in silence. On every face he read his sentence. These men—rakes though they were, professedly—would own him no more for their associate; and what these men thought to-night not a gentleman in town but would be thinking the same tomorrow. He had the stupidity to lay it all to the score of Mr. Caryll, not perceiving that he had brought it upon himself by his own aggressiveness. He paused, his hand upon the doorknob, and turned to loose a last shaft at them.

"As for you others, that follow your bell-wether there," and he indicated his grace, whose shoulder was towards him, "this matter ends not here."

And with that general threat he passed out, and that snug room at White's knew him no more.

Major Gascoigne was gathering up the cards that had been flung down when first the storm arose. Mr. Caryll bent to assist him. And the last voice Lord Rotherby heard as he departed was Mr. Caryll's, and the words it uttered were: "Come, Ned; the deal is with you."

His lordship swore through his teeth, and went downstairs heavily.

CHAPTER X

SPURS TO THE RELUCTANT

Before Mr. Caryll left White's—which he did at a comparatively early hour, that he might be at home to receive Lord Rotherby's friends—not a man present but had offered him his services in the affair he had upon his hands. Wharton, indeed, was not to be denied for one; and for the other Mr. Caryll desired Gascoigne to do him the honor of representing him.

It was a fine, dry night, and feeling the need for exercise, Mr. Caryll set out to walk the short distance from St. James's Street to his lodging, with a link-boy, preceding him, for only attendant. Arrived home, he was met by Leduc with the information that Sir Richard Everard was awaiting him. He went in, and the next moment he was in the arms of his adoptive father.

Greetings and minor courtesies disposed of, Sir Richard came straight to the affair which he had at heart. "Well? How speeds the matter?"

Mr. Caryll's face became overcast. He sat down, a thought wearily.

"So far as Lord Ostermore is concerned, it speeds—as you would wish it. So far as I am concerned"—he paused and sighed—"I would that it sped not at all, or that I was out of it."

Sir Richard looked at him with searching eyes. "How?" he asked. "What would you have me understand?"

"That in spite of all that has been said between us, in spite of all the arguments you have employed, and with which once, for a little while, you convinced me, this task is loathsome to me in the last degree. Ostermore is my father, and I can't forget it."

"And your mother?" Sir Richard's tone was sad, rather than indignant; it spoke of a bitter disappointment, not at the events, but at this man whom he loved with all a father's love.

"It were idle to go over it all again. I know everything that you would—that you could—say. I have said it all to myself again and again, in a vain endeavor to steel myself to the business to which you plighted me. Had Ostermore been different, perhaps it had been easier. I cannot say. As it is, I see in him a weakling, a man of inferior intellect, who does not judge things as you and I judge them, whose life cannot have been guided by the rules that serve for men of stronger purpose."

"You find excuses for him? For his deed?" cried Sir Richard, and his voice was full of horror now; he stared askance at his adoptive son.

"No, no! Oh, I don't know. On my soul and conscience, I don't know!" cried Mr. Caryll, like one in pain. He rose and moved restlessly about the room. "No," he pursued more calmly, "I don't excuse him. I blame him—more bitterly than you can think; perhaps more bitterly even than do you, for I have had a look into his mind and see the exact place held there by my mother's memory. I can judge and condemn him; but I can't execute him; I can't betray him. I don't think I could do it even if he were not my father."

He paused, and leaning his hands upon the table at which Sir Richard sat, he faced him, and spoke in a voice of earnest pleading. "Sir Richard, this was not the task to give me; or, if you had planned to give it me, you should have reared me differently; you should not have sought to make of me a gentleman. You have brought me up to principles of honor, and you ask me now to outrage them, to cast them off, and to become a very Judas. Is't wonderful I should rebel?"

They were hurtful words to Sir Richard—the poor fanatic whose mind was all unsound on this one point, who had lived in contemplation of his vengeance as a fasting monk lives through Lent in contemplation of the Easter plenty. The lines of sorrow deepened in his face.

"Justin," he said slowly, "you forget one thing. Honor is to be used with men of honor; but he who allows his honor to stand a barrier between himself and the man who has wronged him by dishonor, is no better than a fool. You speak of yourself; you think of yourself. And what of me, Justin? The things you say of yourself apply in a like degree—nay, even more—to me."

"Ah, but you are not his son. Oh, believe me, I speak not hastily or lightly. I have been torn this way and that in these past days, until at moments the burden has been heavier than I could bear. Once, for a little while, I thought I could do all and more than you expect of me—the moment, indeed, in which I took the first step, and delivered him the letter. But it was a moment of wild heat. I cooled, and reflection followed, and since then, because so much was done, I have not known an instant's peace of mind; I have endeavored to forget the position in which I am placed; but I have failed. I cannot. And if I go through with this thing, I shall not know another hour in life that is not poisoned by remorse."

"Remorse?" echoed Sir Richard, between consternation and anger. "Remorse?" He laughed bitterly. "What ails thee, boy? Do you pretend that Lord Ostermore should go unpunished? Do you go so far as that?"

"Not so. He has made others suffer, and it is just—as we understand justice—that he should suffer in his turn. Though, when all is said, he is but a poor egotist, too dull-witted to understand the full vileness of his sin. He is suffering, as it is—cursed in his son; for 'the father of a fool hath no joy.' He hates this son of his, and his son despises him. His wife is a shrew, a termagant, who embitters every hour of his existence. Thus he drags out his life, unloving and unloved, a thing to evoke pity."

"Pity?" cried Sir Richard in a voice of thunder. "Pity? Ha! As I've a soul, Justin, he shall be more pitiful yet ere I have done with him."

"Be it so, then. But—if you love me—find some other hand to do the work."

"If I love you, Justin?" echoed the other, and his voice softened, his eyes looked reproachfully upon his adoptive child. "Needs there an 'if' to that? Are you not all I have—my son, indeed?"

He held out his hands, and Justin took them affectionately and pressed them in his own.

"You'll put these weak notions from your mind, Justin, and prove worthy the noble lady who was your mother?"

Mr. Caryll moved aside again, hanging his head, his face pale and troubled. Where Everard's arguments must fail, his own affection for Everard was like to conquer him. It was very weak in him, he told himself; but then his love for Everard was strong, and he would fain spare Everard the pain he knew he must be occasioning him. Still he did battle, his repugnance up in arms.

"I would you could see the matter as I see it," he sighed. "This man grown old, and reaping in his old age the fruits of the egotism he has sown. I do not believe that in all the world there is a single soul would weep his lordship's death—if we except, perhaps, Mistress Winthrop."

"And do you pity him for that?" quoth Sir Richard coldly. "What right has he to expect aught else? Who sows for himself, reaps for himself. I marvel, indeed, that there should be even one to bewail him—to spare him a kind thought."

"And even there," mused Mr. Caryll, "it is perhaps gratitude rather than affection that inspires the kindness."

"Who is Mistress Winthrop?"

"His ward. As sweet a lady, I think, as I have ever seen," said Mr. Caryll, incautious enthusiasm assailing him. Sir Richard's eyes narrowed.

"You have some acquaintance with her?" he suggested.

Very briefly Mr. Caryll sketched for the second time that evening the circumstances of his first meeting with Rotherby.

Sir Richard nodded sardonically. "Hum! He is his father's son, not a doubt of that. 'Twill be a most worthy successor to my Lord Ostermore. But the lady? Tell me of the lady. How comes she linked with them?"

"I scarce know, save from the scraps that I have heard. Her father, it would seem, was Ostermore's friend, and, dying, he appointed Ostermore her guardian. Her fortune, I take it, is very slender. Nevertheless, Ostermore, whatever he may have done by other people, appears in this case to have discharged his trust with zeal and with affection. But, indeed, who could have done other where that sweet lady was concerned? You should see her, Sir Richard!" He was pacing the room now as he spoke, and as he spoke he warmed to his subject more and more. "She is middling tall, of a most dainty slenderness, dark-haired, with a so sweet and saintly beauty of face that it must be seen to be believed. And eyes—Lord! the glory of her eyes! They are eyes that would lead a man into hell and make him believe it heaven,

*"'Love doth to her eyes repair
To help him of his blindness.'"*

Sir Richard watched him, displeasure growing in his face. "So!" he said at last. "Is that the reason?"

"The reason of what?" quoth Mr. Caryll, recalled from his sweet rapture.

"The reason of these fresh qualms of yours. The reason of all this sympathy for Ostermore; this unwillingness to perform the sacred duty that is yours."

"Nay—on my soul, you do me wrong!" cried Mr. Caryll indignantly. "If aught had been needed to spur me on, it had been my meeting with this lady. It needed that to make me realize to the bitter full the wrong my Lord Ostermore has done me in getting me; to make me realize that I am a man without a name to offer any woman."

But Sir Richard, watching him intently, shook his head and fetched a sigh of sorrow and disdain. "Pshaw, Justin! How we befool ourselves! You think it is not so; you try to think it is not so; but to me it is very plain. A woman has arisen in your life, and this woman, seen but once or twice, unknown a week or so ago, suffices to eclipse the memory of your mother and turns your aim in life—the avenging of her bitter wrongs—to water. Oh, Justin, Justin! I had thought you stronger."

"Your conclusions are all wrong. I swear they are wrong!"

88

Sir Richard considered him sombrely. "Are you sure—quite, quite sure?"

Mr. Caryll's eyes fell, as the doubt now entered his mind for the first time that it might be indeed as Sir Richard was suggesting. He was not quite sure.

"Prove it to me, Justin," Everard pleaded. "Prove it by abandoning this weakness where my Lord Ostermore is concerned. Remember only the wrong he has done. You are the incarnation of that wrong, and by your hand must he be destroyed." He rose, and caught the younger man's hands again in his own, forced Mr. Caryll to confront him. "He shall know when the time comes whose hand it was that pulled him down; he shall know the Nemesis that has lain in wait for him these thirty years to smite him at the end. And he shall taste hell in this world before he goes to it in the next. It is God's own justice, boy! Will you be false to the duty that lies before you? Will you forget your mother and her sufferings because you have looked into the eyes of this girl, who—"

"No, no! Say no more!" cried Mr. Caryll, his voice trembling.

"You will do it," said Sir Richard, between question and assertion.

"If Heaven lends me strength of purpose. But it asks much," was the gloomy answer. "I am to see Lord Ostermore to-morrow to obtain his answer to King James' letter."

Sir Richard's eyes gleamed. He released the other's hands, and turned slowly to his chair again. "It is well," he said slowly. "The thing asks dispatch, or else some of his majesty's real friends may be involved."

He proceeded to explain his words. "I have talked in vain with Atterbury. He will not abandon the enterprise even at King James' commands. He urges that his majesty can have no conception of how the matter is advanced; that he has been laboring like Hercules, and that the party is being swelled by men of weight and substance every day; that it is too late to go back, and that he will go forward with the king's consent or without it. Should he or his agents approach Ostermore, in the meantime, it will be too late for us to take such measures as we have concerted. For to deliver up Ostermore then would entail the betrayal of others, which is not to be dreamt of. So you'll use dispatch."

"If I do the thing at all, it shall be done to-morrow," answered Mr. Caryll.

"If at all?" cried Sir Richard, frowning again. "If at all?"

Caryll turned to him. He crossed to the table, and leaning across it, until his face was quite close to his adoptive father's. "Sir Richard," he begged, "let us say no more to-night. My will is all to do the thing. It is my—my instincts that rebel. I think that the day will be carried by my will. I shall strive to that end, believe me. But let us say no more now."

Sir Richard, looking deep into Mr. Caryll's eyes, was touched by something that he saw. "My poor Justin!" he said gently. Then, checking the sympathy as swiftly as it rose: "So be it, then," he said briskly. "You'll come to me to-morrow after you have seen his lordship?"

"Will you not remain here?"

"You have not the room. Besides, Sir Richard Everard—is too well known for a Jacobite to be observed sharing your lodging. I have no right at all in England, and there is always the chance of my being discovered. I would not pull you down with me. I am lodged at the corner of Maiden Lane, next door to the sign of Golden Flitch. Come to me there to-morrow after you have seen Lord Ostermore." He hesitated a moment. He was impelled to recapitulate his injunctions; but he forbore. He put out his hand abruptly. "Good-night, Justin."

Justin took the hand and pressed it. The door opened, and Leduc entered.

"Captain Mainwaring and Mr. Falgate are here, sir, and would speak with you," he announced.

Mr. Caryll knit his brows a moment. His acquaintance with both men was of the slightest, and it was only upon reflection that he bethought him they would, no doubt, be come in the matter of his affair with Rotherby, which in the stress of his interview with Sir Richard had been quite forgotten. He nodded.

"Wait upon Sir Richard to the door, Leduc," he bade his man. "Then introduce these gentlemen."

Sir Richard had drawn back a step. "I trust neither of these gentlemen knows me," he said. "I would not be seen here by any that did. It might compromise you."

But Mr. Caryll belittled Sir Richard's fears. "Pooh! 'Tis very unlike," said he; whereupon Sir Richard, seeing no help for it, went out quickly, Leduc in attendance.

Lord Rotherby's friends in the ante-room paid little heed to him as he passed briskly through. Surveillance came rather from an entirely unsuspected quarter. As he left the house and crossed the square, a figure detached itself from the shadow of the wall, and set out to follow. It hung in his rear through the filthy, labyrinthine streets which Sir Richard took to Charing Cross, followed him along the Strand and up Bedford Street, and took note of the house he entered at the corner of Maiden Lane.

CHAPTER XI

THE ASSAULT-AT-ARMS

The meeting was appointed by my Lord Rotherby for seven o'clock next morning in Lincoln's Inn Fields. It is true that Lincoln's Inn Fields at an early hour of the day was accounted a convenient spot for the transaction of such business as this; yet, considering that it was in the immediate neighborhood of Stretton House, overlooked, indeed, by the windows of that mansion, it is not easy to rid the mind of a suspicion that Rotherby appointed that place of purpose set, and with intent to mark his contempt and defiance of his father, with whom he supposed Mr. Caryll to be in some league.

Accompanied by the Duke of Wharton and Major Gascoigne, Mr. Caryll entered the enclosure promptly as seven was striking from St. Clement Danes. They had come in a coach, which they had left in waiting at the corner of Portugal Row.

As they penetrated beyond the belt of trees they found that they were the first in the field, and his grace proceeded with the major to inspect the ground, so that time might be saved against the coming of the other party.

Mr. Caryll stood apart, breathing the freshness of the sunlit morning, but supremely indifferent to its glory. He was gloomy and preoccupied. He had slept ill that night after his interview with Sir Richard, tormented by the odious choice that lay before him of either breaking with the adoptive father to whom he owed obedience and affection, or betraying his natural father whom he had every reason to hate, yet who remained his father. He had been able to arrive at no solution. Duty seemed to point one way; instinct the other. Down in his heart he felt that when the moment came it would be the behests of instinct that he would obey, and, in obeying them, play false to Sir Richard and to the memory of his mother. It was the only course that went with honor; and yet it was a course that must lead to a break with the one friend he had in the world— the one man who stood to him for family and kin.

And now, as if that were not enough to plague him, there was this quarrel with Rotherby which he had upon his hands. That, too, he had been considering during the wakeful hours of that summer night. Had he reflected he must have seen that no other result could have followed his narrative at White's last night; and yet it was a case in which reflection would not have stayed him. Hortensia Winthrop's fair name was to be cleansed of the smirch that had been cast upon it, and Justin was the only man in whose power it had lain to do it. More than that—if more were needed—it was Rotherby himself, by his aggressiveness, who had thrust Mr. Caryll into a position which almost made it necessary for him to explain himself; and that he could scarcely have done by any other than the means which he had adopted. Under ordinary circumstances the matter would have troubled him not at all; this meeting with such a man as Rotherby would not have robbed him of a moment's sleep. But there came the reflection—belatedly—that Rotherby was his brother, his father's son; and he experienced just the same degree of repugnance at the prospect of crossing swords with him as he did at the prospect of betraying Lord Ostermore. Sir Richard would force upon him a parricide's task; Fate a fratricide's. Truly, he thought, it was an enviable position, his.

Pacing the turf, on which the dew still gleamed and sparkled diamond-like, he pondered his course, and wondered now, at the last moment, was there no way to avert this meeting. Could not the matter be arranged? He was stirred out of his musings by Gascoigne's voice, raised to curse the tardiness of Lord Rotherby.

"'Slife! Where does the fellow tarry? Was he so drunk last night that he's not yet slept himself sober?"

"The streets are astir," put in Wharton, helping himself to snuff. And, indeed, the cries of the morning hawkers reached them now from the four sides of the square. "If his lordship does not come soon, I doubt if we may stay for him. We shall have half the town for spectators."

"Who are these?" quoth Gascoigne, stepping aside and craning his neck to get a better view. "Ah! Here they come." And he indicated a group of three that had that moment passed the palings.

Gascoigne and Wharton went to meet the newcomers. Lord Rotherby was attended by Mainwaring, a militia captain—a great, burly, scarred bully of a man—and a Mr. Falgate, an extravagant young buck of his acquaintance. An odder pair of sponsors he could not have found had he been at pains to choose them so.

"Adso!" swore Mr. Falgate, in his shrill, affected voice. "I vow 'tis a most ungenteel hour, this, for men of quality to be abroad. I had my beauty sleep broke into to be here in time. Lard! I shall be dozing all day for't!" He took off his hat and delicately mopped his brow with a square of lace he called a handkerchief.

"Shall we come to business, gentlemen?" quoth Mainwaring gruffly.

"With all my heart," answered Wharton. "It is growing late."

"Late! La, my dears!" clucked Mr. Falgate in horror. "Has your grace not been to bed yet?"

92

"To save time," said Gascoigne, "we have made an inspection of the ground, and we think that under the trees yonder is a spot not to be bettered."

Mainwaring flashed a critical and experienced eye over the place. "The sun is—So?" he said, looking up. "Yes; it should serve well enough, I—"

"It will not serve at all," cried Rotherby, who stood a pace or two apart. "A little to the right, there, the turf is better."

"But there is no protection," put in the duke. "You will be under observation from that side of the square, including Stretton House."

"What odds?" quoth Rotherby. "Do I care who overlooks us?" And he laughed unpleasantly. "Or is your grace ashamed of being seen in your friend's company?"

Wharton looked him steadily in the face a moment, then turned to his lordship's seconds. "If Mr. Caryll is of the same mind as his lordship, we had best get to work at once," he said; and bowing to them, withdrew with Gascoigne.

"See to the swords, Mainwaring," said Rotherby shortly. "Here, Fanny!" This to Falgate, whose name was Francis, and who delighted in the feminine diminutive which his intimates used toward him. "Come help me with my clothes."

"I vow to Gad," protested Mr. Falgate, advancing to the task. "I make but an indifferent valet, my dear."

Mr. Caryll stood thoughtful a moment when Rotherby's wishes had been made known to him. The odd irony of the situation—the key to which he was the only one to hold—was borne in upon him. He fetched a sigh of utter weariness.

"I have," said he, "the greatest repugnance to meeting his lordship."

"'Tis little wonder," returned his grace contemptuously. "But since 'tis forced upon you, I hope you'll give him the lesson in manners that he needs."

"Is it—is it unavoidable?" quoth Mr. Caryll.

"Unavoidable?" Wharton looked at him in stern wonder.

Gascoigne, too, swung round to stare. "Unavoidable? What can you mean, Caryll?"

"I mean is the matter not to be arranged in any way? Must the duel take place?"

His Grace of Wharton stroked his chin contemplatively, his eye ironical, his lip curling never so slightly. "Why," said he, at length, "you may beg my Lord Rotherby's pardon for having given him the lie. You may retract, and brand yourself a liar and your version of the Maidstone affair a silly invention which ye have not the courage to maintain. You may do that, Mr. Caryll. For my own sake, let me add, I hope you will not do it."

"I am not thinking of your grace at all," said Mr. Caryll, slightly piqued by the tone the other took with him. "But to relieve your mind of such doubts as I see you entertain, I can assure you that it is out of no motives of weakness that I boggle at this combat. Though I confess that I am no ferrailleur, and that I abhor the duel as a means of settling a difference just as I abhor all things that are stupid and insensate, yet I am not the man to shirk an encounter where an encounter is forced upon me. But in this affair—" he paused, then ended—"there is more than meets your grace's eye, or, indeed, anyone's."

He was so calm, so master of himself, that Wharton perceived how groundless must have been his first notion. Whatever might be Mr. Caryll's motives, it was plain from his most perfect composure that they were not motives of fear. His grace's half-contemptuous smile was dissipated.

"This is mere trifling, Mr. Caryll," he reminded his principal, "and time is speeding. Your withdrawal now would not only be damaging to yourself; it would be damaging to the lady of whose fair name you have made yourself the champion. You must see that it is too late for doubts on the score of this meeting."

"Ay—by God!" swore Gascoigne hotly. "What a pox ails you, Caryll?"

Mr. Caryll took off his hat and flung it on the ground behind him. "We must go on, then," said he. "Gascoigne, see to the swords with his lordship's friend there."

With a relieved look, the major went forward to make the final preparations, whilst Mr. Caryll, attended by Wharton, rapidly divested himself of coat and waistcoat, then kicked off his light shoes, and stood ready, a slight, lithe, graceful figure in white Holland shirt and pearl-colored small clothes.

A moment later the adversaries were face to face—Rotherby, divested of his wig and with a kerchief bound about his close-cropped head, all a trembling eagerness; Mr. Caryll with a reluctance lightly masked by a dangerous composure.

There was a perfunctory salute—a mere presenting of arms—and the blades swept round in a half-circle to their first meeting. But Rotherby, without so much as allowing his steel to touch his opponent's, as the laws of courtesy demanded, swirled it away again into the higher lines and lunged. It was almost like a foul attempt to take his adversary unawares and unprepared, and for a second it looked as if it must succeed. It must have succeeded but for the miraculous quickness of Mr. Caryll. Swinging round on the ball of his right foot, lightly and gracefully as a dancing master, and with no sign of haste or fear in his amazing speed, he let the other's hard-driven blade glance past him, to meet nothing but the empty air.

As a result, by the very force of the stroke, Rotherby found himself over-reached and carried beyond his point of aim; while Mr. Caryll's sideward movement brought him not only nearer his opponent, but entirely within his guard.

It was seen by them all, and by none with such panic as Rotherby himself, that, as a consequence of his quasi-foul stroke, the viscount was thrown entirely at the mercy of his opponent thus at the very outset of the encounter, before their blades had so much as touched each other. A straightening of the arm on the part of Mr. Caryll, and the engagement would have been at an end.

Mr. Caryll, however, did not straighten his arm. He was observed to smile as he broke ground and waited for his lordship to recover.

Falgate turned pale. Mainwaring swore softly under his breath, in fear for his principal; Gascoigne did the same in vexation at the opportunity Mr. Caryll had so wantonly wasted. Wharton looked on with tight-pressed lips, and wondered.

Rotherby recovered, and for a moment the two men stood apart, seeming to feel each other with their eyes before resuming. Then his lordship renewed the attack with vigor.

Mr. Caryll parried lightly and closely, plying a beautiful weapon in the best manner of the French school, and opposing to the ponderous force of his antagonist a delicate frustrating science. Rotherby, a fine swordsman in his way, soon saw that here was need for all his skill, and he exerted it. But the prodigious rapidity of his blade broke as upon a cuirass against the other's light, impenetrable guard.

His lordship broke ground, breathed heavily, and sweated under the glare of the morning sun, cursing this swordsman who, so cool and deliberate, husbanded his strength and scarcely seemed to move, yet by sheer skill and address more than neutralized his lordship's advantages of greater strength and length of reach.

"You cursed French dog!" swore the viscount presently, between his teeth, and as he spoke he made a ringing parade, feinted, beat the ground with his foot to draw off the other's attention, and went in again with a full-length lunge. "Parry that, you damned maitre-d'armes" he roared.

Mr. Caryll answered nothing; he parried; parried again; delivered a riposte whenever the opportunity offered, or whenever his lordship grew too pressing, and it became expedient to drive him back; but never once did he stretch out to lunge in his turn. The

95

seconds were so lost in wonder at the beauty of this close play of his that they paid no heed to what was taking place in the square about them. They never observed the opening windows and the spectators gathering at them—as Wharton had feared. Amongst these, had either of the combatants looked up, he would have seen his own father on the balcony of Stretton House. A moment the earl stood there, Lady Ostermore at his side; then he vanished into the house again, to reappear almost at once in the street, with a couple of footmen hurrying after him.

Meanwhile the combat went on. Once Lord Rotherby had attempted to fall back for a respite, realizing that he was winded. But Mr. Caryll denied him this, attacking now for the first time, and the rapidity of his play was such that Rotherby opined—the end to be at hand, appreciated to the full his peril. In a last desperate effort, gathering up what shreds of strength remained him, he repulsed Mr. Caryll by a vigorous counter attack. He saw an opening, feinted to enlarge it, and drove in quickly, throwing his last ounce of strength into the effort. This time it could not be said to have been parried. Something else happened. His blade, coming foible on forte against Mr. Caryll's, was suddenly enveloped. It was as if a tentacle had been thrust out to seize it. For the barest fraction of a second was it held so by Mr. Caryll's sword; then, easily but irresistibly, it was lifted out of Rotherby's hand, and dropped on the turf a half-yard or so from his lordship's stockinged feet.

A cold sweat of terror broke upon him. He caught his breath with a half-shuddering sob of fear, his eyes dilating wildly—for Mr. Caryll's point was coming straight as an arrow at his throat. On it came and on, until it was within perhaps three inches of the flesh.

There it was suddenly arrested, and for a long moment it was held there poised, death itself, menacing and imminent. And Lord Rotherby, not daring to move, rooted where he stood, looked with fascinated eyes along that shimmering blade into two gleaming eyes behind it that seemed to watch him with a solemnity that was grim to the point of mockery.

Time and the world stood still, or were annihilated in that moment for the man who waited.

High in the blue overhead a lark was pouring out its song; but his lordship heard it not. He heard nothing, he was conscious of nothing but that gleaming sword and those gleaming eyes behind it.

Then a voice—the voice of his antagonist—broke the silence. "Is more needed?" it asked, and without waiting for a reply, Mr. Caryll lowered his blade and drew himself upright. "Let this suffice," he said. "To take your life would be to deprive you of the means of profiting by this lesson."

It seemed to Rotherby as if he were awaking from a trance. The world resumed its way. He breathed again, and straightened himself, too, from the arrested attitude of his last lunge. Rage welled up from his black soul; a crimson flood swept into his pallid cheeks; his eyes rolled and blazed with the fury of the mad.

Mr. Caryll moved away. In that quiet voice of his: "Take up your sword," he said to the vanquished, over his shoulder.

Wharton and Gascoigne moved towards him, without words to express the amazement that still held Rotherby glared an instant longer without moving. Then, doing as Mr. Caryll had bidden him, he stooped to recover his blade. A moment he held it, looking after his departing adversary; then with swift, silent stealth he sprang to follow. His fell intent was written on his face.

Falgate gasped—a helpless fool—while Mainwaring hurled himself forward to prevent the thing he saw impended. Too late. Even as he flung out his hands to grapple with his lordship, Rotherby's arm drove straight before him and sent his sword through the undefended back of Mr. Caryll.

All that Mr. Caryll realized at first was that he had been struck a blow between the shoulder blades; and then, ere he could turn to inquire into the cause, he was amazed to see some three inches of steel come through his shirt in front. The next instant an exquisite, burning, searing pain went through and through him as the blade was being withdrawn. He coughed and swayed, then hurtled sideways into the arms of Major Gascoigne. His senses swam. The turf heaved and rolled as if an earthquake moved it; the houses fronting the square and the trees immediately before him leaped and danced as if suddenly launched into grotesque animation, while about him swirled a wild, incoherent noise of voices, rising and falling, now loud, now silent, and reaching him through a murmuring hum that surged about his ears until it shut out all else and consciousness deserted him.

Around him, meanwhile, a wild scene was toward.

His Grace of Wharton had wrenched away the sword from Rotherby, and mastered by an effort his own impulse to use it upon the murderer. Captain Mainwaring—Rotherby's own second, a man of quick, fierce passions—utterly unable to control himself, fell upon his lordship and beat him to the ground with his hands, cursing him and heaping abuse upon him with every blow; whilst delicate Mr. Falgate, in the background, sick to the point of faintness, stood dabbing his lips with his handkerchief and swearing that he would rot before he allowed himself again to be dragged into an affair of honor.

"Ye damned cutthroat!" swore the militia captain, standing

over the man he had felled. "D'ye know what'll be the fruits of this? Ye'll swing at Tyburn like the dirty thief y' are. God help me! I'd give a hundred guineas sooner than be mixed in this filthy business."

"'Tis no matter for that now," said the duke, touching him on the shoulder and drawing him away from his lordship. "Get up, Rotherby."

Heavily, mechanically, Rotherby got to his feet. Now that the fit of rage was over, he was himself all stricken at the thing he had done. He looked at the limp figure on the turf, huddled against the knee of Major Gascoigne; looked at the white face, the closed eyes and the stain of blood oozing farther and farther across the Holland shirt, and, as white himself as the stricken man, he shuddered and his mouth was drawn wide with horror.

But pitiful though he looked, he inspired no pity in the Duke of Wharton, who considered him with an eye of unspeakable severity. "If Mr. Caryll dies," said he coldly, "I shall see to it that you hang, my lord. I'll not rest until I bring you to the gallows."

And then, before more could be said, there came a sound of running steps and labored breathing, and his grace swore softly to himself as he beheld no other than Lord Ostermore advancing rapidly, all out of breath and apoplectic of face, a couple of footmen pressing close upon his heels, and, behind these, a score of sightseers who had followed them.

"What's here?" cried the earl, without glancing at his son. "Is he dead? Is he dead?"

Gascoigne, who was busily endeavoring to stanch the bleeding, answered without looking up: "It is in God's hands. I think he is very like to die."

Ostermore swung round upon Rotherby. He had paled suddenly, and his mouth trembled. He raised his clenched hand, and it seemed that he was about to strike his son; then he let it fall again. "You villain!" he panted, breathless from running and from rage. "I saw it! I saw it all. It was murder, and, as God's my life, if Mr. Caryll dies, I shall see to it that you hang—I, your own father."

Thus assailed on every side, some of the cowering, shrinking manner left the viscount. His antagonism to his father spurred him to a prouder carriage. He shrugged indifferently. "So be it," he said. "I have been told that already. I don't greatly care."

Mainwaring, who had been stooping over Mr. Caryll, and who had perhaps more knowledge of wounds than any present, shook his head ominously.

"'Twould be dangerous to move him far," said he. "'Twill increase the hemorrhage."

"My men shall carry him across to Stretton House," said Lord Ostermore. "Lend a hand here, you gaping oafs."

The footmen advanced. The crowd, which was growing rapidly and was watching almost in silence, awed, pressed as close as it dared upon these gentlemen. Mainwaring procured a couple of cloaks and improvised a stretcher with them. Of this he took one corner himself, Gascoigne another, and the footmen the remaining two. Thus, as gently as might be, they bore the wounded man from the enclosure, through the crowd that had by now assembled in the street, and over the threshold of Stretton House.

A groom had been dispatched for a doctor, and his Grace of Wharton had compelled Rotherby to accompany them into his father's house, sternly threatening to hand him over to a constable at once if he refused.

Within the cool hall of Stretton House they were met by her ladyship and Mistress Winthrop, both pale, but the eyes of each wearing a vastly different expression.

"What's this?" demanded her ladyship, as they trooped in. "Why do you bring him here?"

"Because, madam," answered Ostermore in a voice as hard as iron, "it imports to save his life; for if he dies, your son dies as surely—and on the scaffold."

Her ladyship staggered and flung a hand to her breast. But her recovery was almost immediate. "'Twas a duel—" she began stoutly.

"'Twas murder," his lordship corrected, interrupting— "murder, as any of these gentlemen can and will bear witness. Rotherby ran Mr. Caryll through the back after Mr. Caryll had spared his life."

"'Tis a lie!" screamed her ladyship, her lips ashen. She turned to Rotherby, who stood there in shirt and breeches and shoeless, as he had fought. "Why don't you say that it is a lie?" she demanded.

Rotherby endeavored to master himself. "Madam," he said, "here is no place for you."

"But is it true? Is it true what is being said?"

He half-turned from her, with a despairing movement, and caught the sharp hiss of her indrawn breath. Then she swept past him to the side of the wounded man, who had been laid on a settle. "What is his hurt?" she inquired wildly, looking about her. But no one spoke. Tragedy—more far than the tragedy of that man's possible death—was in the air, and struck them all silent. "Will no one answer me?" she insisted. "Is it mortal? Is it?"

His Grace of Wharton turned to her with an unusual gravity in his blue eyes. "We hope not, ma'am," he said. "But it is as God wills."

Her limbs seemed to fail her, and she sank down on her knees beside the settle. "We must save him," she muttered fearfully. "We must save his life. Where is the doctor? He won't die! Oh, he must not die!"

They stood grouped about, looking on in silence, Rotherby in the background. Behind him again, on the topmost of the three steps that led up into the inner hall, stood Mistress Winthrop, white of face, a wild horror in the eyes she riveted upon the wounded and unconscious man. She realized that he was like to die. There was an infinite pity in her soul—and, maybe, something more. Her impulse was to go to him; her every instinct urged her. But her reason held her back.

Then, as she looked, she saw with a feeling almost of terror that his eyes were suddenly wide open.

"Wha—what?" came in feeble accents from his lips.

There was a stir about him.

"Never move, Justin," said Gascoigne, who stood by his head. "You are hurt. Lie still. The doctor has been summoned."

"Ah!" It was a sigh. The wounded man closed his eyes a moment, then re-opened them. "I remember. I remember," he said feebly. "It is—it is grave?" he inquired. "It went right through me. I remember!" He surveyed himself. "There's been a deal of blood lost. I am like to die, I take it."

"Nay, sir, we hope not—we hope not!" It was the countess who spoke.

A wry smile twisted his lips. "Your ladyship is very good," said he. "I had not thought you quite so much my well-wisher. I—I have done you a wrong, madam." He paused for breath, and it was not plain whether he spoke in sincerity or in sarcasm. Then with a startling suddenness he broke into a soft laugh and to those risen, who could not think what had occasioned it, it sounded more dreadful than any plaint he could have uttered.

He had bethought him that there was no longer the need for him to come to a decision in the matter that had brought him to England, and his laugh was almost of relief. The riddle he could never have solved for himself in a manner that had not shattered his future peace of mind, was solved and well solved if this were death.

"Where—where is Rotherby?" he inquired presently.

There was a stir, and men drew back, leaving an open lane to the place where Rotherby stood. Mr. Caryll saw him, and smiled, and his smile held no tinge of mockery. "You are the best friend I ever had, Rotherby," he startled all by saying. "Let him approach," he begged.

Rotherby came forward like one who walks in his sleep. "I am sorry," he said thickly, "cursed sorry."

"There's scarce the need," said Mr. Caryll. "Lift me up, Tom," he begged Gascoigne. "There's scarce the need. You have cleared up something that was plaguing me, my lord. I am your debtor for—for that. It disposes of something I could never have disposed of had I lived." He turned to the Duke of Wharton. "It was an accident," he said significantly. "You all saw that it was an accident."

A denial rang out. "It was no accident!" cried Lord Ostermore, and swore an oath. "We all saw what it was."

"I'faith, then, your eyes deceived you. It was an accident, I say—and who should know better than I?" He was smiling in that whimsical enigmatic way of his. Smiling still he sank back into Gascoigne's arms.

"You are talking too much," said the Major.

"What odds? I am not like to talk much longer."

The door opened to admit a gentleman in black, wearing a grizzle wig and carrying a gold-headed cane. Men moved aside to allow him to approach Mr. Caryll. The latter, not noticing him, had met at last the gaze of Hortensia's eyes. He continued to smile, but his smile was now changed to wistfulness under that pitiful regard of hers.

"It is better so," he was saying. "Better so!"

His glance was upon her, and she understood what none other there suspected—that those words were for her alone.

He closed his eyes and swooned again, as the doctor stooped to remove the temporary bandages from his wound.

Hortensia, a sob beating in her throat, turned and fled to her own room.

CHAPTER XII

SUNSHINE AND SHADOW

Mr. Caryll was almost happy.

He reclined on a long chair, supported by pillows cunningly set for him by the deft hands of Leduc, and took his ease and indulged his day-dreams in Lord Ostermore's garden. He sat within the cool, fragrant shade of a privet arbor, interlaced with flowering lilac and laburnum, and he looked out upon the long sweep of emerald lawn and the little patch of ornamental water where the water-lilies gaped their ivory chalices to the morning sun.

He looked thinner, paler and more frail than was his habit, which is not wonderful, considering that he had been four weeks abed while his wound was mending. He was dressed, again by the hands of the incomparable Leduc, in a deshabille of some artistry. A dark-blue dressing-gown of flowered satin fell open at the waist; disclosing sky-blue breeches and pearl-colored stockings, elegant shoes of Spanish leather with red heels and diamond buckles. His chestnut hair had been dressed with as great care as though he were attending a levee, and Leduc had insisted upon placing a small round patch under his left eye, that it might—said Leduc—impart vivacity to a countenance that looked over-wan from his long confinement.

He reclined there, and, as I have said, was almost happy.

The creature of sunshine that was himself at heart, had broken through the heavy clouds that had been obscuring him. An oppressive burden was lifted from his mind and conscience. That sword-thrust through the back a month ago had been guided, he opined, by the hand of a befriending Providence; for although he had, as you see, survived it, it had none the less solved for him that hateful problem he could never have solved for himself, that problem whose solution,—no matter which alternative he had adopted—must have brought him untold misery afterwards.

As it was, during the weeks that he had lain helpless, his life attached to him by but the merest thread, the chance of betraying Lord Ostermore was gone, nor—the circumstances being such as they were—could Sir Richard Everard blame him that he had let it pass.

Thus he knew peace; knew it as only those know it who have sustained unrest and can appreciate relief from it.

Nature had made him a voluptuary, and reclining there in an

ease which the languor born of his long illness rendered the more delicious, inhaling the tepid summer air that came to him laden with a most sweet attar from the flowering rose-garden, he realized that with all its cares life may be sweet to live in youth and in the month of June.

He sighed, and smiled pensively at the water-lilies; nor was his happiness entirely and solely the essence of his material ease. This was his third morning out of doors, and on each of the two mornings that were gone Hortensia had borne him company, coming with the charitable intent of lightening his tedium by reading to him, but remaining to talk instead.

The most perfect friendliness had prevailed between them; a camaraderie which Mr. Caryll had been careful not to dispel by any return to such speeches as those which had originally offended but which seemed now mercifully forgotten.

He was awaiting her, and his expectancy heightened for him the glory of the morning, increased the meed of happiness that was his. But there was more besides. Leduc, who stood slightly behind him, fussily, busy about a little table on which were books and cordials, flowers and comfits, a pipe and a tobacco-jar, had just informed him for the first time that during the more dangerous period of his illness Mistress Winthrop had watched by his bedside for many hours together upon many occasions, and once—on the day after he had been wounded, and while his fever was at its height—Leduc, entering suddenly and quietly, had surprised her in tears.

All this was most sweet news to Mr. Caryll. He found that between himself and his half-brother there lay an even deeper debt than he had at first supposed, and already acknowledged. In the delicious contemplation of Hortensia in tears beside him stricken all but to the point of death, he forgot entirely his erstwhile scruples that being nameless he had no name to offer her. In imagination he conjured up the scene. It made, he found, a very pretty picture. He would smoke upon it.

"Leduc, if you were to fill me a pipe of Spanish—"

"Monsieur has smoked one pipe already," Leduc reminded him.

"You are inconsequent, Leduc. It is a sign of advancing age. Repress it. The pipe!" And he flicked impatient fingers.

"Monsieur is forgetting that the doctor—"

"The devil take the doctor," said Mr. Caryll with finality.

"Parfaitement!" answered the smooth Leduc. "Over the bridge we laugh at the saint. Now that we are cured, the devil take the doctor by all means."

A ripple of laughter came to applaud Leduc's excursion into irony. The arbor had another, narrower entrance, on the left. Hortensia had approached this, all unheard on the soft turf, and stood there now, a heavenly apparition in white flimsy garments, head slightly a-tilt, eyes mocking, lips laughing, a heavy curl of her dark hair falling caressingly into the hollow where white neck sprang from whiter shoulder.

"You make too rapid a recovery, sir," said she.

"It comes of learning how well I have been nursed," he answered, making shift to rise, and he laughed inwardly to see the red flush of confusion spread over the milk-white skin, the reproachful shaft her eyes let loose upon Leduc.

She came forward swiftly to check his rising; but he was already on his feet, proud of his return to strength, vain to display it. "Nay," she reproved him. "If you are so headstrong, I shall leave you."

"If you do, ma'am. I vow here, as I am, I hope, a gentleman, that I shall go home to-day, and on foot."

"You would kill yourself," she told him.

"I might kill myself for less, and yet be justified."

She looked her despair of him. "What must I do to make you reasonable?"

"Set me the example by being reasonable yourself, and let there be no more of this wild talk of leaving me the very moment you are come. Leduc, a chair for Mistress Winthrop!" he commanded, as though chairs abounded in a garden nook. But Leduc, the diplomat, had effaced himself.

She laughed at his grand air, and, herself, drew forward the stool that had been Leduc's, and sat down. Satisfied, Mr. Caryll made her a bow, and seated himself sideways on his long chair, so that he faced her. She begged that he would dispose himself more comfortably; but he scorned the very notion.

"Unaided I walked here from the house," he informed her with a boastful air. "I had need to begin to feel my feet again. You are pampering me here, and to pamper an invalid is bad; it keeps him an invalid. Now I am an invalid no longer."

"But the doctor—" she began.

"The doctor, ma'am, is disposed of already," he assured her. "Very definitely disposed of. Ask Leduc. He will tell you."

"Not a doubt of that," she answered. "Leduc talks too much."

"You have a spite against him for the information he gave me on the score of how and by whom I was nursed. So have I. Because he did not tell me before, and because when he told me he would not tell me enough. He has no eyes, this Leduc. He is a dolt, who only sees the half of what happens, and only remembers the half of what he has seen."

"I am sure of it," said she.

He looked surprised an instant. Then he laughed. "I am glad that we agree."

"But you have yet to learn the cause. Had this Leduc used his eyes or his ears to better purpose, he had been able to tell you something of the extent to which I am in your debt."

"Ah?" said he, mystified. Then: "The news will be none the less welcome from your lips, ma'am," said he. "Is it that you are interested in the ravings of delirium, and welcomed the opportunity of observing them at first hand? I hope I raved engagingly, if so be that I did rave. Would it, perchance, be of a lady that I talked in my fevered wanderings?—of a lady pale as a lenten rose, with soft brown eyes, and lips that—"

"Your guesses are all wild," she checked him. "My debt is of a more real kind. It concerns my—my reputation."

"Fan me, ye winds!" he ejaculated.

"Those fine ladies and gentlemen of the town had made my name a by-word," she explained in a low, tense voice, her eyelids lowered. "My foolishness in running off with my Lord Rotherby— that I might at all cost escape the tyranny of my Lady Ostermore" (Mr. Caryll's eyelids flickered suddenly at that explanation)—"had made me a butt and a jest and an object for slander. You remember, yourself, sir, the sneers and oglings, the starings and simperings in the park that day when you made your first attempt to champion my cause, inducing the Lady Mary Deller to come and speak to me."

"Nay, nay—think of these things no more. Gnats will sting; 'tis in their nature. I admit 'tis very vexing at the time; but it soon wears off if the flesh they have stung be healthy. So think no more on't."

"But you do not know what follows. Her ladyship insisted that I should drive with her a week after your hurt, when the doctor first proclaimed you out of danger, and while the town was still all agog with the affair. No doubt her ladyship thought to put a fresh and greater humiliation upon me; you would not be present to blunt the edge of the insult of those creatures' glances. She carried me to Vauxhall, where a fuller scope might be given to the pursuit of my shame and mortification. Instead, what think you happened?"

"Her ladyship, I trust, was disappointed."

"The word is too poor to describe her condition. She broke a fan, beat her black boy and dismissed a footman, that she might vent some of the spleen it moved in her. Never was such respect, never such homage shown to any woman as was shown to me that evening. We were all but mobbed by the very people who had earlier slighted me.

"'Twas all so mysterious that I must seek the explanation of it. And I had it, at length, from his Grace of Wharton, who was at my side for most of the time we walked in the gardens. I asked him frankly to what was this change owing. And he told me, sir."

She looked at him as though no more need be said. But his brows were knit. "He told you, ma'am?" he questioned. "He told you what?"

"What you had done at White's. How to all present and to my Lord Rotherby's own face you had related the true story of what befell at Maidstone—how I had gone thither, an innocent, foolish maid, to be married to a villain, whom, like the silly child I was, I thought I loved; how that villain, taking advantage of my innocence and ignorance, intended to hoodwink me with a mock-marriage.

"That was the story that was on every lip; it had gone round the town like fire; and it says much for the town that what between that and the foul business of the duel, my Lord Rotherby was receiving on every hand the condemnation he deserves, while for me there was once more—and with heavy interest for the lapse from it—the respect which my indiscretion had forfeited, and which would have continued to be denied me but for your noble championing of my cause.

"That, sir, is the extent to which. I am in your debt. Do you think it small? It is so great that I have no words in which to attempt to express my thanks."

Mr. Caryll looked at her a moment with eyes that were very bright. Then he broke into a soft laugh that had a note of slyness.

"In my time," said he, "I have seen many attempts to change an inconvenient topic. Some have been artful; others artless; others utterly clumsy. But this, I think, is the clumsiest of them all. Mistress Winthrop, 'tis not worthy in you."

She looked puzzled, intrigued by his mood.

"Mistress Winthrop," he resumed, with an entire change of voice. "To speak of this trifle is but a subterfuge of yours to prevent me from expressing my deep gratitude for your care of me."

"Indeed, no—" she began.

"Indeed, yes," said he. "How can this compare with what you have done for me? For I have learnt how greatly it is to you, yourself, that I owe my recovery—the saving of my life."

"Ah, but that is not true. It—"

"Let me think so, whether it be true or not," he implored her, eyes between tenderness and whimsicality intent upon her face. "Let me believe it, for the belief has brought me happiness—the

106

greatest happiness, I think, that I have ever known. I can know but one greater, and that—"

He broke off suddenly, and she observed that the hand he had stretched out trembled a moment ere it was abruptly lowered again. It was as a man who had reached forth to grasp something that he craves, and checked his desire upon a sudden thought.

She felt oddly stirred, despite herself, and oddly constrained. It may have been to disguise this that she half turned to the table, saying: "You were about to smoke when I came." And she took up his pipe and tobacco—jar to offer them.

"Ah, but since you've come, I would not dream," he said.

She looked at him. The complete change of topic permitted it. "If I desired you so to do?" she inquired, and added: "I love the fragrance of it."

He raised his brows. "Fragrance?" quoth he. "My Lady Ostermore has another word for it." He took the pipe and jar from her. "'Tis no humoring, this, of a man you imagine sick—no silly chivalry of yours?" he questioned doubtfully. "Did I think that, I'd never smoke another pipe again."

She shook her head, and laughed at his solemnity. "I love the fragrance," she repeated.

"Ah! Why, then, I'll pleasure you," said he, with the air of one conferring favors, and filled his pipe. Presently he spoke again in a musing tone. "In a week or so, I shall be well enough to travel."

"'Tis your intent to travel?" she inquired.

He set down the jar, and reached for the tinderbox. "It is time I was returning home," he explained.

"Ah, yes. Your home is in France."

"At Maligny; the sweetest nook in Normandy. 'Twas my mother's birthplace, and 'twas there she died."

"You have felt the loss of her, I make no doubt."

"That might have been the case if I had known her," answered he. "But as it is, I never did. I was but two years old—she, herself, but twenty—when she died."

He pulled at his pipe in silence a moment or two, his face overcast and thoughtful. A shallower woman would have broken in with expressions of regret; Hortensia offered him the nobler sympathy of silence. Moreover, she had felt from his tone that there was more to come; that what he had said was but the preface to some story that he desired her to be acquainted with. And presently, as she expected, he continued.

"She died, Mistress Winthrop, of a broken heart. My father had abandoned her two years and more before she died. In those years of repining—ay, and worse, of actual want—her health was broken so that, poor soul, she died."

"O pitiful!" cried Hortensia, pain in her face.

"Pitiful, indeed—the more pitiful that her death was a source of some slight happiness to those who loved her; the only happiness they could have in her was to know that she was at rest."

"And—and your father?"

"I am coming to him. My mother had a friend—a very noble, lofty-minded gentleman who had loved her with a great and honest love before the profligate who was my father came forward as a suitor. Recognizing in the latter—as he thought in his honest heart—a man in better case to make her happy, this gentleman I speak of went his ways. He came upon her afterwards, broken and abandoned, and he gathered up the poor shards of her shattered life, and sought with tender but unavailing hands to piece them together again. And when she died he vowed to stand my friend and to make up to me for the want I had of parents. 'Tis by his bounty that to-day I am lord of Maligny that was for generations the property of my mother's people. 'Tis by his bounty and loving care that I am what I am, and not what so easily I might have become had the seed sown by my father been allowed to put out shoots."

He paused, as if bethinking himself, and looked at her with a wistful, inquiring smile. "But why plague you," he cried, "with this poor tale of yesterday that will be forgot to-morrow?"

"Nay—ah, nay," she begged, and put out a hand in impulsive sympathy to touch his own, so transparent now in its emaciation. "Tell me; tell me!"

His smile softened. He sighed gently and continued. "This gentleman who adopted me lived for one single purpose, with one single aim in view—to avenge my mother, whom he had loved, upon the man whom she had loved and who had so ill repaid her. He reared me for that purpose, as much, I think, as out of any other feeling. Thirty years have sped, and still the hand of the avenger has not fallen upon my father. It should have fallen a month ago; but I was weak; I hesitated; and then this sword-thrust put me out of all case of doing what I had crossed from France to do."

She looked at him with something of horror in her face. "Were you—were you to have been the instrument?" she inquired. "Were you to have avenged this thing upon your own father?"

He nodded slowly. "'Twas to that end that I was reared," he answered, and put aside his pipe, which had gone out. "The spirit of revenge was educated into me until I came to look upon revenge as the best and holiest of emotions; until I believed that if I failed to wreak it I must be a craven and a dastard. All this seemed so until the moment came to set my hand to the task. And then—" He shrugged.

"And then?" she questioned.

"I couldn't. The full horror of it burst upon me. I saw the thing in its true and hideous proportions, and it revolted me."

"It must have been so," she approved him.

"I told my foster-father; but I met with neither sympathy nor understanding. He renewed his old-time arguments, and again he seemed to prove to me that did I fail I should be false to my duty and to my mother's memory—a weakling, a thing of shame."

"The monster! Oh, the monster! He is an evil man for all that you have said of him."

"Not so. There is no nobler gentleman in all the world. I who know him, know that. It is through the very nobility of it that this warp has come into his nature. Sane in all things else, he is—I see it now, I understand it at last—insane on this one subject. Much brooding has made him mad upon this matter—a fanatic whose gospel is Vengeance, and, like all fanatics, he is harsh and intolerant when resisted on the point of his fanaticism. This is something I have come to realize in these past days, when I lay with naught else to do but ponder.

"In all things else he sees as deep and clear as any man; in this his vision is distorted. He has looked at nothing else for thirty years; can you wonder that his sight is blurred?"

"He is to be pitied then," she said, "deeply to be pitied."

"True. And because I pitied him, because I valued his regard—however mistaken he might be—above all else, I was hesitating again—this time between my duty to myself and my duty to him. I was so hesitating—though I scarce can doubt which had prevailed in the end—when came this sword-thrust so very opportunely to put me out of case of doing one thing or the other."

"But now that you are well again?" she asked.

"Now that I am well again—I thank Heaven that it will be too late. The opportunity that was ours is lost. His—my father should now be beyond our power."

There ensued a spell of silence. He sat with eyes averted from her face—those eyes which she had never known other than whimsical and mocking, now full of gloom and pain—riveted upon the glare of sunshine on the pond out yonder. A great sympathy welled up from her heart for this man whom she was still far from understanding, and who, nevertheless—because of it, perhaps, for there is much fascination in that which puzzles—was already growing very dear to her. The story he had told her drew her infinitely closer to him, softening her heart for him even more

109

perhaps than it had already been softened when she had seen him—
as she had thought—upon the point of dying. A wonder flitted
through her mind as to why he had told her; then another question
surged. She gave it tongue.

"You have told me so much, Mr. Caryll," she said, "that I am
emboldened to ask something more." His eyes invited her to put her
question. "Your—your father? Was he related to Lord Ostermore?"

Not a muscle of his face moved. "Why that?" he asked.

"Because your name is Caryll," said she.

"My name?" he laughed softly and bitterly. "My name?" He
reached for an ebony cane that stood beside his chair. "I had
thought you understood." He heaved himself to his feet, and she
forgot to caution him against exertion. "I have no right to any
name," he told her. "My father was a man too full of worldly affairs
to think of trifles. And so it befell that before he went his ways he
forgot to marry the poor lady who was my mother. I might take
what name I chose. I chose Caryll. But you will understand, Mistress
Winthrop," and he looked her fully in the face, attempting in vain to
dissemble the agony in his eyes—he who a little while ago had been
almost happy—"that if ever it should happen that I should come to
love a woman who is worthy of being loved, I who am nameless
have no name to offer her."

Revelation illumined her mind as in a flash. She looked at
him.

"Was—was that what you meant, that day we thought you
dying, when you said to me—for it was to me you spoke, to me
alone—that it was better so?"

He inclined his head. "That is what I meant," he answered.

Her lids drooped; her cheeks were very white, and he
remarked the swift, agitated surge of her bosom, the fingers that
were plucking at one another in her lap. Without looking up, she
spoke again. "If you had the love to offer, what would the rest
matter? What is a name that it should weigh so much?"

"Heyday!" He sighed, and smiled very wistfully. "You are
young, child. In time you will understand what place the world
assigns to such men as I. It is a place I could ask no woman to share.
Such as I am, could I speak of love to any woman?"

"Yet you spoke of love once to me," she reminded him,
scarcely above her breath, and stabbed him with the recollection.

"In an hour of moonshine, an hour of madness, when I was a
reckless fool that must give tongue to every impulse. You reproved
me then in just the terms my case deserved. Hortensia," he bent
towards her, leaning on his cane, "'tis very sweet and merciful in you
to recall it without reproach. Recall it no more, save to think with

110

scorn of the fleering coxcomb who was so lost to the respect that is due to so sweet a lady. I have told you so much of myself to-day that you may."

"Decidedly," came a shrill, ironical voice from the arbor's entrance, "I may congratulate you, sir, upon the prodigious strides of your recovery."

Mr. Caryll straightened himself from his stooping posture, turned and made Lady Ostermore a bow, his whole manner changed again to that which was habitual to him. "And no less decidedly, my lady," said he with a tight-lipped smile, "may I congratulate your ladyship's son upon that happy circumstance, which is—as I have learned—so greatly due to the steps your ladyship took—for which I shall be ever grateful—to ensure that I should be made whole again."

CHAPTER XIII

THE FORLORN HOPE

Her ladyship stood a moment, leaning upon her cane, her head thrown back, her thin lip curling, and her eyes playing over Mr. Caryll with a look of dislike that she made no attempt to dissemble.

Mr. Caryll found the situation redolent with comedy. He had a quick eye for such matters; so quick an eye that he deplored on the present occasion her ladyship's entire lack of a sense of humor. But for that lamentable shortcoming, she might have enjoyed with him the grotesqueness of her having—she, who disliked him so exceedingly—toiled and anguished, robbed herself of sleep, and hoped and prayed with more fervor, perhaps, than she had ever yet hoped and prayed for anything, that his life might be spared.

Her glance shifted presently from him to Hortensia, who had risen and who stood in deep confusion at having been so found by her ladyship, and in deep agitation still arising from the things he had said and from those which he had been hindered from adding by the coming of the countess.

The explanations that had been interrupted might never be renewed; she felt they never would be; he would account that he had said enough; since he was determined to ask for nothing. And unless the matter were broached again, what chance had she of combatting his foolish scruples; for foolish she accounted them; they were of no weight with her, unless, indeed, to heighten the warm feeling that already she had conceived for him.

Her ladyship moved forward a step or two, her fan going gently to and fro, stirring the barbs of the white plume that formed part of her tall head-dress.

"What were you doing here, child?" she inquired, very coldly.

Mistress Winthrop looked up—a sudden, almost scared glance it was.

"I, madam? Why—I was walking in the garden, and seeing Mr. Caryll here, I came to ask him how he did; to offer to read to him if he would have me."

"And the Maidstone matter not yet cold in its grave!" commented her ladyship sourly. "As I'm a woman, it is monstrous I should be inflicted with the care of you that have no care for yourself."

Hortensia bit her lip, controlling herself bravely, a spot of red in either cheek. Mr. Caryll came promptly to her rescue.

"Your ladyship must confess that Mistress Winthrop has assisted nobly in the care of me, and so, has placed your ladyship in her debt."

"In my debt?" shrilled the countess, eyebrows aloft, head-dress nodding. "And what of yours?"

"In my clumsy way, ma'am, I have already attempted to convey my thanks to her. It might be graceful in your ladyship to follow my example."

Mentally Mr. Caryll observed that it is unwise to rouge so heavily as did Lady Ostermore when prone to anger and to paling under it. The false color looks so very false on such occasions.

Her ladyship struck the ground with her cane. "For what have I to thank her, sir? Will you tell me that, you who seem so very well informed."

"Why, for her part in saving your son's life, ma'am, if you must have it. Heaven knows," he continued in his characteristic, half-bantering manner, under which it was so difficult to catch a glimpse of his real feelings, "I am not one to throw services done in the face of folk, but here have Mistress Winthrop and I been doing our best for your son in this matter; she by so diligently nursing me; I by responding to her nursing—and your ladyship's—and so, recovering from my wound. I do not think that your ladyship shows us a becoming gratitude. It is but natural that we fellow-workers in your ladyship's and Lord Rotherby's interests, should have a word to say to each other on the score of those labors which have made us colleagues."

Her ladyship measured him with a malignant eye. "Are you quite mad, sir?" she asked him.

He shrugged and smiled. "It has been alleged against me on occasion. But I think it was pure spite." Then he waved his hand towards the long seat that stood at the back of the arbor. "Will your ladyship not sit? You will forgive that I urge it in my own interest. They tell me that it is not good for me to stand too long just yet."

It was his hope that she would depart. Not so. "I cry you mercy!" said she acidly, and rustled to the bench. "Be seated, pray." She continued to watch them with her baleful glance. "We have heard fine things from you, sir, of what you have both done for my Lord Rotherby," she gibed, mocking him with the spirit of his half-jest. "Shall I tell you more precisely what 'tis he owes you?"

"Can there be more?" quoth Mr. Caryll, smiling so amiably that he must have disarmed a Gorgon.

Her ladyship ignored him. "He owes it to you both that you

113

have estranged him from his father, set up a breach between them that is never like to be healed. 'Tis what he owes you."

"Does he not owe it, rather, to his abandoned ways?" asked Hortensia, in a calm, clear voice, bravely giving back her ladyship look for look.

"Abandoned ways?" screamed the countess. "Is't you that speak of abandoned ways, ye shameless baggage? Faith, ye may be some judge of them. Ye fooled him into running off with you. 'Twas that began all this. Just as with your airs and simpers, and prettily-played innocences you fooled this other, here, into being your champion."

"Madam, you insult me!" Hortensia was on her feet, eyes flashing, cheeks aflame.

"I am witness to that," said Lord Ostermore, coming in through the side-entrance.

Mr. Caryll was the only one who had seen him approach. The earl's face that had wont to be so florid, was now pale and careworn, and he seemed to have lost flesh during the past month. He turned to her ladyship.

"Out on you!" he said testily, "to chide the poor child so!"

"Poor child!" sneered her ladyship, eyes raised to heaven to invoke its testimony to this absurdity. "Poor child."

"Let there be an end to it, madam," he said with attempted sternness. "It is unjust and unreasonable in you."

"If it were that—which it is not—it would be but following the example that you set me. What are you but unreasonable and unjust—to treat your son as you are treating him?"

His lordship crimsoned. On the subject of his son he could be angry in earnest, even with her ladyship, as already we have seen.

"I have no son," he declared, "there is a lewd, drunken, bullying profligate who bears my name, and who will be Lord Ostermore some day. I can't strip him of that. But I'll strip him of all else that's mine, God helping me. I beg, my lady, that you'll let me hear no more of this, I beg it. Lord Rotherby leaves my house to-day—now that Mr. Caryll is restored to health. Indeed, he has stayed longer than was necessary. He leaves to-day. He has my orders, and my servants have orders to see that he obeys them. I do not wish to see him again—never. Let him go, and let him be thankful—and be your ladyship thankful, too, since it seems you must have a kindness for him in spite of all he has done to disgrace and discredit us—that he goes not by way of Holborn Hill and Tyburn."

She looked at him, very white from suppressed fury. "I do believe you had been glad had it been so."

"Nay," he answered, "I had been sorry for Mr. Caryll's sake."

"And for his own?"

"Pshaw!"

"Are you a father?" she wondered contemptuously.

"To my eternal shame, ma'am!" he flung back at her. He seemed, indeed, a changed man in more than body since Mr. Caryll's duel with Lord Rotherby. "No more, ma'am—no more!" he cried, seeming suddenly to remember the presence of Mr. Caryll, who sat languidly drawing figures on the ground with the ferrule of his cane. He turned to ask the convalescent how he did. Her ladyship rose to withdraw, and at that moment Leduc made his appearance with a salver, on which was a bowl of soup, a flask of Hock, and a letter. Setting this down in such a manner that the letter was immediately under his master's eyes, he further proceeded to draw Mr. Caryll's attention to it. It was addressed in Sir Richard Everard's hand. Mr. Caryll took it, and slipped it into his pocket. Her ladyship's eyebrows went up.

"Will you not read your letter, Mr. Caryll?" she invited him, with an amazingly sudden change to amiability.

"It will keep, ma'am, to while away an hour that is less pleasantly engaged." And he took the napkin Leduc was proffering.

"You pay your correspondent a poor compliment," said she.

"My correspondent is not one to look for them or need them," he answered lightly, and dipped his spoon in the broth.

"Is she not?" quoth her ladyship.

Mr. Caryll laughed. "So feminine!" said he. "Ha, ha! So very feminine—to assume the sex so readily."

"'Tis an easy assumption when the superscription is writ in a woman's hand."

Mr. Caryll, the picture of amiability, smiled between spoonfuls. "Your ladyship's eyes preserve not only their beauty but a keenness beyond belief."

"How could you have seen it from that distance, Sylvia?" inquired his practical lordship.

"Then again," said her ladyship, ignoring both remarks, "there is the assiduity of this fair writer since Mr. Caryll has been in case to receive letters. Five billets in six days! Deny it if you can, Mr. Caryll."

Her playfulness, so ill-assumed, sat more awkwardly upon her than her usual and more overt malice towards him.

"To what end should I deny it?" he replied, and added in his most ingratiating manner another of his two-edged compliments. "Your ladyship is the model chatelaine. No happening in your household can escape your knowledge. His lordship is greatly to be envied."

115

"Yet, you see," she cried, appealing to her husband, and even to Hortensia, who sat apart, scarce heeding this trivial matter of which so much was being made, "you see that he evades the point, avoids a direct answer to the question that is raised."

"Since your ladyship perceives it, it were more merciful to spare my invention the labor of fashioning further subterfuges. I am a sick man still, and my wits are far from brisk." He took up the glass of wine Leduc had poured for him.

The countess looked at him again through narrowing eyelids, the playfulness all vanished. "You do yourself injustice, sir, as I am a woman. Your wits want nothing more in briskness." She rose, and looked down upon him engrossed in his broth. "For a dissembler, sir," she pronounced upon him acidly, "I think it would be difficult to meet your match."

He dropped his spoon into the bowl with a clatter. He looked up, the very picture of amazement and consternation.

"A dissembler, I?" quoth he in earnest protest; then laughed and quoted, adapting,

"'Tis not my talent to conceal my thoughts
Or carry smiles and sunshine in my face
Should discontent sit heavy at my heart."

She looked him over, pursing her lips. "I've often thought you might have been a player," said she contemptuously.

"I'faith," he laughed, "I'd sooner play than toil."

"Ay; but you make a toil of play, sir."

"Compassionate me, ma'am," he implored in the best of humors. "I am but a sick man. Your ladyship's too keen for me."

She moved across to the exit without answering him. "Come, child," she said to Hortensia. "We are tiring Mr. Caryll, I fear. Let us leave him to his letter, ere it sets his pocket afire."

Hortensia rose. Loath though she might be to depart, there was no reason she could urge for lingering.

"Is not your lordship coming?" said she.

"Of course he is," her ladyship commanded. "I need to speak with you yet concerning Rotherby," she informed him.

"Hem!" His lordship coughed. Plainly he was not at his ease. "I will follow soon. Do not stay for me. I have a word to say to Mr. Caryll."

"Will it not keep? What can you have to say to him that is so pressing?"

"But a word—no more."

"Why, then, we'll stay for you," said her ladyship, and threw him into confusion, hopeless dissembler that he was.

"Nay, nay! I beg that you will not."

Her ladyship's brows went up; her eyes narrowed again, and a frown came between them. "You are mighty mysterious," said she, looking from one to the other of the men, and bethinking her that it was not the first time she had found them so; bethinking her, too—jumping, woman-like, to rash conclusions—that in this mystery that linked them might lie the true secret of her husband's aversion to his son and of his oath a month ago to see that same son hang if Mr. Caryll succumbed to the wound he had taken. With some women, to suspect a thing is to believe that thing. Her ladyship was of these. She set too high value upon her acumen, upon the keenness of her instincts.

And if aught were needed to cement her present suspicions, Mr. Caryll himself afforded that cement, by seeming to betray the same eagerness to be alone with his lordship that his lordship was betraying to be alone with him; though, in truth, he no more than desired to lend assistance to the earl out of curiosity to learn what it was his lordship might have to say.

"Indeed," said he, "if you could give his lordship leave, ma'am, for a few moments, I should myself be glad on't."

"Come, Hortensia," said her ladyship shortly, and swept out, Mistress Winthrop following.

In silence they crossed the lawn together. Once only ere they reached the house, her ladyship looked back. "I would I knew what they are plotting," she said through her teeth.

"Plotting?" echoed Hortensia.

"Ay—plotting, simpleton. I said plotting. I mind me 'tis not the first time I have seen them so mysterious together. It began on the day that first Mr. Caryll set foot at Stretton House. There's a deal of mystery about that man—too much for honesty. And then these letters touching which he is so close—one a day—and his French lackey always at hand to pounce upon them the moment they arrive. I wonder what's at bottom on't! I wonder! And I'd give these ears to know," she snapped in conclusion as they went indoors.

In the arbor, meanwhile, his lordship had taken the rustic seat her ladyship had vacated. He sat down heavily, like a man who is weary in body and in mind, like a man who is bearing a load too heavy for his shoulders. Mr. Caryll, watching him, observed all this.

"A glass of Hock?" he suggested, waving his hand towards the flask. "Let me play host to you out of the contents of your own cellar."

His lordship's eye brightened at the suggestion, which confirmed the impression Mr. Caryll had formed that all was far from well with his lordship. Leduc brimmed a glass, and handed it to my lord, who emptied it at a draught. Mr. Caryll waved an

117

impatient hand. "Away with you, Leduc. Go watch the goldfish in the pond. I'll call you if I need you."

After Leduc had departed a silence fell between them, and endured some moments. His lordship was leaning forward, elbows on knees, his face in shadow. At length he sat back, and looked at his companion across the little intervening space.

"I have hesitated to speak to you before, Mr. Caryll, upon the matter that you know of, lest your recovery should not be so far advanced that you might bear the strain and fatigue of conversing upon serious topics. I trust that that cause is now so far removed that I may put aside my scruples."

"Assuredly—I am glad to say—thanks to the great care you have had of me here at Stretton House."

"There is no debt between us on that score," answered his lordship shortly, brusquely almost. "Well, then—" He checked, and looked about him. "We might be approached without hearing any one," he said.

Mr. Caryll smiled, and shook his head. "I am not wont to neglect such details," he observed. "The eyes of Argus were not so vigilant as my Leduc's; and he understands that we are private. He will give us warning should any attempt to approach. Be assured of that, and believe, therefore, that we are more snug here than we should be even in your lordship's closet."

"That being so, sir—hem! You are receiving letters daily. Do they concern the business of King James?"

"In a measure; or, rather, they are from one concerned in it."

Ostermore's eyes were on the ground again. There fell a pause, Mr. Caryll frowning slightly and full of curiosity as to what might be coming.

"How soon, think you," asked his lordship presently, "you will be in case to travel?"

"In a week, I hope," was the reply.

"Good." The earl nodded thoughtfully. "That may be in time. I pray it may be. 'Tis now the best that we can do. You'll bear a letter for me to the king?"

Mr. Caryll passed a hand across his chin, his face very grave. "Your answer to the letter that I brought you?"

"My answer. My acceptance of his majesty's proposals."

"Ha!" Mr. Caryll seemed to be breathing hard.

"Your letters, sir—the letters that you have been receiving will have told you, perhaps, something of how his majesty's affairs are speeding here?"

"Very little; and from that little I fear that they speed none too well. I would counsel your lordship," he continued slowly—he was thinking as he went—"to wait a while before you burn your boats. From what I gather, matters are in the air just now."

The earl made a gesture, brusque and impatient. "Your information is very scant, then," said he.

Mr. Caryll looked askance at him.

"Pho, sir! While you have been abed, I have been up and doing; up and doing. Matters are being pushed forward rapidly. I have seen Atterbury. He knows my mind. There lately came an agent from the king, it seems, to enjoin the bishop to abandon this conspiracy, telling him that the time was not yet ripe. Atterbury scorns to act upon that order. He will work in the king's interests against the king's own commands even."

"Then, 'tis possible he may work to his own undoing," said Mr. Caryll, to whom this was, after all, no news.

"Nay, nay; you have been sick; you do not know how things have sped in this past month. Atterbury holds, and he is right, I dare swear—he holds that never will there be such another opportunity. The finances of the country are still in chaos, in spite of all Walpole's efforts and fine promises. The South Sea bubble has sapped the confidence in the government of all men of weight. The very Whigs themselves are shaken. 'Tis to King James, England begins to look for salvation from this topsy-turveydom. The tide runs strongly in our favor. Strongly, sir! If we stay for the ebb, we may stay for good; for there may never be another flow within our lifetime."

"Your lordship is grown strangely hot upon this question," said Caryll, very full of wonder.

As he understood Ostermore, the earl was scarcely the sentimentalist to give way to such a passion of loyalty for a weaker side. Yet his lordship had spoken, not with the cold calm of the practical man who seeks advantage, but with all the fervor of the enthusiast.

"Such is my interest," answered his lordship. "Even as the fortunes of the country are beggared by the South Sea Company, so are my own; even as the country must look to King James for its salvation, so must I. At best 'tis but a forlorn hope, I confess; yet 'tis the only hope I see."

Mr. Caryll looked at him, smiled to himself, and nodded. So! All this fire and enthusiasm was about the mending of his personal fortunes—the grubbing of riches for himself. Well, well! It was good matter wasted on a paltry cause. But it sorted excellently with what Mr. Caryll knew of the nature of this father of his. It never could transcend the practical; there was no imagination to carry it beyond those narrow sordid confines, and Mr. Caryll had been a fool to have

119

supposed that any other springs were pushing here. Egotism, egotism, egotism! Its name, he thought, was surely Ostermore. And again, as once before, under the like circumstances, he found more pity than scorn awaking in his heart. The whole wasted, sterile life that lay behind this man; the unhappy, loveless home that stood about him now in his declining years were the fruits he had garnered from that consuming love of self with which the gods had cursed him.

The only ray to illumine the black desert of Ostermore's existence was the affection of his ward, Hortensia Winthrop, because in that one instance he had sunk his egotism a little, sparing a crumb of pity—for once in his life—for the child's orphanhood. Had Ostermore been other than the man he was, his existence must have proved a burden beyond his strength. It was so barren of good deeds, so sterile of affection. Yet encrusted as he was in that egotism of his—like the limpet in its shell—my lord perceived nothing of this, suffered nothing of it, understanding nothing. He was all-sufficient to himself. Giving nothing, he looked for nothing, and sought his happiness—without knowing the quest vain—in what he had. The fear of losing this had now in his declining years cast, at length, a shadow upon his existence.

Mr. Caryll looked at him almost sorrowfully. Then he put by his thoughts, and broke the silence. "All this I had understood when first I sought you out," said he. "Yet your lordship did not seem to realize it quite so keenly. Is it that Atterbury and his friends—?"

"No, no," Ostermore broke in. "Look'ee! I will be frank—quite frank and open with you, Mr. Caryll. Things were bad when first you came to me. Yet not so bad that I was driven to a choice of evils. I had lost heavily. But enough remained to bear me through my time, though Rotherby might have found little enough left after I had gone. While that was so, I hesitated to take a risk. I am an old man. It had been different had I been young with ambitions that craved satisfying. I am an old man; and I desired peace and my comforts. Deeming these assured, I paused ere I risked their loss against the stake which in King James's name you set upon the board. But it happens to-day that these are assured no longer," he ended, his voice breaking almost, his eyes haggard. "They are assured no longer."

"You mean?" inquired Caryll.

"I mean that I am confronted by the danger of beggary, ruin, shame, and the sponging-house, at best."

Mr. Caryll was stirred out of his calm. "My lord!" he cried. "How is this possible? What can have come to pass?"

The earl was silent for a long while. It was as if he pondered how he should answer, or whether he should answer at all. At last, in a low voice, a faint tinge reddening his face, his eyes averted, he explained. It shamed him so to do, yet must he satisfy that craving of weak minds to unburden, to seek relief in confession. "Mine is the case of Craggs, the secretary of state," he said. "And Craggs, you'll remember, shot himself."

"My God," said Mr. Caryll, and opened wide his eyes. "Did you-?" He paused, not knowing what euphemism to supply for the thing his lordship must have done.

His lordship looked up, sneering almost in self-derision. "I did," he answered. "To tell you all—I accepted twenty thousand pounds' worth of South Sea stock when the company was first formed, for which I did not pay other than by lending the scheme the support of my name at a time when such support was needed. I was of the ministry, then, you will remember."

Mr. Caryll considered him again, and wondered a moment at the confession, till he understood by intuition that the matter and its consequences were so deeply preying upon the man's mind that he could not refrain from giving vent to his fears.

"And now you know," his lordship added, "why my hopes are all in King James. Ruin stares me in the face. Ruin and shame. This forlorn Stuart hope is the only hope remaining me. Therefore, am I eager to embrace it. I have made all plain to you. You should understand now."

"Yet not quite all. You did this thing. But the inspection of the company's books is past. The danger of discovery, at least, is averted. Or is it that your conscience compels you to make restitution?"

His lordship stared and gaped. "Do you suppose me mad?" he inquired, quite seriously. "Pho! Others were overlooked at the time. We did not all go the way of Craggs and Aislabie and their fellow-sufferers. Stanhope was assailed afterward, though he was innocent. That filthy fellow, the Duke of Wharton, from being an empty fop turned himself on a sudden into a Crown attorney to prosecute the peculators. It was an easy road to fame for him, and the fool had a gift of eloquence. Stanhope's death is on his conscience—or would be if he had one. That was six months ago. When he discovered his error in the case of Stanhope and saw the fatal consequences it had, he ceased his dirty lawyer's work. But he had good grounds upon which to suspect others as highly placed as Stanhope, and had he followed his suspicions he might have turned them into certainties and discovered evidence. As it was, he let the matter lie, content with the execution he had done, and the esteem into which he had so suddenly hoisted himself—the damned profligate!"

Mr. Caryll let pass, as typical, the ludicrous want of logic in Ostermore's strictures of his Grace of Wharton, and the application by him to the duke of opprobrious terms that were no whit less applicable to himself.

"Then, that being so, what cause for these alarms some six months later?"

"Because," answered his lordship in a sudden burst of passion that brought him to his feet, empurpled his face and swelled the veins of his forehead, "because I am cursed with the filthiest fellow in England for my son."

He said it with the air of one who throws a flood of light where darkness has been hitherto, who supplies the key that must resolve at a turn a whole situation. But Mr. Caryll blinked foolishly.

"My wits are very dull, I fear," said he. "I still cannot understand."

"Then I'll make it all clear to you," said his lordship.

Leduc appeared at the arbor entrance.

"What now?" asked Mr. Caryll.

"Her ladyship is approaching, sir," answered Leduc the vigilant.

CHAPTER XIV

LADY OSTERMORE

Lord Ostermore and Mr. Caryll looked across the lawn towards the house, but failed to see any sign of her ladyship's approach.

Mr. Caryll raised questioning eyes to his servant's stolid face, and in that moment caught the faintest rustle of a gown behind the arbor. He half-turned to my lord, and nodded slightly in the direction of the sound, a smile twisting his lips. With a gesture he dismissed Leduc, who returned to the neighborhood of the pond.

His lordship frowned, angered by the interruption. Then: "If your ladyship will come inside," said he, "you will hear better and with greater comfort."

"Not to speak of dignity," said Mr. Caryll.

The stiff gown rustled again, this time without stealth. The countess appeared, no whit abashed. Mr. Caryll rose politely.

"You sit with spies to guard your approaches," said she.

"As a precaution against spies," was his lordship's curt answer.

She measured him with a cool eye. "What is't ye hide?" she asked him.

"My shame," he answered readily. Then after a moment's pause, he rose and offered her his seat. "Since you have thrust yourself in where you were not bidden, you may hear and welcome, ma'am," said he. "It may help you to understand what you term my injustice to my son."

"Are these matters wherewith to importune a stranger—a guest?"

"I am proposing to say in your presence what I was about to say in your absence," said he, without answering her question. "Be seated, ma'am."

She sniffed, closed her fan with a clatter, and sat down. Mr. Caryll resumed his long chair, and his lordship took the stool.

"I am told," the latter resumed presently, recapitulating in part for her ladyship's better understanding, "that his Grace of Wharton is intending to reopen the South Sea scandal, as soon as he can find evidence that I was one of those who profited by the company's charter."

"Profited?" she echoed, between scorn and bitter amusement. "Profited, did ye say? I think your dotage is surely upon you—you

123

that have sunk nigh all your fortune and all that you had with me in this thieving venture—d'ye talk of profits?"

"At the commencement I did profit, as did many others. Had I been content with my gains, had I been less of a trusting fool, it had been well. I was dazzled, maybe, by the glare of so much gold. I needed more; and so I lost all. That is evil enough. But there is worse. I may be called upon to make restitution of what I had from the company without paying for it—I may give all that's left me and barely cover the amount, and I may starve and be damned thereafter."

Her ladyship's face was ghastly. Horror stared from her pale eyes. She had known, from the beginning, of that twenty thousand pounds' worth of stock, and she had had—with his lordship—her anxious moments when the disclosures were being made six months ago that had brought the Craggses, Aislabie and a half-dozen others to shame and ruin.

His lordship looked at her a moment. "And if this shipwreck comes, as it now threatens," he continued, "it is my son I shall have to thank for't."

She found voice to ask: "How so?" courage to put the question scornfully. "Is it not rather Rotherby you have to thank that the disclosures did not come six months ago? What was it saved you but the friendship his Grace of Wharton had for Charles?"

"Why, then," stormed his lordship, "did he not see to't that he preserved that friendship? It but needed a behavior of as much decency and honor as Wharton exacts in his associates—and the Lord knows how much that is!" he sneered. "As it is, he has gone even lower than that abandoned scourer; so low that even this rakehell duke must become his enemy for his own credit's sake. He attempts mock-marriages with ladies of quality; and he attempts murder by stabbing through the back a gentleman who has spared his worthless life. Not even the president of the Hell Fire Club can countenance these things, strong stomach though he have for villainy. It is something to have contrived to come so low that even his Grace of Wharton must turn upon him, and swear his ruin. And so that he may ruin him, his grace is determined to ruin me. Now you understand, madam—and you, Mr. Caryll."

Mr. Caryll understood. He understood even more than his lordship meant him to understand; more than his lordship understood, himself. So, too, did her ladyship, if we may judge from the reply she made him.

"You fool," she railed. "You vain, blind, selfish fool! To blame Rotherby for this. Rather should Rotherby, blame you that by your damned dishonesty have set a weapon against him in his enemy's hands."

"Madam!" he roared, empurpling, and coming heavily to his feet. "Do you know who I am?"

"Ay—and what you are, which is something you will never know. God! Was there ever so self-centered a fool? Compassionate me, Heaven!" She rose, too, and turned to Mr. Caryll. "You, sir," she said to him, "you have been dragged into this, I know not why."

She broke off suddenly, looking at him, her eyes a pair of gimlets now for penetration. "Why have you been dragged into it?" she demanded. "What is here? I demand to know. What help does my lord expect from you that he tells you this? Does he—" She paused an instant, a cunning smile breaking over her wrinkled, painted face. "Does he propose to sell himself to the king over the water, and are you a secret agent come to do the buying? Is that the answer to this riddle?"

Mr. Caryll, imperturbable outwardly, but very ill at ease within, smiled and waved the delicate hand that appeared through the heavy ruffle at his wrist. "Madam, indeed—ah—your ladyship goes very fast. You leap so at conclusions for which no grounds can exist. His lordship is so overwrought—as well he may be, alas!—that he cares not before whom he speaks. Is it not plainly so?"

She smiled very sourly. "You are a very master of evasion, sir. But your evasion gives me the answer that I lack—that and his lordship's face. I drew my bow at a venture; yet look, sir, and tell me, has my quarrel missed its mark?"

And, indeed, the sudden fear and consternation written on my lord's face was so plain that all might read it. He was—as Mr. Caryll had remarked on the first occasion that they met—the worst dissembler that ever set hand to a conspiracy. He betrayed himself at every step, if not positively, by incautious words, why then by the utter lack of control he had upon his countenance.

He made now a wild attempt to bluster. "Lies! Lies!" he protested. "Your ladyship's a-dreaming. Should I be making bad worse by plotting at my time of life? Should I? What can King James avail me, indeed?"

"'Tis what I will ask Rotherby to help me to discover," she informed him.

"Rotherby?" he cried. "Would you tell that villain what you suspect? Would you arm him with another weapon for my undoing?"

"Ha!" said she. "You admit so much, then?" And she laughed disdainfully. Then with a sudden sternness, a sudden nobility almost in the motherhood which she put forward—"Rotherby is my son," she said, "and I'll not have my son the victim of your follies as well as of your injustice. We may curb the one and the other yet, my lord."

And she swept out, fan going briskly in one hand, her long ebony cane swinging as briskly in the other.

"O God!" groaned Ostermore, and sat down heavily.

Mr. Caryll helped himself copiously to snuff. "I think," said he, his voice so cool that it had an almost soothing influence, "I think your lordship has now another reason why you should go no further in this matter."

"But if I do not—what other hopes have I? Damn me! I'm a ruined man either way."

"Nay, nay," Mr. Caryll reminded him. "Assuming even that you are correctly informed, and that his Grace of Wharton is determined to move against you, it is not to be depended that he will succeed in collecting such evidence as he must need. At this date much of the evidence that may once have been available will have been dissipated. You are rash to despair so soon."

"There is that," his lordship admitted thoughtfully, a little hopefully, even; "there is that." And with the resilience of his nature—of men who form opinions on slight grounds, and, therefore, are ready to change them upon grounds as slight—"I' faith! I may have been running to meet my trouble. 'Tis but a rumor, after all, that Wharton is for mischief, and—as you say—as like as not there'll be no evidence by now. There was little enough at the time.

"Still, I'll make doubly sure. My letter to King James can do no harm. We'll talk of it again, when you are in case to travel."

It passed through Mr. Caryll's mind at the moment that Lady Ostermore and her son might between them brew such mischief as might seriously hinder him from travelling, and he was very near the truth. For already her ladyship was closeted with Rotherby in her boudoir.

The viscount was dressed for travelling, intent upon withdrawing to the country, for he was well-informed already of the feeling of the town concerning him, and had no mind to brave the slights and cold-shoulderings that would await him did he penetrate to any of the haunts of people of quality and fashion. He stood before his mother now, a tall, lank figure, his black face very gloomy, his sensual lips thrust forward in a sullen pout. She, in a gilt arm-chair before her toilet-table, was telling him the story of what had passed, his father's fear of ruin and disgrace. He swore between his teeth when he heard that the danger threatened from the Duke of Wharton.

"And your father's destitution means our destitution—yours and mine; for his gambling schemes have consumed my portion long since."

He laughed and shrugged. "I marvel I should concern myself," said he. "What can it avail me to save the rags that are left him of his fortune? He's sworn I shall never touch a penny that he may die possessed of."

"But there's the entail," she reminded him. "If restitution is demanded, the Crown will not respect it. 'Twill be another sop to throw the whining curs that were crippled by the bubble, and who threaten to disturb the country if they are not appeased. If Wharton carries out this exposure, we're beggars—utter beggars, that may ask an alms to quiet hunger."

"'Tis Wharton's present hate of me," said he thoughtfully, and swore. "The damned puppy! He'd make a sacrifice of me upon the altar of respectability, just as he made a sacrifice of the South Sea bubblers. What else was the stinking rakehell seeking but to put himself right again in the eyes of a town that was nauseated with him and his excesses? The self-seeking toad that makes virtue his profession—the virtue of others—and profligacy his recreation!" He smote fist into palm. "There's a way to silence him."

"Ah?" she looked up quickly, hopefully.

"A foot or so of steel," Rotherby explained, and struck the hilt of his sword. "I might pick a quarrel with him. 'Twould not be difficult. Come upon him unawares, say, and strike him. That should force a fight."

"Tusk, fool! He's all empanoplied in virtue where you are concerned. He'd use the matter of your affair with Caryll as a reason not to meet you, whatever you might do, and he'd set his grooms to punish any indignity you might put upon him."

"He durst not."

"Pooh! The town would all approve him in it since your running Caryll through the back. What a fool you were, Charles."

He turned away, hanging his head, full conscious, and with no little bitterness, of how great had been his folly.

"Salvation may lie for you in the same source that has brought you to the present pass—this man Caryll," said the countess presently. "I suspect him more than ever of being a Jacobite agent."

"I know him to be such."

"You know it?"

"All but; and Green is assured of it, too." He proceeded to tell her what he knew. "Ever since Green met Caryll at Maidstone has he suspected him, yet but that I kept him to the task he would have abandoned it. He's in my pay now as much as in Lord Carteret's, and if he can run Caryll to earth he receives his wages from both sides."

"Well—well? What has he discovered? Anything?"

"A little. This Caryll frequented regularly the house of one Everard, who came to town a week after Caryll's own arrival. This Everard—Sir Richard Everard is known to be a Jacobite. He is the Pretender's Paris agent. They would have laid him by the heels before, but that by precipitancy they feared to ruin their chances of discovering the business that may have brought him over. They are giving him rope at present. Meanwhile, by my cursed folly, Caryll's visits to him were interrupted. But there has been correspondence between them."

"I know," said her ladyship. "A letter was delivered him just now. I tried to smoke him concerning it. But he's too astute."

"Astute or not," replied her son, "once he leaves Stretton House it should not be long ere he betrays himself and gives us cause to lay him by the heels. But how will that help us?"

"Do you ask how? Why, if there is a plot, and we can discover it, we might make terms with the secretary of state to avoid any disclosure Wharton may intend concerning the South Sea matter."

"But that would be to discover my father for a Jacobite! What advantage should we derive from that? 'Twould be as bad as t'other matter."

"Let me die, but ye're a slow-witted clod, Charles. D'ye think we can find no way to disclose the plot and Mr. Caryll—and Everard, too, if you choose—without including your father? My lord is timidly cautious, and you may depend he'll not have put himself in their hands to any extent just yet."

The viscount paced the chamber slowly in long strides, head bent in thought, hands clasped behind him. "It will need consideration," said he. "But it may serve, and I can count upon Green. He is satisfied that Caryll befooled him at Maidstone, and that he kept the papers he carried despite the thoroughness of Green's investigations. Moreover, he was handled with some roughness by Caryll. For that and the other matter he asks redress—thirsts for it. He's a very willing tool, as I have found."

"Then see that you use him adroitly to your work," said his mother. "Best not leave town at present, Charles."

"Why, no," said he. "I'll find me a lodging somewhere at hand, since my fond sire is determined I shall pollute no longer the sacrosanctity of his dwelling. Perhaps when I have pulled him out of this quicksand, he will deign to mitigate the bitterness of his feelings for me. Though, faith, I find life endurable without the affection he should have consecrated to me."

128

"Ay," she said, looking up at him. "You are his son; too much his son, I fear. 'Tis why he dislikes you so intensely. He sees in you the faults to which he is blind in himself."

"Sweet mother!" said his lordship, bowing.

She scowled at him. She could deal in irony herself—and loved to—but she detested to have it dealt to her.

He bowed again; gained the door, and would have passed out but that she detained him.

"'Tis a pity, on some scores, to dispose so utterly of this Caryll," she said. "The pestilent coxcomb has his uses, and his uses, like adversity's, are sweet."

He paused to question her with his eyes.

"He might have made a husband for Hortensia, and rid me of the company of that white-faced changeling."

"Might he so?" quoth the viscount, face and voice, expressionless.

"They were made for each other," her ladyship opined.

"Were they so?"

"Ay—were they. And faith they've discovered it. I would you had seen the turtles in the arbor an hour ago, when I surprised them."

His lordship attempted a smile, but achieved nothing more than a wry face and a change of color. His mother's eyes, observing these signs, grew on a sudden startled.

"Why, fool," quoth she, "do you hold there still? Art not yet cured of that folly?"

"What folly, ma'am?"

"This folly that already has cost you so much. 'Sdeath! As I'm a woman, if you'd so much feeling for the girl, I marvel ye did not marry her honestly and in earnest when the chance was yours."

The pallor of his face increased. He clenched his hands. "I marvel myself that I did not," he answered passionately—and went out, slamming the door after him, and leaving her ladyship agape and angry.

CHAPTER XV

LOVE AND RAGE

Lord Rotherby, descending from that interview with his mother, espied Hortensia crossing the hall below. Forgetting his dignity, he quickened his movements, and took the remainder of the stairs two at a stride. But, then, his lordship was excited and angry, and considerations of dignity did not obtain with him at the time. For that matter, they seldom did.

"Hortensia! Hortensia!" he called to her, and at his call she paused.

Not once during the month that was past—and during which he had, for the most part, kept his room, to all intents a prisoner—had she exchanged so much as a word with him. Thus, not seeing him, she had been able, to an extent, to exclude him from her thoughts, which, naturally enough, were reluctant to entertain him for their guest.

Her calm, as she paused now in acquiescence to his bidding, was such that it almost surprised herself. She had loved him once—or thought so, a little month ago—and at a single blow he had slain that love. Now love so slain has a trick of resurrecting in the guise of hate; and so, she had thought at first had been the case with her. But this moment proved to her now that her love was dead, indeed, since of her erstwhile affection not even a recoil to hate remained. Dislike she may have felt; but it was that cold dislike that breeds a deadly indifference, and seeks no active expression, asking no more than the avoidance of its object.

Her calm, reflected in her face of a beauty almost spiritual, in every steady line of her slight, graceful figure, gave him pause a moment, and his hot glance fell abashed before the chill indifference that met him from those brown eyes.

A man of deeper sensibilities, of keener perceptions, would have bowed and gone his way. But then a man of deeper sensibilities would never have sought this interview that the viscount was now seeking. Therefore, it was but natural that he should recover swiftly from his momentary halt, and step aside to throw open the door of a little room on the right of the hall. Bowing slightly, he invited her to enter.

"Grant me a moment ere I go, Hortensia," he said, between command and exhortation.

She stood cogitating him an instant, with no outward sign of what might be passing in her mind; then she slightly inclined her head, and went forward as he bade her.

It was a sunny room, gay with light color and dainty furnishings, having long window-doors that opened to the garden. An Aubusson carpet of palest green, with a festoon pattern of pink roses, covered two-thirds of the blocked, polished floor. The empanelled walls were white, with here a gilt mirror, flanked on either side by a girandole in ormolu. A spinet stood open in mid-chamber, and upon it were sheets of music, a few books and a bowl of emerald-green ware, charged now with roses, whose fragrance lay heavy on the air. There were two or three small tables of very dainty, fragile make, and the chairs were in delicately-tinted tapestry illustrating the fables of La Fontaine.

It was an apartment looked upon by Hortensia as her own withdrawing-room, set apart for her own use, and as that the household—her very ladyship included—had ever recognized it.

His lordship closed the door with care. Hortensia took her seat upon the long stool that stood at the spinet, her back to the instrument, and with hands idle in her lap—the same cold reserve upon her countenance-she awaited his communication.

He advanced until he was close beside her, and stood leaning an elbow on the corner of the spinet, a long and not ungraceful figure, with the black curls of his full-bottomed wig falling about his swarthy, big-featured face.

"I have but my farewells to make, Hortensia," said he. "I am leaving Stretton House, to-day, at last."

"I am glad," said she, in a formal, level voice, "that things should have fallen out so as to leave you free to go your ways."

"You are glad," he answered, frowning slightly, and leaning farther towards her. "Ay, and why are you glad? Why? You are glad for Mr. Caryll's sake. Do you deny it?"

She looked up at him quite calm and fearlessly. "I am glad for your own sake, too."

His dark brooding eyes looked deep into hers, which did not falter under his insistent gaze. "Am I to believe you?" he inquired.

"Why not? I do not wish your death."

"Not my death—but my absence?" he sneered. "You wish for that, do you not? You would prefer me gone? My room is better than my company just now? 'Tis what you think, eh?"

"I have not thought of it at all," she answered him with a pitiless frankness.

He laughed, soft and wickedly. "Is it so very hopeless, then? You have not thought of it at all by which you mean that you have not thought of me at all."

131

"Is't not best so? You have given me no cause to think of you to your advantage. I am therefore kind to exclude you from my thoughts."

"Kind?" he mocked her. "You think it kind to put me from your mind—I who love you, Hortensia!"

She rose upon the instant, her cheeks warming faintly. "My lord," said she, "I think there is no more to be said between us."

"Ah, but there is," he cried. "A deal more yet." And he left his place by the spinet to come and stand immediately before her, barring her passage to the door. "Not only to say farewell was it that I desired to speak with you alone here." His voice softened amazingly. "I want your pardon ere I go. I want you to say that you forgive me the vile thing I would have done, Hortensia." Contrition quivered in his lowered voice. He bent a knee to her, and held out his hand. "I will not rise until you speak my pardon, child."

"Why, if that be all, I pardon you very readily," she answered, still betraying no emotion.

He frowned. "Too readily!" he cried. "Too readily for sincerity. I will not take it so."

"Indeed, my lord, for a penitent, you are very difficult to please. I pardon you with all my heart."

"You are sincere?" he cried, and sought to take her hands; but she whipped them away and behind her. "You bear me no ill-will?"

She considered him now with a calm, critical gaze, before which he was forced to lower his bold eyes. "Why should I bear you an ill-will?" she asked him.

"For the thing I did—the thing I sought to do."

"I wonder do you know all that you did?" she asked him, musingly. "Shall I tell you, my lord? You cured me of a folly. I had been blind, and you made me see. I had foolishly thought to escape one evil, and you made me realize that I was rushing into a worse. You saved me from myself. You may have made me suffer then; but it was a healing hurt you dealt me. And should I bear you an ill-will for that?"

He had risen from his knee. He stood apart, pondering her from under bent brows with eyes that were full of angry fire.

"I do not think," she ended, "that there needs more between us. I have understood you, sir, since that day at Maidstone—I think we were strangers until then; and perhaps now you may begin to understand me. Fare you well, my lord."

She made shift to go, but he barred her passage now in earnest, his hands clenched beside him in witness of the violence he did himself to keep them there. "Not yet," he said, in a deep, concentrated voice. "Not yet. I did you a wrong, I know. And what

132

you say—cruel as it is—is no more than I deserve. But I desire to make amends. I love you, Hortensia, and desire to make amends."

She smiled wistfully. "'Tis overlate to talk of that."

"Why?" he demanded fiercely, and caught her arms, holding her there before him. "Why is it overlate?"

"Suffer me to go," she commanded, rather than begged, and made to free herself of his grasp.

"I want you to be my wife, Hortensia—my wedded wife."

She looked at him, and laughed; a cold laugh, disdainful, yet not bitter. "You wanted that before, my lord; yet you neglected the opportunity my folly gave you. I thank you—you, after God—for that same neglect."

"Ah, do not say that!" he begged, a very suppliant again. "Do not say that! Child, I love you. Do you understand?"

"Who could fail to understand, after the abundant proof you have afforded me of your sincerity and your devotion?"

"Do you rally me?" he demanded, letting through a flash of the anger that was mounting in him. "Am I so poor a thing that you whet your little wit upon me?"

"My lord, you are paining me. What can you look to gain by this? Suffer me to go."

A moment yet he stood, holding her wrists and looking down into her eyes with a mixture of pleading and ferocity in his. Then he made a sound in his throat, and caught her bodily to him; his arms, laced about her, held her bound and crushed against him. His dark, flushed face hovered above her own.

Fear took her at last. It mounted and grew to horror. "Let me go, my lord," she besought him, her voice trembling. "Oh, let me go!"

"I love you, Hortensia! I need you!" he cried, as if wrung by pain, and then hot upon her brow and cheeks and lips his kisses fell, and shame turned her to fire from head to foot as she fought helplessly within his crushing grasp.

"You dog!" she panted, and writhing harder, wrenched free a hand and arm. Blindly she beat upwards into that evil satyr's face. "You beast! You toad! You coward!"

They fell apart, each panting; she leaning faint against the spinet, her bosom galloping; he muttering oaths decent and other—for in the upward thrusting of her little hand one of its fingers had prodded at an eye, and the pain of it—which had caused him to relax his hold of her—stripped what little veneer remained upon the man's true nature.

"Will you go?" she asked him furiously, outraged by the vileness of his ravings. "Will you go, or must I summon help?"

He stood looking at her, straightening his wig, which had become disarranged in the struggle, and forcing himself to an outward calm. "So," he said. "You scorn me? You will not marry me? You realise the chance, eh? And why? Why?"

"I suppose it is because I am blind to the honor of the alliance," she controlled herself to answer him. "Will you go?"

He did not move. "Yet you loved me once—"

"'Tis a lie!" she blazed. "I thought I did—to my undying shame. No more than that, my lord—as I've a soul to be saved."

"You loved Me," he insisted. "And you would love me still but for this damned Caryll—this French coxcomb, who has crawled into your regard like the slimy, creeping thing he is."

"It sorts well with your ways, my lord, that you could say these things behind his back. You are practiced at stabbing men behind."

The gibe, with all the hurtful, stinging quality that only truth possesses, struck his anger from him, leaving him limp and pale. Then he recovered.

"Do you know who he is—what he is?" he asked. "I will tell you. He's a spy—a damned Jacobite spy, whom a word from me will hang."

Her eyes lashed him with her scorn. "I were a fool did I believe you," was her contemptuous answer.

"Ask him," he said, and laughed. He turned and strode to the door. Paused there, sardonic, looking back. "I shall be quits with you, ma'am. Quits! I'll hang this pretty turtle of yours at Tyburn. Tell him so from me."

He wrenched the door open, and went out on that, leaving her cold and sick with dread.

Was it but an idle threat to terrorize her? Was it but that? Her impulse was to seek Mr. Caryll upon the instant that she might ask him and allay her fears. But what right had she? Upon what grounds could she set a question upon so secret a matter? She conceived him raising his brows in that supercilious way of his, and looking her over from head to toe as though seeking a clue to the nature of this quaint thing that asked him questions. She pictured his smile and the jest with which he would set aside her inquiry. She imagined, indeed, just what she believed would happen did she ask him; which was precisely what would not have happened. Imagining thus, she held her peace, and nursed her secret dread. And on the following day, his weakness so far overcome as to leave him no excuse to linger at Stretton House, Mr. Caryll took his departure and returned to his lodging in Old Palace Yard.

One more treasonable interview had he with Lord Ostermore in the library ere he departed. His lordship it was who reopened again the question, to repeat much of what he had said in the arbor on the previous day, and Mr. Caryll replied with much the same arguments in favor of procrastination that he had already employed.

"Wait, at least," he begged, "until I have been abroad a day or two, and felt for myself how the wind Is setting."

"'Tis a prodigiously dangerous document," he declared. "I scarce see the need for so much detail."

"How can it set but one way?"

"'Tis a question I shall be in better case to answer when I have had an opportunity of judging. Meanwhile, be assured I shall not sail for France without advising you. Time enough then to give me your letter should you still be of the same mind."

"Be it so," said the earl. "When all is said, the letter will be safer here, meantime, than in your pocket." And he tapped the secretaire. "But see what I have writ his majesty, and tell me should I alter aught."

He took out a drawer on the right—took it out bodily—then introduced his hand into the opening, running it along the inner side of the desk until, no doubt, he touched a spring; for suddenly a small trap was opened. From this cavity he fished out two documents—one the flimsy tissue on which King James' later was penned; the other on heavier material Lord Ostermore's reply. He spread the latter before him, and handed it to Mr. Caryll, who ran an eye over it.

It was indited with stupid, characteristic incaution; concealment was never once resorted to; everywhere expressions of the frankest were employed, and every line breathed the full measure of his lordship's treason and betrays the existence of a plot.

Mr. Caryll returned it. His countenance was grave.

"I desire his majesty to know how whole-heartedly I belong to him."

"'Twere best destroyed, I think. You can write another when the time comes to dispatch it."

But Ostermore was never one to take sensible advice. "Pooh! 'Twill be safe in here. 'Tis a secret known to none." He dropped it, together with King James' letter, back into the recess, snapped down the trap, and replaced the drawer. Whereupon Mr. Caryll took his leave, promising to advise his lordship of whatever he might glean, and so departed from Stretton House.

My Lord Rotherby, meanwhile, was very diligent in the business upon which he was intent. He had received in his interview with Hortensia an added spur to such action as might be scatheful to Mr. Caryll. His lordship was lodged in Portugal Row, within a stone's throw of his father's house, and there, on that same evening of his moving thither, he had Mr. Green to see him, desiring news.

Mr. Green had little to impart, but strong hope of much to be garnered presently. His little eyes twinkling, his chubby face suffused in smiles, as though it were an excellent jest to be hunting knowledge that should hang a man, the spy assured Lord Rotherby that there was little doubt Mr. Caryll could be implicated as soon as he was about again.

"And that's the reason—after your lordship's own express wishes—why so far I have let Sir Richard Everard be. It may come to trouble for me with my Lord Carteret should it be smoked that I have been silent on the matters within my knowledge. But—"

"Oh, a plague on that!" said his lordship. "You'll be well paid for your services when you've rendered them. And, meanwhile, I understand that not another soul in London—that is, on the side of the government—is aware of Sir Richard's presence in town. So where is your danger?"

"True," said Mr. Green, plump hand caressing plumper chin. "Had it not been so, I should have been forced to apply to the secretary for a warrant before this."

"Then you'll wait," said his lordship, "and you'll act as I may direct you. It will be to your credit in the end. Wait until Caryll has enmeshed himself by frequent visits to Sir Richard's. Then get your warrant—when I give the word—and execute it one fine night when Caryll happens to be closeted with Everard. Whether we can get further evidence against him or not, that circumstance of his being found with the Pretender's agent should go some way towards hanging him. The rest we must supply."

Mr. Green smiled seraphically. "Ecod! I'd give my ears to have the slippery fellow safe. Codso! I would. He bubbled me at Maidstone, and I limped a fortnight from the kick he gave me."

"He shall do a little more kicking—with both feet," said his lordship with unction.

CHAPTER XVI

MR. GREEN EXECUTES HIS WARRANT

Five days later, Mr. Caryll—whose recovery had so far progressed that he might now be said to be his own man again—came briskly up from Charing Cross one evening at dusk, to the house at the corner of Maiden Lane where Sir Richard Everard was lodged. He observed three or four fellows lounging about the corner of Chandos street and Bedford street, but it did not occur to him that from that point they could command Sir Richard's door—nor that such could be their object—until, as he swung sharply round the corner, he hurtled violently into a man who was moving in the opposite direction without looking whither he was going. The man stepped quickly aside with a murmured word of apology, to give Mr. Caryll the wall that he might pass on. But Mr. Caryll paused.

"Ah, Mr. Green!" said he very pleasantly. "How d'ye? Have ye been searching folk of late?"

Mr. Green endeavored to dissemble his startled expression in a grin that revealed his white teeth. "Ye can't forgive me that blunder, Mr. Caryll," said he.

Mr. Caryll smiled fondly upon him. "From your manner I take it that on your side you practice a more Christian virtue. It is plain that you forgive me the sequel."

Mr. Green shrugged and spread his hands. "You were in the right, sir; you were in the right," he explained. "Those are the risks a man of my calling must run. I must suffer for my blunders."

Mr. Caryll continued to smile. But that the light was failing, the spy might have observed a certain hardening in the lines of his mouth. "Here is a very humble mood," said he. "It is like the crouch before the spring. In whom do you design to plant your claws?— yours and your friends yonder." And he pointed with his cane across the street towards the loungers he had observed.

"My friends?" quoth Mr. Green, in a voice of disgust. "Nay, your honor! No friends of mine, ecod! Indeed, no!"

"No? I am at fault, then. Yet they look as if they might be bumbailiffs. 'Tis the kind ye herd with, is't not? Give you good-even, Mr. Green." And he went on, cool and unconcerned, and turned in through the narrow doorway by the glover's shop to mount the stairs to Sir Richard's lodging.

Mr. Green stood still to watch him go. Then he swore through his teeth, and beckoned one of those whose acquaintance he had disclaimed.

"'Tis like him, ecod! to have gone in in spite of seeing me and you! He's cool! Damned cool! But he'll be cooler yet, codso!" Then, briskly questioning his satellite: "Is Sir Richard within, Jerry?"

"Ay," answered Jerry—a rough, heavily-built tatterdemalion. "He's been there these two hours."

"'Tis our chance to nab 'em both, then-our last chance, maybe. The game is up. That fine gentleman has smoked it." He was angry beyond measure. Their plans were far from ripe, and yet to delay longer now that their vigilance was detected was, perhaps, to allow Sir Richard to slip through their fingers, as well as the other. "Have ye your barkers?" he asked harshly.

Jerry tapped a heavily bulging pocket, and winked. Mr. Green thrust his three-cornered hat a-cock over one eye, and with his hands behind the tails of his coat, stood pondering. "Ay, pox on't!" he grumbled. "It must be done to-night. I dursn't delay longer. We'll give the gentlemen time to settle comfortably; then up we go to make things merry for 'em." And he beckoned the others across.

Meanwhile Mr. Caryll had gone up with considerable misgivings. The last letter he had received from Sir Richard—that day at Stretton House—had been to apprise him that his adoptive father was on the point of leaving town but that he would be returned within the week. The business that had taken him had been again concerned with Atterbury the obstinate. Upon another vain endeavor to dissuade the bishop from a scheme his king did not approve had Sir Richard journeyed to Rochester. He had had his pains for nothing. Atterbury had kept him there, entertaining him, and seeking in his turn to engulf the agent in the business that was toward—business which was ultimately to suck down Atterbury and his associates. Sir Richard, however, was very firm. And when at last he left Rochester to return to town and his adoptive son, a coolness marked the parting of those two adherents of the Stuart dynasty.

Returned to London—whence his absence had been marked with alarm by Mr. Green—Sir Richard had sent a message to Mr. Caryll, and the latter made haste to answer it in person.

His adoptive father received him with open arms, and such a joy in his face, such a light in his old eyes as should have gladdened his visitor, yet only served sadden him the more. He sighed as Sir Richard thrust him back that he might look at him.

"Ye're pale, boy," he said, "and ye look thinner." And with that he fell to reviling the deed that was the cause of this, Rotherby and the whole brood of Ostermore.

"Let be," said Mr. Caryll, as he dropped into a chair.

"Rotherby is undergoing his punishment. The town looks on him as a cut-throat who has narrowly escaped the gallows. I marvel that he tarries here. An I were he, I think I'd travel for a year or two."

"What weakness made you spare him when ye had him at the point of your sword?"

"That which made me regret that I had him there; the reflection that he is my brother."

Sir Richard looked at him in some surprise. "I thought you of sterner stuff, Justin," he said presently, and sighed, passing a long white hand across his bony brow. "I thought I had reared you to a finer strength. But there! What of Ostermore himself?"

"What of him?"

"Have you not talked again with him of the matter of going over to King James?"

"To what end, since the chance is lost? His betrayal now would involve the betrayal of Atterbury and the others—for he has been in touch with them."

"Has he though? The bishop said naught of this."

"I have it from my lord himself—and I know the man. Were he taken they'd wring out of him whatever happened to be in him. He has no discretion. Indeed, he's but a clod, too stupid even to be aware of his own stupidity."

"Then what is to be done?" inquired Sir Richard, frowning.

"We'd best get home to France again."

"And leave matters thus?" He considered a moment, and shook his head, smiling bitterly. "Could that content you, Justin? Could you go as you have come—taking no more than you brought; leaving that man as you found him? Could you?"

Mr. Caryll looked at the baronet, and wondered for a moment whether he should persevere in the rule of his life and deal quite frankly with him, telling him precisely what he felt. Then he realized that he would not be understood. He could not combat the fanaticism that was Sir Richard's in this matter. If he told him the truth; how he loathed the task; how he rejoiced that circumstances had now put it beyond his reach—all he would achieve would be to wound Sir Richard in his tenderest place and to no purpose.

"It is not a matter of what I would," he answered slowly, wearily almost. "It is a matter of what I must. Here in England is no more to be done. Moreover, there's danger for you in lingering, or I'm much mistaken else."

"Danger of what?" asked Sir Richard, with indifference.

"You are being spied upon."

"Pho! I am accustomed to it. I have been spied upon all my life."

"Like enough. But this time the spies are messengers from the secretary of state. I caught a glimpse of them lurking about your doorway—three or four at least—and as I entered I all but fell over a Mr. Green—a most pertinacious gentleman with whom I have already some acquaintance. He is the very man who searched me at Maidstone; he has kept his eye upon me ever since, which has not troubled me. But that he should keep an eye on you means that your identity is suspected, and if that be so—well, the sooner we are out of England the better for your health."

Sir Richard shook his head calmly. The fine-featured, lean old face showed no sign of uneasiness. "A fig for all that!" said he. "I go not thus—empty-handed as I came. After all these years of waiting."

A knock fell upon the door, and Sir Richard's man entered. His face was white, his eyes startled.

"Sir Richard," he announced, his voice lowered portentously, "there are some men here who insist upon seeing you."

Mr. Caryll wheeled in his chair. "Surely they did not ask for him by name?" he inquired in the same low key employed by the valet.

The man nodded in silence. Mr. Caryll swore through his teeth. Sir Richard rose.

"I am occupied at present," he said in a calm voice. "I can receive nobody. Desire to know their business. If it imports, bid them come again to-morrow."

"It is over-urgent for that, Sir Richard Everard," came the soft voice of Mr. Green, who thrust himself suddenly forward past the servant. Other figures were seen moving behind him in the ante-room.

"Sir," cried Sir Richard angrily. "This is a most insolent intrusion. Bentley, show this fellow the door."

Bentley set a hand on Mr. Green's shoulder. Mr. Green nimbly twisted out of it, and produced a paper. "I have here a warrant for your apprehension, Sir Richard, from my Lord Carteret, the secretary of state."

Mr. Caryll advanced menacingly upon the tipstaff. Mr. Green stepped back, and fell into a defensive attitude, balancing a short but formidable-looking life-preserver.

"Keep your distance, sir, or 'twill be the worse for you," he threatened. "Hi!" he called. "Jerry! Beattie!"

Jerry, Beattie, and two other ruffians crowded to the doorway, but advanced little beyond the threshold. Mr. Caryll turned to Sir Richard. But Mr. Green was the first to speak.

"Sir Richard," said he, "you'll see that we are but instruments of the law. It grieves me profoundly to have you for our object. But ye'll see that 'tis no affair of ours, who have but to do the duty that we're ordered. Ye'll not give these poor fellows trouble, I trust. Ye'll surrender quietly."

Sir Richard's answer was to pull open a drawer in the writing-table, by which he was standing, and whip out a pistol.

What exactly he may have intended, he was never allowed to announce. An explosion shook the room, coming from the doorway, upon which Mr. Caryll had turned his shoulder; there was a spurt of flame, and Sir Richard collapsed forward onto the table, and slithered thence to the ground.

Jerry, taking fright at the sight of the pistol Sir Richard had produced, had forestalled what he supposed to be the baronet's intentions by firing instantly upon him, with this disastrous result.

Confusion ensued. Mr. Caryll, with no more thought for the tipstaves than he had for the smoke in his eyes or the stench of powder in his nostrils, sped to Sir Richard. In a passion of grief and anxiety, he raised his adoptive father, aided by Bentley, what time Mr. Green was abusing Jerry, and Jerry was urging in exculpation how he had acted purely in Mr. Green's interest, fearing that Sir Richard might have been on the point of shooting him.

The spy went forward to Mr. Caryll. "I am most profoundly sorry—" he began.

"Take your sorrow to hell," snarled Mr. Caryll, his face livid, his eyes blazing uncannily. "I believe ye've murdered him."

"Ecod! the fool shall smart for't if Sir Richard dies," grumbled Mr. Green.

"What's that to me? You may hang the muckworm, and what shall that profit any one? Will it restore me Sir Richard's life? Send one of your ruffians for a doctor, man. And bid him hasten."

Mr. Green obeyed with alacrity. Apart from his regrets at this happening for its own sake, it would suit his interests not at all that Sir Richard should perish thus. Meanwhile, with the help of the valet, who was blubbering like a child—for he had been with Sir Richard for over ten years, and was attached to him as a dog to its master—they opened the wounded man's sodden waistcoat and shirt, and reached the hurt, which was on the right side of the breast.

Between them they lifted him up gently. Mr. Green would have lent a hand, but a snarl from Mr. Caryll drove him back in sheer terror, and alone those two bore the baronet into the next room and laid him on his bed. Here they did the little that they could; propping him up and stemming the bleeding, what time they waited through what seemed a century for the doctor's coming, Mr. Caryll mad—stark mad for the time—with grief and rage.

The physician arrived at last—a small, bird-like man under a great gray periwig, with pointed features and little eyes that beamed brightly behind horn-rimmed spectacles.

In the ante-room he was met by Mr. Green, who in in a few words told him what had happened. Then the doctor entered the bedchamber alone, and deposing hat and cane, went forward to make his examination.

Mr. Caryll and Bentley stood aside to give place to him. He stooped, felt the pulse, examined the lips of the wound, estimating the locality and direction of the bullet, and his mouth made a clucking sound as of deprecation.

"Very deplorable, very deplorable!" he muttered. "So hale a man, too, despite his years. Very deplorable!" He looked up. "A Jacobite, ye say he is, sir?"

"Will he live?" inquired Mr. Caryll shortly, by way of recalling the man of medicine to the fact that politics was not the business on which he had been summoned.

The doctor pursed his lips, and looked at Mr. Caryll over the top of his spectacles. "He will live—"

"Thank God!" breathed Mr. Caryll.

"—perhaps an hour," the doctor concluded, and never knew how near was Mr. Caryll to striking him. He turned again to his patient, producing a probe. "Very deplorable!" Mr. Caryll heard him muttering, parrot-like.

A pause ensued, and a silence broken only by occasional cluckings from the little doctor, and Mr. Caryll stood by, a prey to an anguish more poignant than he had ever known. At last there was a groan from the wounded man. Mr. Caryll started forward.

Sir Richard's eyes were open, and he was looking about him at the doctor, the valet, and, lastly, at his adopted son. He smiled faintly at the latter. Then the doctor touched Mr. Caryll's sleeve, and drew him aside.

"I cannot reach the bullet," he said. "But 'tis no matter for that." He shook his head solemnly. "The lung has been pierced. A little time now, and—I can do nothing more."

Mr. Caryll nodded in silence, his face drawn with pain. With a gesture he dismissed the doctor, who went out with Bentley.

When the valet returned, Mr. Caryll was on his knees beside the bed, Sir Richard's hand in his, and Sir Richard was speaking in a feeble, hoarse voice—gasping and coughing at intervals.

"Don't—don't grieve, Justin," he was saying. "I am an old man. My time must have been very near. I—I am glad that it is thus. It is much better than if they had taken me. They'd ha' shown me no mercy. 'Tis swifter thus, and—and easier."

Silently Justin wrung the hand he held.

"You'll miss me a little, Justin," the old man resumed presently. "We have been good friends, lad—good friends for thirty years."

"Father!" Justin cried, a sob in his voice.

Sir Richard smiled. "I would I were your father in more than name, Justin. Hast been a good son to me—no son could have been more than you."

Bentley drew nigh with a long glass containing a cordial the doctor had advised. Sir Richard drank avidly, and sighed content when he returned the glass. "How long yet, Justin?" he inquired.

"Not long, father," was the gloomy answer.

"It is well. I am content. I am happy, Justin. Believe me, I am happy. What has my life been? Dissipated in the pursuit of a phantom." He spoke musingly, critically calm, as one who already upon the brink of dissolution takes already but an impersonal interest in the course he has run in life.

Judging so, his judgment was clearer than it had yet been; it grew sane, and was freed at last from the hackles of fanaticism; and there was something that he saw in its true proportions. He sighed heavily.

"This is a judgment upon me," he said presently. He turned his great eyes full upon Justin, and their dance was infinitely wistful. "Do you remember, Justin, that night at your lodging—that first night on which we talked here in London of the thing you were come to do—the thing to which I urged you? Do you recall how you upbraided me for having set you a task that was unworthy and revolting?"

"I remember," answered Justin, with an inward shudder, fearful of what might follow.

"Oh, you were right, Justin; right, and I was entirely wrong— wickedly wrong. I should have left vengeance to God. He is wreaking it. Ostermore's whole life has been a punishment; his end will be a punishment. I understand it now. We do no wrong in life, Justin, for which in this same life payment is not exacted. Ostermore has been paying. I should have been content with that. After all, he is your father in the flesh, and it was not for you to raise your hand against him. 'Tis what you have felt, and I am glad you should have felt it, for it proves your worthiness. Can you forgive me?"

"Nay, nay, father! Speak not of forgiveness."

"I have sore need of it."

"Ah, but not from me; not from me! What is there I should forgive? There is a debt between us I had hoped to repay some day

143

when you were grown truly old. I had looked to tend you in your old age, to be the comfort of it, and the support that you were to my infancy."

"It had been sweet, Justin," sighed Sir Richard, smiling upon his adopted son, and putting forth an unsteady hand to stroke the white, drawn face. "It had been sweet. It is sweet to hear that you so proposed."

A shudder convulsed him. He sank back coughing, and there was froth and blood on his lips. Reverently Justin wiped them, and signed for the cordial to Bentley, who stood, numbed, in the background.

"It is the end," said Sir Richard feebly. "God has been good to me beyond my deserts, and this is a crowning mercy. Consider, Justin, it might have been the gibbet and a crowd—instead of this snug bed, and you and Bentley here—just two good friends."

Bentley, losing all self-control at this mention of himself, sank weeping to his knees. Sir Richard put out a hand, and touched his head.

"You will serve Mr. Caryll, Bentley. You'll find him a good master if you are as good a servant to him as you have been to me."

Then suddenly he made the quick movement of one who bethinks himself of something. He waved Bentley away.

"There is a case in the drawer yonder," he said, when the servant was beyond earshot. "It contains papers that concern you— certificates of your birth and of your mothers death. I brought them with me as proofs of your identity, against the time when the hour of vengeance upon Ostermore should strike. They twill serve no purpose now. Burn them. They are best destroyed."

Mr. Caryll nodded understanding, and on Sir Richard's part there followed another fight for breath, another attack of coughing, during which Bentley instinctively approached again.

When the paroxysm was past, Sir Richard turned once more to Justin, who was holding him in his arms, upright, to ease his breathing. "Be good to Bentley," he murmured, his voice very faint and exhausted now. "You are my heir, Justin. All that I have—I set all in order ere I left Paris. It—it is growing dark. You have not snuffed the candles, Bentley. They are burning very low."

Suddenly he started forward, held as he was in Justin's arms. He half-raised his arms, holding out his hands toward the foot of the bed. His eyes dilated; the expression of his livid face grew first surprised, then joyous—beatific. "Antoinette!" he cried in a loud voice. "Antoi—"

And thus, abruptly, but in great happiness, he passed.

144

CHAPTER XVII

AMID THE GRAVES

What time Sir Richard had been dying in the inner room, Mr. Green and two of his acolytes had improved the occasion by making a thorough search in Sir Richard's writing-table and a thorough investigation of every scrap of paper found there. From which you will understand how much Mr. Green was a gentleman who set business above every other consideration.

The man who had shot Sir Richard had been ordered by Mr. Green to take himself off, and had been urged to go down on his knees, for once in a way, and pray Heaven that his rashness might not bring him to the gallows as he so richly deserved.

His fourth myrmidon Mr. Green had dispatched with a note to my Lord Rotherby, and it was entirely upon the answer he should receive that it must depend whether he proceeded or not, forthwith, to the apprehension of Mr. Caryll. Meanwhile the search went on amain, and was extended presently to the very bedroom where the dead Sir Richard lay. Every nook and cranny was ransacked; the very mattress under the dead man was removed, and investigated, and even Mr. Caryll and Bentley had to submit to being searched. But it all proved fruitless. Not a line of treasonable matter was to be found anywhere. To the certificates upon Mr. Caryll the searcher made the mistake of paying but little heed in view of their nature.

But if there were no proofs of plots and treasonable dealings, there was, at least, abundant proof of Sir Richard's identity, and Mr. Green appropriated these against any awkward inquiries touching the manner in which the baronet had met his death.

Of such inquiries, however, there were none. It was formally sworn to Lord Carteret by Green and his men that the secretary's messenger, Jerry—the fellow owned no surname—had shot Sir Richard in self-defence, when Sir Richard had produced firearms upon being arrested on a charge of high treason, for which they held the secretary's own warrant.

At first Lord Carteret considered it a thousand pities that they should not have contrived matters better so as to take Sir Richard alive; but upon reflection he was careful not to exaggerate to himself the loss occasioned by his death, for Sir Richard, after all, was a notoriously stubborn man, not in the least likely to have made any avowals worth having. So that his trial, whilst probably resulting sterile of such results as the government could desire, would have given publicity to the matter of a plot that was hatching; and such publicity at a time of so much unrest was the last thing the government desired. Where Jacobitism was concerned, Lord Carteret had the wise discretion to proceed with the extremest caution. Publicity might serve to fan the smouldering embers into a blaze, whereas it was his cunning aim quietly to stifle them as he came upon them.

So, upon the whole, he was by no means sure but that Jerry had done the state the best possible service in disposing thus summarily of that notorious Jacobite agent, Sir Richard Everard. And his lordship saw to it that there was no inquiry and that nothing further was heard of the matter.

As for Lord Rotherby, had the affair transpired twenty-four hours earlier, he would certainly have returned Mr. Green a message to effect the arrest of Mr. Caryll upon suspicion. But as it chanced, he had that very afternoon received a visit from his mother, who came in great excitement to inform him that she had forced from Lord Ostermore an acknowledgment that he was plotting with Mr. Caryll to go over to King James.

So, before they could move further against Mr. Caryll, it behooved them to ascertain precisely to what extent Lord Ostermore might not be incriminated, as otherwise the arrest of Caryll might lead to exposures that would ruin the earl more thoroughly than could any South Sea bubble revelations. Thus her ladyship to her son. He turned upon her.

"Why, madam," said he, "these be the very arguments I used t'other day when we talked of this; and all you answered me then was to call me a dull-witted clod, for not seeing how the thing might be done without involving my lord."

"Tcha!" snapped her ladyship, beating her knuckles impatiently with her fan. "A dull-witted clod did I call you? 'Twas flattery—sheer flattery; for I think ye're something worse. Fool, can ye not see the difference that lies betwixt your disclosing a plot to the secretary of state, and causing this Caryll to disclose it—as might happen if he were seized? First discover the plot—find out in what it may consist, and then go to Lord Carteret to make your terms."

He looked at her, out of temper by her rebuke. "I may be as dull as your ladyship says—but I do not see in what the position now is different from what it was."

"It isn't different—but we thought it was different," she explained impatiently. "We assumed that your father would not have betrayed himself, counting upon his characteristic caution. But it seems we are mistook. He has betrayed himself to Caryll. And before we can move in this matter, we must have proofs of a plot to lay before the secretary of state."

Lord Rotherby understood, and accounted himself between Scylla and Charybdis, and when that evening Green's messenger found him, he gnashed his teeth in rage at having to allow this chance to pass, at being forced to temporize until he should be less parlously situated. He returned Mr. Green an urgent message to take no steps concerning Mr. Caryll until they should have concerted together.

Mr. Green was relieved. Mr. Caryll arrested might stir up matters against the slayer of Sir Richard, and this was a business which Mr. Green had prevision enough to see his master, Lord Carteret, would prefer should not be stirred up. He had a notion, for the rest, that if Mr. Caryll were left to go his ways, he would not be likely to give trouble touching that same matter. And he was right in this. Before his overwhelming sense of loss, Mr. Caryll had few thoughts to bestow upon the manner in which that loss had been sustained. Moreover, if he had a quarrel with any one on that account, it was with the government whose representative had issued the warrant for Sir Richard's arrest, and no more with the wretched tipstaff who had fired the pistol than with the pistol itself. Both alike were but instruments, of slightly different degrees of insensibility.

For twenty-four hours Mr. Caryll's grief was overwhelming in its poignancy. His sense of solitude was awful. Gone was the only living man who had stood to him for kith and kin. He was left alone in the world; utterly alone. That was the selfishness of his sorrow— the consideration of Sir Richard's death as it concerned himself.

Presently an alloy of consolation was supplied by the reflection of Sir Richard's own case—as Sir Richard himself had stated it upon his deathbed. His life had not been happy; it had been poisoned by a monomania, which, like a worm in the bud, had consumed the sweetness of his existence. Sir Richard was at rest. And since he had been discovered, that shot was, indeed, the most merciful end that could have been measured out to him. The alternative might have been the gibbet and the gaping crowd, and a moral torture to precede the end. Better—a thousand times better— as it was.

So much did all this weigh with him that when on the following Monday he accompanied the body to its grave, he found his erstwhile passionate grief succeeded by an odd thankfulness that things were as they were, although it must be confessed that a pang of returning anguish smote him when he heard the earth clattering down upon the wooden box that held all that remained of the man who had been father, mother, brother and all else to him.

He turned away at last, and was leaving the graveyard, when some one touched him on the arm. It was a timid touch. He turned sharply, and found himself looking into the sweet face of Hortensia Winthrop, wondering how came she there. She wore a long, dark cloak and hood, but her veil was turned back. A chair was waiting not fifty paces from them along the churchyard wall.

"I came but to tell you how much I feel for you in this great loss," she said.

He looked at her in amazement. "How did you know?" he asked her.

"I guessed," said she. "I heard that you were with him at the end, and I caught stray words from her ladyship of what had passed. Lord Rotherby had the information from the tipstaff who went to arrest Sir Richard Everard. I guessed he was your—your foster-father, as you called him; and I came to tell you how deeply I sorrow for you in your sorrow."

He caught her hands in his and bore them to his lips, reckless of who might see the act. "Ah, this is sweet and kind in you," said he.

She drew him back into the churchyard again. Along the wall there was an avenue of limes—a cool and pleasant walk wherein idlers lounged on Sundays in summer after service. Thither she drew him. He went almost mechanically. Her sympathy stirred his sorrow again, as sympathy so often does.

"I have buried my heart yonder, I think," said he, with a wave of his hand towards that spot amid the graves where the men were toiling with their shovels. "He was the only living being that loved me."

"Ah, surely not," said she, sorrow rather than reproach in her gentle voice.

"Indeed, yes. Mine is a selfish grief. It is for myself that I sorrow, for myself and my own loneliness. It is thus with all of us. When we argue that we weep the dead, it would be more true to say that we bewail the living. For him—it is better as it is. No doubt it is better so for most men, when all is said, and we do wrong to weep their passing."

"Do not talk so," she said. "It hurts."

"Ay—it is the way of truth to hurt, which is why, hating pain, we shun truth so often." He sighed. "But, oh, it was good in you to seek me, to bring me word with your own lips of your sweet sympathy. If aught could lighten the gloom of my sorrow, surely it is that."

They stepped along in silence until they came to the end of the avenue, and turned. It was no idle silence: the silence of two beings who have naught to say. It was a grave, portentous silence, occasioned by the unutterable much in the mind of one, and by the other's apprehension of it. At last she spoke, to ask him what he meant to do.

"I shall return to France," he said. "It had perhaps been better had I never crossed to England."

"I cannot think so," she said, simply, frankly and with no touch of a coquetry that had been harshly at discord with time and place.

He shot her a swift, sidelong glance; then stopped, and turned. "I am glad on't," said he. "'Twill make my going the easier."

"I mean not that," she cried, and held out her hands to him. "I meant not what you think—you know, you know what 'twas I meant. You know—you must—what impulse brought me to you in this hour, when I knew you must need comfort. And in return how cruel, were you not—to tell me that yonder lay buried the only living being that—that loved you?"

His fingers were clenched upon her arm. "Don't—don't!" he implored hoarsely, a strange fire in his eyes, a hectic flush on either cheek. "Don't! Or I'll forget what I am, and take advantage of this midsummer folly that is upon you."

"Is it no more than folly, Justin?" she asked him, brown eyes looking up into gray-green.

"Ay, something more—stark madness. All great emotions are. It will pass, and you will be thankful that I was man enough—strong enough—to allow it the chance of passing."

She hung her head, shaking it sorrowfully. Then very softly: "Is it no more than the matter of—of that, that stands between us?" she inquired.

"No more than that," he answered, "and yet more than enough. I have no name to offer any woman."

"A name?" she echoed scornfully. "What store do you think I lay by that? When you talk so, you obey some foolish prejudice; no more."

"Obedience to prejudices is the whole art of living," he answered, sighing.

She made a gesture of impatience, and went on. "Justin, you said you loved me; and when you said so much, you gave me the right—or so I understood it—to speak to you as I am doing now. You are alone in the world, without kith or kin. The only one you had— the one who represented all for you—lies buried there. Would you return thus, lonely and alone, to France?"

"Ah, now I understand!" he cried. "Now I understand. Pity is the impulse that has urged you—pity for my loneliness, is't not, Hortensia?"

"I'll not deny that without the pity there might not have been the courage. Why should I—since it is a pity that gives you no offense, a pity that is rooted firmly in—in love for you, my Justin?"

He set his hands upon her shoulders, and with glowing eyes regarded her. "Ah, sweet!" said he, "you make me very, very proud."

And then his arms dropped again limply to his sides. He sighed, and shook his head drearily. "And yet—reflect. When I come to beg your hand in marriage of your guardian, what shall I answer him of the questions he will ask me of myself—touching my family, my parentage and all the rest that he will crave to know?"

She observed that he was very white again. "Need you enter into that? A man is himself; not his father or his family." And then she checked. "You make me plead too much," she said, a crimson flood in her fair cheeks. "I'll say no more than I have said. Already have I said more than I intended. And you have wanted mercy that you could drive me to it. You know my mind—my—my inmost heart. You know that I care nothing for your namelessness. It is yours to decide what you will do. Come, now; my chair is staying for me."

He bowed; he sought again to convey some sense of his appreciation of her great nobility; then led her through the gate and to her waiting chair.

"Whatever I may decide, Hortensia" was the last thing he said to her, "and I shall decide as I account best for you, rather than for myself; and for myself there needs no thought or hesitation— whatever I may decide, believe me when I say from my soul that all my life shall be the sweeter for this hour."

CHAPTER XVIII

THE GHOST OF THE PAST

Temptation had seized Mr. Caryll in a throttling grip, and for two whole days he kept the house, shunning all company and wrestling with that same Temptation. In the end he took a whimsical resolve, entirely worthy of himself.

He would go to Lord Ostermore formally to ask in marriage the hand of Mistress Winthrop, and he would be entirely frank with the earl, stating his exact condition, but suppressing the names of his parents.

He was greatly taken with the notion. It would create a situation ironical beyond any, grotesque beyond belief; and its development should be stupendously interesting. It attracted him irresistibly. That he should leave it to his own father to say whether a man born as he was born might aspire to marry his father's ward, had in it something that savored of tragi-comedy. It was a pretty problem, that once set could not be left unsolved by a man of Mr. Caryll's temperament. And, indeed, no sooner was the idea conceived than it quickened into a resolve upon which he set out to act.

He bade Leduc call a chair, and, dressed in mourning, but with his habitual care, he had himself carried to Lincoln's Inn Fields.

Engrossed as he was in his own thoughts, he paid little heed to the hum of excitement about the threshold of Stretton House. Within the railed enclosure that fronted the mansion two coaches were drawn up, and a little knot of idlers stood by one of these in busy gossip.

Paying no attention to them, Mr. Caryll mounted the steps, nor noticed the gravity of the porter's countenance as he passed within.

In the hall he found a little flock of servants gathered together, and muttering among themselves like conspirators in a tragedy; and so engrossed that they paid no heed to him as he advanced, nor until he had tapped one of them on the shoulder with his cane—and tapped him a thought peremptorily.

"How now?" said he. "Does no one wait here?"

They fell apart a little, and stood at attention, with something curious in their bearing, one and all.

"My service to his lordship, and say that I desire to speak with him."

151

They looked at one another in hesitation for a moment; then Humphries, the butler, came forward. "Your honor'll not have heard the news?" said he, a solemn gravity in face and tone.

"News?" quoth Mr. Caryll sharply, intrigued by so much show of mystery. "What news?"

"His lordship is very ill, sir. He had a seizure this morning when they came for him."

"A seizure?" said Mr. Caryll. And then: "When they came for him?" he echoed, struck by something odd in the man's utterance of those five words. "When who came for him?"

"The messengers, sir," replied the butler dejectedly. "Has your honor not heard?" And seeing the blank look on Mr. Caryll's face, he proceeded without waiting for an answer: "His lordship was impeached yesterday by his Grace of Wharton on a matter concerning the South Sea Company, and Lord Carteret—the secretary of state, your honor—sent this morning to arrest him."

"'Sdeath!" ejaculated Mr. Caryll in his surprise, a surprise that was tempered with some dismay. "And he had a seizure, ye say?"

"An apoplexy, your honor. The doctors are with him now; Sir James, himself, is here. They're cupping him—so I hear from Mr. Tom, his lordship's man. I'd ha' thought your honor would ha' heard. 'Tis town talk, they say."

Mr. Caryll would have found it difficult to have said exactly what impression this news made upon him. In the main, however, he feared it left him cold.

"'Tis very regrettable," said he. He fell thoughtful a moment. Then: "Will you send word to Mistress Winthrop that I am here, and would speak with her, Humphries?"

Humphries conducted Mr. Caryll to the little white and gold withdrawing-room that was Hortensia's. There, in the little time that he waited, he revolved the situation as it now stood, and the temptation that had been with him for the past three days rose up now with a greater vigor. Should Lord Ostermore die, Temptation argued, he need no longer hesitate. Hortensia would be as much alone in the world as he was; worse, for life at Stretton House with her ladyship—from which even in the earl's lifetime she had been led to attempt to escape—must be a thing unbearable, and what alternative could he suggest but that she should become his wife?

She came to him presently, white-faced and with startled eyes. As she took his outstretched hands, she attempted a smile. "It is kind in you to come to me at such a time," she said.

"You mistake," said he, "as is but natural. I had not heard what had befallen. I came to ask your hand in marriage of his lordship."

Some faint color tinged her cheeks. "You had decided, then?"

"I had decided that his lordship must decide," he answered.

"And now?"

"And now it seems we must decide for ourselves if his lordship dies."

Her mind swung to the graver matter. "Sir James has every hope," she said, and added miserably: "I know not which to pray for, his recovery or his death."

"Why that?"

"Because if he survive it may be for worse. The secretary's agent is even now seeking evidence against him among his own papers. He is in the library at this moment, going through his lordship's desk."

Mr. Caryll started. That mention of Ostermore's desk brought vividly before his mind the recollection of the secret drawer wherein the earl had locked away the letter he had received from King James and his own reply, all packed as it was, with treason. If that drawer were discovered, and those papers found, then was Ostermore lost indeed, and did he survive this apoplexy, it would be to surrender his head upon the scaffold.

A moment he considered this, dispassionately. Then it broke upon his mind that were this to happen, Ostermore's blood would indirectly be upon his own head, since for the purpose of betrayal had he sought him out with that letter from the exiled Stuart—which, be it remembered, King James himself had no longer wished delivered.

It turned him cold with horror. He could not remain idle and let matters run their course. He must avert these discoveries if it lay within his power to do so, or else he must submit to a lifetime of remorse should Ostermore survive to be attainted of treason. He had made an end—a definite end—long since of his intention of working Ostermore's ruin; he could not stand by now and see that ruin wrought as a result of the little that already he had done towards encompassing it.

"His papers must be saved," he said shortly. "I'll go to the library at once."

"But the secretary's agent is there already," she repeated.

"'Tis no matter for that," said he, moving towards the door. "His desk contains that which will cost him his head if discovered. I know it," he assured her, and left her cold with fear.

"But, then, you—you?" she cried. "Is it true that you are a Jacobite?"

"True enough," he answered.

"Lord Rotherby knows it," she informed him. "He told me it was so. If—if you interfere in this, it—it may mean your ruin." She came to him swiftly, a great fear written or her winsome face.

"Sh," said he. "I am not concerned to think of that at present. If Lord Ostermore perishes through his connection with the cause, it will mean worse than ruin for me—though not the ruin that you are thinking of."

"But what can you do?"

"That I go to learn."

"I will come with you, then."

He hesitated a moment, looking at her; then he opened the door, and held it for her, following after. He led the way across the hall to the library, and they went in together.

Lord Ostermore's secretaire stood open, and leaning over it, his back towards them was a short, stiffly-built man in a snuff-colored coat. He turned at the sound of the closing door, and revealed the pleasant, chubby face of Mr. Green.

"Ha!" said Mr. Caryll. "Mr. Green again. I declare, sir, ye've the gift of ubiquity."

The spy stood up to regard him, and for all that his voice inclined to sharpness when he spoke, the habitual grin sat like a mask upon the mobile features. "What d'ye seek here?"

"Tis what I was about to ask you—what you are seeking; for that you seek is plain. I thought perhaps I might assist you."

"I nothing doubt you could," answered Mr. Green with a fresh leer, that contained this time something ironic. "I nothing doubt it! But by your leave, I'll pursue my quest without your assistance."

Mr. Caryll continued, nevertheless, to advance towards him, Mistress Hortensia remaining in the background, a quiet spectator, betraying nothing of the anxieties by which she was being racked.

"Ye're mighty curt this morning, Mr. Green," said Mr. Caryll, very airy. "Ye're mighty curt, and ye're entirely wrong so to be. You might find me a very useful friend."

"I've found you so before," said Mr. Green sourly.

"Ye've a nice sense of humor," said Mr. Caryll, head on one side, contemplating the spy with admiration in his glance.

"And a nicer sense of a Jacobite," answered Mr. Green.

"He will have the last word, you perceive," said Mr. Caryll to Hortensia.

"Harkee, Mr. Caryll," quoth Mr. Green, quite grimly now. "I'd ha' laid you by the heels a month or more ago, but for certain friends o' mine who have other ends to serve."

"Sir, what you tell me shocks me. It shakes the very foundations of my faith in human nature. I have esteemed you an honest man, Mr. Green, and it seems—on your own confessing—that ye're no better than a damned rogue who neglects his duty to the state. I've a mind to see Lord Carteret, and tell him the truth of the matter."

"Ye shall have an opportunity before long, ecod!" said Mr. Green. "Good-morning to you! I've work to do." And he turned back to the desk.

"'Tis wasted labor," said Mr. Caryll, producing his snuff-box, and tapping it. "You might seek from now till the crack of doom, and not find what ye seek—not though you hack the desk to pieces. It has a secret, Mr. Green. I'll make a bargain with you for that secret."

Mr. Green turned again, and his shrewd, bright eyes scanned more closely that lean face, whose keenness was all dissembled now in an easy, languid smile. "A bargain?" grumbled the spy. "I' faith, then, the secret's worthless."

"Ye think that? Pho! 'Tis not like your usual wit, Mr. Green. The letter that I carried into England, and that you were at such splendid pains to find at Maidstone, is in here." And he tapped the veneered top of the secretaire with his forefinger. "But ye'll not find it without my help. It is concealed as effectively—as effectively as it was upon my person when ye searched me. Now, sir, will ye treat with me? It'll save you a world of labor."

Mr. Green still looked at him. He licked his lips thoughtfully, cat-like. "What terms d'ye make?" he inquired, but his tone was very cold. His busy brain was endeavoring to conjecture what exactly might be Mr. Caryll's object in this frankness which Mr. Green was not fool enough to believe sincere.

"Ah," said Mr. Caryll. "That is more the man I know." He tapped his snuff-box, and in that moment memory rather than inspiration showed him the thing he needed. "Did ye ever see 'The Constant Couple,' Mr. Green?" he inquired.

"'The Constant Couple'?" echoed Mr. Green, and though mystified, he must air his little jest. "I never saw any couple that was constant—leastways, not for long."

"Ha! Ye're a roguish wag! But 'The Constant Couple' I mean is a play."

"Oh, a play! Ay, I mind me I saw it some years ago, when 'twas first acted. But what has that to do with—"

"Ye'll understand in a moment," said Mr. Caryll, with a smile the spy did not relish. "D'ye recall a ruse of Sir Harry Wildairs to rid himself of the company of an intrusive old fool who was not wanted? D'ye remember what 'twas he did?"

Mr. Green, his head slightly on one side, was watching Mr. Caryll very closely, and not without anxiety. "I don't," said he, and dropped a hand to the pocket where a pistol lay, that he might be prepared for emergencies. "What did he do?"

"I'll show you," said Mr. Caryll. "He did this." And with a swift

155

upward movement, he emptied his snuff-box full into the face of Mr. Green.

Mr. Green leapt back, with a scream of pain, hands to his eyes, and quite unconsciously set himself to play to the life the part of the intrusive old fellow in the comedy. Dancing wildly about the room, his eyes smarting and burning so that he could not open them, he bellowed of hell-fire and other hot things of which he was being so intensely reminded.

"'Twill pass," Mr. Caryll consoled him. "A little water, and all will be well with you." He stepped to the door as he spoke, and flung it open. "Ho, there! Who waits?" he called.

Two or three footmen sprang to answer him. He took Mr. Green, still blind and vociferous, by the shoulders, and thrust him into their care. "This gentleman has had a most unfortunate accident. Get him water to wash his eyes—warm water. So! Take him. 'Twill pass, Mr. Green. 'Twill soon pass, I assure you."

He shut the door upon them, locked it, and turned to Hortensia, smiling grimly. Then he crossed quickly to the desk, and Hortensia followed him. He sat down, and pulled out bodily the bottom drawer on the right inside of the upper part of the desk, as he had seen Lord Ostermore do that day, a little over a week ago. He thrust his hand into the opening, and felt along the sides for some moments in vain. He went over the ground again slowly, inch by inch, exerting constant pressure, until he was suddenly rewarded by a click. The small trap disclosed itself. He pulled it up, and took some papers from the recess. He spread them before him. They were the documents he sought—the king's letter to Ostermore, and Ostermore's reply, signed and ready for dispatch. "These must be burnt," he said, "and burnt at once, for that fellow Green may return, or he may send others. Call Humphries. Get a taper from him."

She sped to the door, and did his bidding. Then she returned. She was plainly agitated. "You must go at once," she said, imploringly. "You must return to France without an instant's delay."

"Why, indeed, it would mean my ruin to remain now," he admitted. "And yet—" He held out his hands to her.

"I will follow you," she promised him. "I will follow you as soon as his lordship is recovered, or—or at peace."

"You have well considered, sweetheart?" he asked her, holding her to him, and looking down into her gentle eyes.

"There is no happiness for me apart from you."

Again his scruples took him. "Tell Lord Ostermore—tell him all," he begged her. "Be guided by him. His decision for you will represent the decision of the world."

"What is the world to me? You are the world to me," she cried.

There was a rap upon the door. He put her from him, and went to open. It was Humphries with a lighted taper. He took it, thanked the man with a word, and shut the door in his face, ignoring the fact that the fellow was attempting to tell him something.

He returned to the desk. "Let us make quite sure that this is all," he said, and held the taper so that the light shone into the recess. It seemed empty at first; then, as the light penetrated farther, he saw something that showed white at the back of the cachette. He thrust in his hand, and drew out a small package bound with a ribbon that once might have been green but was faded now to yellow. He set it on the desk, and returned to his search. There was nothing else. The recess was empty. He closed the trap and replaced the drawer. Then he sat down again, the taper at his elbow, Mistress Winthrop looking on, facing him across the top of the secretaire, and he took up the package.

The ribbon came away easily, and some half-dozen sheets fell out and scattered upon the desk. They gave out a curious perfume, half of age, half of some essence with which years ago they had been imbued. Something took Mr. Caryll in the throat, and he could never explain whether it was that perfume or some premonitory emotion, some prophetic apprehension of what he was about to see.

He opened the first of those folded sheets, and found it to be a letter written in French and in an ink that had paled to yellow with the years that were gone since it had been penned. The fine, pointed writing was curiously familiar to Mr. Caryll. He looked at the signature at the bottom of the page. It swam before his eyes— ANTOINETTE-"Celle qui l'adore, Antoinette," he read, and the whole world seemed blotted out for him; all consciousness, his whole being, his every sense, seemed concentrated into his eyes as they gazed upon that relic of a deluded woman's dream.

He did not read. It was not for him to commit the sacrilege of reading what that girl who had been his mother had written thirty years ago to the man she loved—the man who had proved false as hell.

He turned the other letters over; opened them one by one, to make sure that they were of the same nature as the first, and what time he did so he found himself speculating upon the strangeness of Ostermore's having so treasured them. Perhaps he had thrust them into that secret recess, and there forgotten them; 'twas an explanation that sorted better with what Mr. Caryll knew of his father, than the supposition that so dull and practical and self-centered a nature could have been irradiated by a gleam of such tenderness as the hoarding of those letters might have argued.

He continued to turn them over, half-mechanically, forgetful of the urgent need to burn the treasonable documents he had secured, forgetful of everything, even Hortensia's presence. And meantime she watched him in silence, marvelling at this delay, and still more at the gray look that had crept into his face.

"What have you found?" she asked at last.

"A ghost," he answered, and his voice had a strained, metallic ring. He even vented an odd laugh. "A bundle of old love-letters."

"From her ladyship?"

"Her ladyship?" He looked up, an expression on his face which seemed to show that he could not at the moment think who her ladyship might be. Then as the picture of that bedaubed, bedizened and harsh-featured Jezebel arose in his mind to stand beside the sweet girl—image of his mother—as he knew her from the portrait that hung at Maligny—he laughed again. "No, not from her ladyship," said he. "From a woman who loved him years ago." And he turned to the seventh and last of those poor ghosts-the seventh, a fateful number.

He spread it before him; frowned down on it a moment with a sharp hiss of indrawn breath. Then he twisted oddly on his chair, and sat bolt upright, staring straight before him with unseeing eyes. Presently he passed a hand across his brow, and made a queer sound in his throat.

"What is it?" she asked.

But he did not answer; he was staring at the paper again. A while he sat thus; then with swift fevered fingers he took up once more the other letters. He unfolded one, and began to read. A few lines he read, and then—"O God!" he cried, and flung out his arms under stress of 'his emotions. One of them caught the taper that stood upon the desk; and swept it, extinguished, to the floor. He never heeded it, never gave a thought to the purpose for which it had been fetched, a purpose not yet served. He rose. He was white as the dead are white, and she observed that he was trembling. He took up the bundle of old letters, and thrust them into an inside pocket of his coat.

"What are you doing?" she cried, seeking at last to arouse him from the spell under which he appeared to have fallen. "Those letters—"

"I must see Lord Ostermore," he answered wildly, and made for the door, reeling like a drunkard in his walk.

CHAPTER XIX

THE END OF LORD OSTERMORE

In the ante-room communicating with Lord Ostermore's bedroom the countess was in consultation with Rotherby, who had been summoned by his mother when my lord was stricken.

Her ladyship occupied the window-seat; Rotherby stood beside her, leaning slightly against the frame of the open window. Their conversation was earnest and conducted in a low key, and one would naturally have conjectured that it had for subject the dangerous condition of the earl. And so it had—the dangerous condition of the earl's political, if not physical, affairs. To her ladyship and her son, the matter of their own future was of greater gravity than the matter of whether his lordship lived or died— which, whatever it may be, is not unreasonable. Since the impeachment of my lord and the coming of the messengers to arrest him, the danger of ruin and beggary were become more imminent— indeed, they impended, and measures must be concerted to avert these evils. By comparison with that, the earl's succumbing or surviving was a trivial matter; and the concern they had manifested in Sir James' news—when the important, well-nourished physician who had bled his lordship came to inform them that there was hope—was outward only, and assumed for pure decorum's sake.

"Whether he lives or dies," said the viscount pertinently, after the doctor had departed to return to his patient, "the measures to be taken are the same." And he repeated the substance of their earlier discussions upon this same topic. "If we can but secure the evidence of his treason with Caryll," he wound up, "I shall be able to make terms with Lord Carteret to arrest the proceedings the government may intend, and thus avert the restitution it would otherwise enforce."

"But if he were to die," said her ladyship, as coldly, horribly calculating as though he were none of hers, "there would be an end to this danger. They could not demand restitution of the dead, nor impose fines upon him."

Rotherby shook his head. "Believe not that, madam," said he. "They can demand restitution of his heirs and impose their fines upon the estate. 'Twas done in the case of Chancellor Craggs, though he shot himself."

She raised a haggard face to his. "And do you dream that Lord Carteret would make terms with you?"

"If I can show him—by actual proof—that a conspiracy does exist, that the Stuart supporters are plotting a rising. Proof of that should be of value to Lord Carteret, of sufficient value to the government to warrant the payment of the paltry price I ask—that the impeachment against my father for his dealings with the South Sea Company shall not be allowed.

"But it might involve the worse betrayal of your father, Charles, and if he were to live—"

"'Sdeath, mother, why must you harp on that? I a'n't the fool you think me," he cried. "I shall make it a further condition that my father have immunity. There will be no lack of victims once the plot is disclosed; and they may begin upon that coxcomb Caryll—the damned meddler who is at the bottom of all this garboil."

She sat bemused, her eyes upon the sunlit gardens below, where a faint breeze was stirring the shrub tops.

"There is," she said presently, "a secret drawer somewhere in his desk. If he has papers they will, no doubt, be there. Had you not best be making search for them?"

He smiled darkly. "I have seen to that already," he replied.

"How?" excitedly. "You have got the papers?"

"No; but I have set an experienced hand to find them, and one, moreover, who has the right by virtue of his warrant—the messenger of the secretary of state."

She sat up, rigid. "'Sdeath! What is't ye mean?"

"No need for alarm," he reassured her. "This fellow Green is in my pay, as well as in the secretary's, and it will profit him most to keep faith with me. He's a self-seeking dog, content to run with the hare and hunt with the hounds, so that there be profit in it, and he'd sacrifice his ears to bring Mr. Caryll to the gallows. I have promised him that and a thousand pounds if we save the estates from confiscation."

She looked at him, between wonder and fear. "Can ye trust him?" she asked breathlessly.

He laughed softly and confidently. "I can trust him to earn a thousand pounds," he answered. "When he heard of the impeachment, he used such influence as he has to be entrusted with the arrest of his lordship; and having obtained his warrant, he came first to me to tell me of it. A thousand pounds is the price of him, body and soul. I bade him seek not only evidence of my lord's having received that plaguey stock, but also papers relating to this Jacobite plot into which his lordship has been drawn by our friend Caryll. He is at his work at present. And I shall hear from him when it is accomplished."

She nodded slowly, thoughtfully. "You have very well

160

disposed, Charles," she approved him. "If your father lives, it should not be a difficult matter—"

She checked suddenly and turned, while Rotherby, too, looked up and stepped quickly from the window-embrasure where he had stood.

The door of the bedroom had been suddenly pulled open, and Sir James came out, very pale and discomposed.

"Madam—your ladyship—my lord!" he gasped, his mouth working, his hands waving foolishly.

The countess rose to confront him, tall, severe and harsh. The viscount scowled a question. Sir James quailed before them, evidently in affliction.

"Madam—his lordship," he said, and by his eloquent gesture of dejection announced what he had some difficulty in putting into words.

She stepped forward, and took him by the wrist. "Is he dying?" she inquired.

"Have courage, madam," the doctor besought her.

The apparent irrelevancy of the request at such a moment, angered her. Her mood was dangerously testy. And had the doctor but known it, sympathy was a thing she had not borne well these many years.

"I asked you was he dying," she reminded him, with a cold sternness that beat aside all his attempts at subterfuge.

"Your ladyship—he is dead," he faltered, with lowered eyes.

"Dead?" she echoed dully, and her hand went to the region of her heart, her face turned livid under its rouge. "Dead?" she said again, and behind her, Rotherby echoed the dread word in a stupor almost equal to her own. Her lips moved to speak, but no words came. She staggered where she stood, and put her hand to her brow. Her son's arms were quickly about her. He supported her to a chair, where she sank as if all her joints were loosened.

Sir James flew for restoratives; bathed her brow with a dampened handkerchief; held strong salts to her nostrils, and murmured words of foolish, banal consolation, whilst Rotherby, in a half-dreaming condition, stunned by the suddenness of the blow, stood beside her, mechanically lending his assistance and supporting her.

Gradually she mastered her agitation. It was odd that she should feel so much at losing what she valued so little. Leastways, it would have been odd, had it been that. It was not—it was something more. In the awful, august presence of death, stepped so suddenly into their midst, she felt herself appalled.

For nigh upon thirty years she had been bound by legal and

161

churchly ties in a loveless union with Lord Ostermore—married for the handsome portion that had been hers, a portion which he had gamed away and squandered until, for their station, their circumstances were now absolutely straitened. They had led a harsh, discordant life, and the coming of a son, which should have bridged the loveless gulf between them, seemed but to have served to dig it wider. And the son had been just the harsh, unfeeling offspring that might be looked for from such a union. Thirty years of slavery had been her ladyship's, and in those thirty years her nature had been soured and warped, and what inherent sweetness it may once have known had long since been smothered and destroyed. She had no cause to love that man who had never loved her, never loved aught of hers beyond her jointure. And yet, there was the habit of thirty years. For thirty years they had been yoke-fellows, however detestable the yoke. But yesterday he had been alive and strong, a stupid, querulous thing maybe, but a living. And now he was so much carrion that should be given to the earth. In some such channel ran her ladyship's reflections during those few seconds in which she was recovering. For an instant she was softened. The long-since dried-up springs of tenderness seemed like to push anew under the shock of this event. She put out a hand to take her son's.

"Charles!" she said, and surprised him by the tender note.

A moment thus; then she was herself again. "How did he die?" she asked the doctor; and the abruptness of the resumption of her usual manner startled Sir James more than aught in his experience of such scenes.

"It was most sudden, madam," answered he. "I had the best grounds for hope. I was being persuaded we should save him. And then, quite suddenly, without an instant's warning, he succumbed. He just heaved a sigh, and was gone. I could scarcely believe my senses, madam."

He would have added more particulars of his feelings and emotions—for he was of those who believe that their own impressions of a phenomenon are that phenomenon's most interesting manifestations—but her ladyship waved him peremptorily into silence.

He drew back, washing his hands in the air, an expression of polite concern upon his face. "Is there aught else I can do to be of service to your ladyship?" he inquired, solicitous.

"What else?" she asked, with a fuller return to her old self. "Ye've killed him. What more is there you can do?"

"Oh, madam—nay, madam! I am most deeply grieved that my—my—"

"His lordship will wait upon you to the door," said she, designating her son.

The eminent physician effaced himself from her ladyship's attention. It was his boast that he could take a hint when one was given him; and so he could, provided it were broad enough, as in the present instance.

He gathered up his hat and gold-headed cane—the unfailing insignia of his order—and was gone, swiftly and silently.

Rotherby closed the door after him, and returned slowly, head bowed, to the window where his mother was still seated. They looked at each other gravely for a long moment.

"This makes matters easier for you," she said at length.

"Much easier. It does not matter now how far his complicity may be betrayed by his papers. I am glad, madam, to see you so far recovered from your weakness."

She shivered, as much perhaps at his tone as at the recollections he evoked. "You are very indifferent, Charles," said she.

He looked at her steadily, then slightly shrugged. "What need to wear a mask? Bah! Did he ever give me cause to feel for him?" he asked. "Mother, if one day I have a son of my own, I shall see to it that he loves me."

"You will be hard put to it, with your nature, Charles," she told him critically. Then she rose. "Will you go to him with me?" she asked.

He made as if to acquiesce, then halted. "No," he said, and there was repugnance in his tone and face. "Not—not now."

There came a knocking at the door, rapid, insistent. Grateful for the interruption, Rotherby went to open.

Mr. Green staggered forward with swollen eyes, his face inflamed with rage, and with something else that was not quite apparent to Rotherby.

"My lord!" he cried in a loud, angry voice.

Rotherby caught his wrist and checked him. "Sh! sir," he said gravely. "Not here." And he pushed him out again, her ladyship following them.

It was in the gallery—above the hall, in which the servants still stood idly about—that Mr. Green spattered out his wrathful tale of what had befallen in the library.

Rotherby shook him as if he had been a rat. "You cursed fool!" he cried. "You left him there—at the desk?"

"What help had I?" demanded Green with spirit. "My eyes were on fire. I couldn't see, and the pain of them made me helpless."

"Then why did ye not send word to me at once, you fool?"

163

"Because I was concerned only to stop my eyes from burning," answered Mr. Green, in a towering rage at finding reproof where he had come in quest of sympathy. "I have come to you at the first moment, damn you!" he burst out, in full rebellion. "And you'll use me civilly now that I am come, or—ecod!—it'll be the worse for your lordship."

Rotherby considered him through a faint mist that rage had set before his eyes. To be so spoken to—damned indeed!—by a dirty spy! Had he been alone with the man, there can be little doubt but that he would have jeopardized his very precarious future by kicking Mr. Green downstairs. But his mother saved him from that rashness. It may be that she saw something of his anger in his kindling eye, and thought it well to intervene.

She set a hand on his sleeve. "Charles!" she said to him in a voice that was dead cold with warning.

He responded to it, and chose discretion. He looked Green over, nevertheless. "I vow I'm very patient with you," said he, and Green had the discretion on his side to hold his tongue. "Come, man, while we stand talking here that knave may be destroying precious evidence."

And his lordship went quickly down the stairs, Mr. Green following hard upon his heels, and her ladyship bringing up the rear.

At the door of the library Rotherby came to a halt, and turned the handle. The door was locked. He beckoned a couple of footmen across the hall, and bade them break it open.

CHAPTER XX

Mr. CARYLL'S IDENTITY

"I must see Lord Ostermore!" had been Mr. Caryll's wild cry, as he strode to the door.

From the other side of it there came a sound of steps and voices. Some one was turning the handle.

Hortensia caught Mr. Caryll by the sleeve. "But the letters!" she cried frantically, and pointed to the incriminating papers which he had left, forgotten, upon the desk.

He stared at her a moment, and memory swept upon him in a flood. He mastered the wild agitation that had been swaying him, thrust the paper that he was carrying into his pocket, and turned to go back for the treasonable letters.

"The taper!" he exclaimed, and pointed to the extinguished candle on the floor. "What can we do?"

A sharp blow fell upon the lock of the door. He stood still, looking over his shoulder.

"Quick! Make haste!" Hortensia admonished him in her excitement. "Get them! Conceal them, at least! Do the best you can since we have not the means to burn them."

A second blow was struck, succeeded instantly by a third, and something was heard to snap. The door swung open, and Green and Rotherby sprang into the room, a brace of footmen at their heels. They were followed more leisurely by the countess; whilst a little flock of servants brought up the rear, but checked upon the threshold, and hung there to witness events that held out such promise of being unusual.

Mr. Caryll swore through set teeth, and made a dash for the desk. But he was too late to accomplish his object. His hand had scarcely closed upon the letters, when he was, himself, seized. Rotherby and Green, on either side of him, held him in their grasp, each with one hand upon his shoulder and the other at his wrist. Thus stood he, powerless between them, and, after the first shock of it, cool and making no effort to disengage himself. His right hand was tightly clenched upon the letters.

Rotherby called a servant forward. "Take those papers from the thief's hand," he commanded.

"Stop!" cried Mr. Caryll. "Lord Rotherby, may I speak with you alone before you go further in a matter you will bitterly regret?"

"Take those papers from him," Rotherby repeated, swearing;

165

and the servant bent to the task. But Mr. Caryll suddenly wrenched the hand away from the fellow and the wrist out of Lord Rotherby's grip.

"A moment, my lord, as you value your honor and your possessions!" he insisted. "Let me speak with Lord Ostermore first. Take me before him."

"You are before him now," said Rotherby. "Say on!"

"I demand to see Lord Ostermore."

"I am Lord Ostermore," said Rotherby.

"You? Since when?" said Mr. Caryll, not even beginning to understand.

"Since ten minutes ago," was the callous answer that first gave that household the news of my lord's passing.

There was a movement, a muttering among the servants. Old Humphries broke through the group by the door, his heavy chops white and trembling, and in that moment Hortensia turned, awe-stricken, to ask her ladyship was this true. Her ladyship nodded in silence. Hortensia cried out, and sank to a chair as if beaten down by the news, whilst the old servant, answered, too, withdrew, wringing his hands and making foolish laments; and the tears of those were the only tears that watered the grave of John Caryll, fifth Earl of Ostermore.

As for Mr. Caryll, the shock of that announcement seemed to cast a spell upon him. He stood still, limp and almost numbed. Oh, the never-ceasing irony of things! That his father should have died at such a moment.

"Dead?" quoth he. "Dead? Is my lord dead? They told me he was recovering."

"They told you false," answered Rotherby. "So now—those papers!"

Mr. Caryll relinquished them. "Take them," he said. "Since that is so—take them."

Rotherby received them himself. "Remove his sword," he bade a footman.

Mr. Caryll looked sharply round at him. "My sword?" quoth he. "What do you mean by that? What right?"

"We mean to keep you by us, sir," said Mr. Green on his other side, "until you have explained what you were doing with those papers—what is your interest in them."

Meanwhile a servant had done his lordship's bidding, and Mr. Caryll stood weaponless amid his enemies. He mastered himself at once. Here it was plain that he must walk with caution, for the ground, he perceived, was of a sudden grown most insecure and treacherous. Rotherby and Green in league! It gave him matter for much thought.

"There's not the need to hold me," said he quietly. "I am not likely to tire myself by violence. There's scarcely necessity for so much."

Rotherby looked up sharply. The cool, self-possessed tone had an intimidating note. But Mr. Green laughed maliciously, as he continued to mop his still watering eyes. He was acquainted with Mr. Caryll's methods, and knew that, probably, the more at ease he seemed, the less at ease he was.

Rotherby spread the letters on the desk, and scanned them with a glowing eye, Mr. Green at his elbow reading with him. The countess swept forward that she, too, might inspect this find.

"They'll serve their turn," said her son, and added to Caryll: "And they'll help to hang you."

"No doubt you find me mentioned in them," said Mr. Caryll.

"Ay, sir," snapped Green, "if not by name, at least as the messenger who is to explain that which the writers—the royal writer and the other—have out of prudence seen fit to exclude."

Hortensia looked up and across the room at that, a wild fear clutching at her heart. But Mr. Caryll laughed pleasantly, eyebrows raised as if in mild surprise. "The most excellent relations appear to prevail between you," said he, looking from Rotherby to Green. "Are you, too, my lord, in the secretary's pay."

His lordship flushed darkly. "You'll clown it to the end," he sneered.

"And that's none so far off," snarled Mr. Green, who since the peppering of his eyes, had flung aside his usual cherubic air. "Oh, you may sneer, sir," he mocked the prisoner. "But we have you fast. This letter was brought hither by you, and this one was to have been carried hence by you."

"The latter, sir, was a matter for the future, and you can hardly prove what a man will do; so we'll let that pass. As for the former—the letter which you say I brought—you'll remember that you searched me at Maidstone—"

"And I have your admission that the letter was upon you at the time," roared the spy, interrupting him—"your admission in the presence of that lady, as she can be made to witness."

Mistress Winthrop rose. "'Tis a lie," she said firmly. "I can not be made to witness."

Mr. Caryll smiled, and nodded across to her. "'Tis vastly kind in you, Mistress Winthrop. But the gentleman is mistook." He turned to Green. "Harkee, sirrah did I admit that I had carried that letter?"

Mr. Green shrugged. "You admitted that you carried a letter. What other letter should it have been but that?"

"Nay," smiled Mr. Caryll. "'Tis not for you to ask me. Rather is it for you to prove that the letter I admitted having carried and that letter are one and the same. 'Twill take a deal of proving, I dare swear."

"Ye'll be forsworn, then," put in her ladyship sourly. "For I can witness to the letter that you bore. Not only did I see it—a letter on that same fine paper—in my husband's hands on the day you came here and during your visit, but I have his lordship's own word for it that he was in the plot and that you were the go-between."

"Ah!" chuckled Mr. Green. "What now, sir? What now? By what fresh piece of acrobatics will you get out of that?"

"Ye're a fool," said Mr. Caryll with calm contempt, and fetched out his snuff-box. "D'ye dream that one witness will suffice to establish so grave a charge? Pah!" He opened his snuff-box to find it empty, and viciously snapped down the lid again. "Pah!" he said again, "ye've cost me a whole boxfull of Burgamot."

"Why did ye throw it in my face?" demanded Mr. Green. "What purpose did ye look to serve but one of treason? Answer me that!"

"I didn't like the way ye looked at me. 'Twas wanting respect, and I bethought me I would lessen the impudence of your expression. Have ye any other foolish questions for me?" And he looked again from Green to Rotherby, including both in his inquiry. "No?" He rose. "In that case, if you'll give me leave, and—"

"You do not leave this house," Rotherby informed him.

"I think you push hospitality too far. Will you desire your lackey to return me my sword? I have affairs elsewhere."

"Mr. Caryll, I beg that you will understand," said his lordship, with a calm that he was at some pains to maintain, "that you do not leave this house save in the care of the messengers from the secretary of state."

Mr. Caryll looked at him, and yawned in his face. "Ye're prodigiously tiresome," said he, "did ye but know how I detest disturbances. What shall the secretary of state require of me?"

"He'll require you on a charge of high treason," said Mr. Green.

"Have you a warrant to take me?"

"I have not, but—"

"Then how do you dare detain me, sir?" demanded Mr. Caryll sharply. "D'ye think I don't know the law?"

"I think you'll know a deal more of it shortly," countered Mr. Green.

"Meanwhile, sirs, I depart. Offer me violence at your peril."
He moved a step, and then, at a sign from Rotherby, the lackey's hands fell on him again, and forced him back and down into his chair.

"Away with you for the warrant," said Rotherby to Green. "We'll keep him here till you return."

Mr. Green grinned at the prisoner, and was gone in great haste.

Mr. Caryll lounged back in his chair, and threw one leg over the other. "I have always endeavored," said he, "to suffer fools as gladly as a Christian should. So since you insist, I'll be patient until I have the ear of my Lord Carteret—who, I take it, is a man of sense. But if I were you, my lord, and you, my lady, I should not insist. Believe me, you'll cut poor figures. As for you, my lord, ye're in none such good odor, as it is."

"Let that be," snarled his lordship.

"If I mention it at all, I but do so in your lordship's own interests. It will be remembered that ye attempted to murder me once, and that will not be of any great help to such accusations as you may bring against me. Besides which, there is the unfortunate circumstance that it's widely known ye're not a man to be believed."

"Will you be silent?" roared his lordship, in a towering passion.

"If I trouble myself to speak at all, it is out of concern for your lordship," Mr. Caryll insisted sweetly. "And in your own interest, and your ladyship's, too, I'd counsel you to hear me a moment without witnesses."

His tone was calculatedly grave. Lord Rotherby looked at him, sneering; not so her ladyship. Less acquainted with his ways, the absolute confidence and unconcern of his demeanor was causing her uneasiness. A man who was perilously entrammelled would not bear himself so easily, she opined. She rose, and crossed to her son's side.

"What have you to say?" she asked Mr. Caryll.

"Nay, madam," he replied, "not before these." And he indicated the servants.

"'Tis but a pretext to have them out of the room," said Rotherby.

Mr. Caryll laughed the notion to scorn. "If you think that—I give you my word of honor to attempt no violence, nor to depart until you shall give me leave," said he.

Rotherby, judging Mr. Caryll by his knowledge of himself, still hesitated. But her ladyship realized, in spite of her detestation of the man, that he was not of the temper of those whose word is to be doubted. She signed to the footmen.

"Go," she bade them. "Wait within call."

They departed, and Mr. Caryll remained seated for all that her ladyship was standing; it was as if by that he wished to show how little he was minded to move.

Her ladyship's eye fell upon Hortensia. "Do you go, too, child," she bade her.

Instead, Hortensia came forward. "I wish to remain, madam," she said.

"Did I ask you what you wished?" demanded the countess.

"My place is here," Hortensia explained. "Unless Mr. Caryll should, himself, desire me to depart."

"Nay, nay," he cried, and smiled upon her fondly—so fondly that the countess's eyes grew wider. "With all my heart, I desire you to remain. It is most fitting you should hear that which I have to say."

"What does it mean?" demanded Rotherby, thrusting himself forward, and scowling from one to the other of them. "What d'ye mean, Hortensia?"

"I am Mr. Caryll's betrothed wife," she answered quietly.

Rotherby's mouth fell open, but he made no sound. Not so her ladyship. A peal of shrill laughter broke from her. "La! What did I tell you, Charles?" Then to Hortensia: "I'm sorry for you, ma'am," said she. "I think ye've been a thought too long in making up your mind." And she laughed again.

"Lord Ostermore lies above stairs," Hortensia reminded her, and her ladyship went white at the reminder, the indecency of her laughter borne in upon her.

"Would ye lesson me, girl?" she cried, as much to cover her confusion as to vent her anger at the cause of it. "Ye've an odd daring, by God! Ye'll be well matched with his impudence, there."

Rotherby, singularly self-contained, recalled her to the occasion.

"Mr. Caryll is waiting," said he, a sneer in his voice.

"Ah, yes," she said, and flashing a last malignant glance upon Hortensia, she sank to a chair beside her, but not too near her.

Mr. Caryll sat back, his legs crossed, his elbows on his chair-arms, his finger-tips together. "The thing I have to tell you is of some gravity," he announced by way of preface.

Rotherby took a seat by the desk, his hand upon the treasonable letters. "Proceed, sir," he said, importantly. Mr. Caryll nodded, as in acknowledgment of the invitation.

"I will admit, before going further, that in spite of the cheerful countenance I maintained before your lordship's friend, the bumbailiff, and your lackeys, I recognize that you have me in a very dangerous position."

"Ah!" from his lordship in a breath of satisfaction, and

"Ah!" from Hortensia in a gasp of apprehension.

Her ladyship retained a stony countenance, and a silence that sorted excellently with it.

"There is," Mr. Caryll proceeded, marking off the points on his fingers, "the incident at Maidstone; there is your ladyship's evidence that I was the bearer of just such a letter on the day that first I came here; there is the dangerous circumstance—of which Mr. Green, I am sure, will not fail to make a deal—of my intimacy with Sir Richard Everard, and my constant visits to his lodging, where I was, in fact, on the occasion when he met his death; there is the fact that I committed upon Mr. Green an assault with my snuff box for motives that, after all, admit of but one acceptable explanation; and, lastly, there is the circumstance that, apparently, if interrogated, I can show no good reason why I should be in England at all, where no apparent interest has called me or keeps me.

"Now, these matters are so trivial that taken separately they have no value whatever; taken conjointly, their value is not great; they do not contain evidence enough to justify the hanging of a dog. And yet, I realize that disturbed as the times are, fearful of sedition as the government finds itself in consequence of the mischief done to public credit by the South Sea disaster, and ready as the ministry is to see plots everywhere and to make examples, pour discourager les autres, if the accusation you intend is laid against me, backed by such evidence as this, it is not impossible—indeed, it is not improbable—that it may—ah—tend to shorten my life."

"Sir," sneered Rotherby, "I declare you should have been a lawyer. We haven't a pleader of such parts and such lucidity at the whole bar."

Mr. Caryll nodded his thanks. "Your praise is very flattering, my lord," said he, with a wry smile, and then proceeded: "It is because I see my case to be so very nearly desperate, that I venture to hope you will not persevere in the course you are proposing to adopt."

Lord Rotherby laughed noiselessly. "Can you urge me any reasons why we should not?"

"If you could urge me any reasons why you should," said Mr. Caryll, "no doubt I should be able to show you under what misapprehensions you are laboring." He shot a keen glance at his lordship, whose face had suddenly gone blank. Mr. Caryll smiled quietly. "There is in this something that I do not understand," he resumed. "It does not satisfy me to suppose, as at first might seem, that you are acting out of sheer malice against me. You have scarcely cause to do that, my lord; and you, my lady, have none. That fool Green—patience—he conceives that he has suffered at my hands. But without your assistance Mr. Green would be powerless to hurt me. What, then, is it that is moving you?"

He paused, looking from one to the other of his declared enemies. They exchanged glances—Hortensia watching them, breathless, her own mind working, too, upon this question that Mr. Caryll had set, yet nowhere finding an answer.

"I had thought," said her ladyship at last, "that you promised to tell us something that it was in our interest to hear. Instead, you appear to be asking questions."

Mr. Caryll shifted in his chair. One glance he gave the countess, then smiled. "I have sought at your hands the reasons why you should desire my death," said he slowly. "You withhold them. Be it so. I take it that you are ashamed of them; and so, their nature is not difficult to conjecture."

"Sir—" began Rotherby, hotly, half-starting from his seat.

"Nay, let him trundle on, Charles," said his mother. "He'll be the sooner done."

"Instead," proceeded Mr. Caryll, as if there had been no interruption, "I will now urge you my reasons why you should not so proceed."

"Ha!" snapped Rotherby. "They will need to be valid."

Mr. Caryll twisted farther round, to face his lordship more fully. "They are as valid," said he very impressively—so impressively and sternly that his hearers felt themselves turning cold under his words, filled with some mysterious apprehension. "They are as valid as were my reasons for holding my hand in the field out yonder, when I had you at the mercy of my sword, my lord. Neither more nor less. From that, you may judge them to be very valid."

"But ye don't name them," said her ladyship, attempting to conquer her uneasiness.

"I shall do so," said he, and turned again to his lordship. "I had no cause to love you that morning, nor at any time, my lord; I had no cause to think—as even you in your heart must realize, if so be that you have a heart, and the intelligence to examine it—I had no cause to think, my lord, that I should be doing other than a good deed by letting drive my blade. That such an opinion was well founded was proven by the thing you did when I turned my back upon you after sparing your useless life."

Rotherby broke in tempestuously, smiting the desk before him. "If you think to move us to mercy by such—"

"Oh, not to mercy would I move you," said Mr. Caryll, his hand raised to stay the other, "not to mercy, but to horror of the thing you contemplate." And then, in an oddly impressive manner, he launched his thunderbolt. "Know, then, that if that morning I would not spill your blood, it was because I should have been spilling the same blood that flows in my own veins; it was because you are my brother; because your father was my father. No less than that was the reason that withheld my hand."

He had announced his aim of moving them to horror; and it was plain that he had not missed it, for in frozen horror sat they all, their eyes upon him, their cheeks ashen, their mouths agape—even Hortensia, who from what already Mr. Caryll had told her, understood now more than any of them.

After a spell Rotherby spoke. "You are my brother?" he said, his voice colorless. "My brother? What are you saying?"

And then her ladyship found her voice. "Who was your mother?" she inquired, and her very tone was an insult, not to the man who sat there so much as to the memory of poor Antoinette de Maligny. He flushed to the temples, then paled again.

"I'll not name her to your ladyship," said he at, last, in a cold, imperious voice.

"I'm glad ye've so much decency," she countered.

"You mistake, I think," said he. "'Tis respect for my mother that inspires me." And his green eyes flashed upon the painted hag. She rose up a very fury.

"What are you saying?" she shrilled. "D'ye hear the filthy fellow, Rotherby? He'll not name the wanton in my presence out of respect for her."

"For shame, madam! You are speaking of his mother," cried Hortensia, hot with indignation.

"Pshaw! 'Tis all an impudent lie—a pack of lies!" cried Rotherby. "He's crafty as all the imps of hell."

Mr. Caryll rose. "Here in the sight of God and by all that I hold most sacred, I swear that what I have said is true. I swear that Lord Ostermore—your father—was my father. I was born in France, in the year 1690, as I have papers upon me that will prove, which you may see, Rotherby."

His lordship rose. "Produce them," said he shortly.

Mr. Caryll drew from an inner pocket of his coat the small leather case that Sir Richard Everard had given him. From this he took a paper which he unfolded. It was a certificate of baptism, copied from the register of the Church of St. Antoine in Paris.

Rotherby held out his hand for it. But Mr. Caryll shook his head. "Stand here beside me, and read it," said he.

173

Obeying him, Rotherby went and read that authenticated copy, wherein it was declared that Sir Richard Everard had brought to the Church of St. Antoine for baptism a male child, which he had declared to be the son of John Caryll, Viscount Rotherby, and Antoinette de Maligny, and which had received in baptism the name of Justin.

Rotherby drew away again, his head sunk on his breast. Her ladyship was seated, her eyes upon her son, her fingers drumming absently at the arms of her chair. Then Rotherby swung round again.

"How do I know that you are the person designated there—this Justin Caryll?"

"You do not; but you may. Cast your mind back to that night at White's when you picked your quarrel with me, my lord. Do you remember how Stapleton and Collis spoke up for me, declared that they had known me from boyhood at Oxford, and had visited me at my chateau in France? What was the name of that chateau, my lord—do you remember?"

Rotherby looked at him, searching his memory. But he did not need to search far. At first glance the name of Maligny had seemed familiar to him. "It was Maligny," he replied, "and yet—"

"If more is needed to convince you, I can bring a hundred witnesses from France, who have known me from infancy. You may take it that I can establish my identity beyond all doubt."

"And what if you do?" demanded her ladyship suddenly. "What if you do establish your identity as my lord's bastard? What claim shall that be upon us?"

"That, ma'am," answered Mr. Caryll very gravely, "I wait to learn from my brother here."

CHAPTER XXI

THE LION'S SKIN

For a spell there was utter silence in that spacious, pillared chamber. Mr. Caryll and her ladyship had both resumed their chairs: the former spuriously calm; the latter making no attempt to conceal her agitation. Hortensia leant forward, an eager spectator, watching the three actors in this tragicomedy.

As for Rotherby, he stood with bent head and furrowed brow. It was for him to speak, and yet he was utterly at a loss for words. He was not moved at the news he had received, so much as dismayed. It dictated a course that would interfere with all his plans, and therefore a course unthinkable. So he remained puzzled how to act, how to deal with this unexpected situation.

It was her ladyship who was the first to break the silence. She had been considering Mr. Caryll through narrowing eyes, the corners of her mouth drawn down. She had caught the name of Maligny when it was uttered, and out of the knowledge which happened to be hers—though Mr. Caryll was ignorant of this—it set her thinking.

"I do not believe that you are the son of Mademoiselle de Maligny," she said at last. "I never heard that my lord had a son; I cannot believe there was so much between them."

Mr. Caryll stared, startled out of his habitual calm. Rotherby turned to her with an exclamation of surprise. "How?" he cried. "You knew, then? My father was—"

She laughed mirthlessly. "Your father would have married her had he dared," she informed them. "'Twas to beg his father's consent that he braved his banishment and came to England. But his father was as headstrong as himself; held just such views as he, himself, held later where you were concerned. He would not hear of the match. I was to be had for the asking. My father was a man who traded in his children, and he had offered me, with a jointure that was a fortune, to the Earl of Ostermore as a wife for his son."

Mr. Caryll was listening, all ears. Some light was being shed upon much that had lain in darkness.

"And so," she proceeded, "your grandfather constrained your father to forget the woman he had left in France, and to marry me. I know not what sins I had committed that I should have been visited with such a punishment. But so it befell. Your father resisted, dallying with the matter for a whole year. Then there was a duel

175

fought. A cousin of Mademoiselle de Maligny's crossed to England, and forced a quarrel upon your father. They met, and M. de Maligny was killed. Then a change set in in my lord's bearing, and one day, a month or so later, he gave way to his father's insistence, and we were wed. But I do not believe that my lord had left a son in France—I do not believe that had he done so, I should not have known it; I do not believe that under such circumstances, unfeeling as he was, he would have abandoned Mademoiselle de Maligny."

"You think, then," said Rotherby, "that this man has raked up this story to—"

"Consider what you are saying," cut in Mr. Caryll, with a flash of scorn. "Should I have come prepared with documents against such a happening as this?"

"Nay, but the documents might have been intended for some other purpose had my lord lived—some purpose of extortion," suggested her ladyship.

"But consider again, madam, that I am wealthy—far wealthier than was ever my Lord Ostermore, as my friends Collis, Stapleton and many another can be called to prove. What need, then, had I to extort?"

"How came you by your means, being what you say you are?" she asked him.

Briefly he told her how Sir Richard Everard had cared for him, for his mother's sake; endowed him richly upon adopting him, and since made him heir to all his wealth, which was considerable. "And for the rest, madam, and you, Rotherby, set doubts on one side. Your ladyship says that had my lord had a son you must have heard of it. But my lord, madam, never knew he had a son. Tell me—can you recall the date, the month at least, in which my lord returned to England?"

"I can, sir. It was at the end of April of '89. What then?"

Mr. Caryll produced the certificate again. He beckoned Rotherby, and held the paper under his eyes. "What date is there—the date of birth?"

Rotherby read: "The third of January of 1690."

Mr. Caryll folded the paper again. "That will help your ladyship to understand how it might happen that my lord remained in ignorance of my birth." He sighed as he replaced the case in his pocket. "I would he had known before he died," said he, almost as if speaking to himself.

And now her ladyship lost her temper. She saw Rotherby wavering, and it angered her; and angered, she committed a grave error. Wisdom lay in maintaining the attitude of repudiation; it would at least have afforded some excuse for her and Rotherby.

Instead, she now recklessly flung off that armor, and went naked down into the fray.

"A fig for't all!" she cried, and snapped her fingers. She had risen, and she towered there, a lean and malevolent figure, her head-dress nodding foolishly. "What does it matter that you be what you claim to be? Is it to weigh with you, Rotherby?"

Rotherby turned grave eyes upon her. He was, it seemed, not quite rotten through and through; there was still in him—in the depths of him—a core that was in a measure sound; and that core was reached. Most of all had the story weighed with him because it afforded the only explanation of why Mr. Caryll had spared his life that morning of the duel. It was a matter that had puzzled him, as it had puzzled all who had witnessed the affront that led to the encounter.

Between that and the rest—to say nothing of the certificate he had seen, which he could not suppose a forgery—he was convinced that Mr. Caryll was the brother that he claimed to be. He gathered from his mother's sudden anger that she, too, was convinced, in spite of herself, by the answers Mr. Caryll had returned to all her arguments against the identity he claimed.

He hated Mr. Caryll no whit less for what he had learnt; if anything, he hated him more. And yet a sense of decency forbade him from persecuting him now, as he had intended, and delivering to the hangman. From ordinary murder, once in the heat of passion—as we have seen—he had not shrunk. But fratricide appeared—such is the effect of education—a far, far graver thing, even though it should be indirect fratricide of the sort that he had contemplated before learning that this man was his brother.

There seemed to be one of two only courses left him: to provide Mr. Caryll with the means of escape, or else to withhold such evidence as he intended to supply against him, and to persuade—to compel, if necessary—his mother to do the same. When all was said, his interests need not suffer very greatly. His position would not be quite so strong, perhaps, if he but betrayed a plot without delivering up any of the plotters; still, he thought, it should be strong enough. His father dead, out of consideration of the signal loyalty his act must manifest, he thought the government would prove grateful and forbear from prosecuting a claim for restitution against the Ostermore estates.

He had, then, all but resolved upon the cleaner course, when, suddenly, something that in the stress of the moment he had gone near to overlooking, was urged upon his attention.

Hortensia had risen and had started forward at her ladyship's last words. She stood before his lordship now with pleading eyes,

177

and hands held out. "My lord," she cried, "you cannot do this thing! You cannot do it!"

But instead of moving him to generosity, by those very words she steeled his heart against it, and proved to him that, after all, his potentialities for evil were strong enough to enable him to do the very thing she said he could not. His brow grew black as midnight; his dark eyes raked her face, and saw the agony of apprehension for her lover written there. He drew breath, hissing and audible, glanced once at Caryll; then: "A moment!" said he.

He strode to the door and called the footmen, then turned again.

"Mr. Caryll," he said in a formal voice, "will you give yourself the trouble of waiting in the ante-room? I need to consider upon this matter."

Mr. Caryll, conceiving that it was with his mother that Rotherby intended to consider, rose instantly. "I would remind you, Rotherby, that time is pressing," said he.

"I shall not keep you long," was Rotherby's cold reply, and Mr. Caryll went out.

"What now, Charles?" asked his mother. "Is this child to remain?"

"It is the child that is to remain," said his lordship. "Will your ladyship do me the honor, too, of waiting in the ante-room?" and he held the door for her.

"What folly are you considering?" she asked.

"Your ladyship is wasting time, and time, as Mr. Caryll has said, is pressing."

She crossed to the door, controlled almost despite herself by the calm air of purpose that was investing him. "You are not thinking of—"

"You shall learn very soon of what I am thinking, ma'am. I beg that you will give us leave."

She paused almost upon the threshold. "If you do a rashness, here, remember that I can still act without you," she reminded him. "You may choose to believe that that man is your brother, and so, out of that, and"—she added with a cruel sneer at Hortensia—"other considerations, you may elect to let him go. But remember that you still have me to reckon with. Whether he prove of your blood or not, he cannot prove himself of mine—thank God!"

His lordship bowed in silence, preserving an unmoved countenance, whereupon she cursed him for a fool, and passed out. He closed the door, and turned the key, Hortensia watching him in a sort of horror. "Let me go!" she found voice to cry at last, and advanced towards the door herself. But Rotherby came to meet her, his face white, his eyes glowing. She fell away before his opening arms, and he stood still, mastering himself.

"That man," he said, jerking a backward thumb at the closed door, "lives or dies, goes free or hangs, as you shall decide, Hortensia."

She looked at him, her face haggard, her heart beating high in her throat as if to suffocate her. "What do you mean?" she asked.

"You love him!" he growled. "Pah! I see it in your eyes—in your tremors—that you do. It is for him that you are afraid, is't not?"

"Why do you mock me with it?" she inquired with dignity.

"I do not mock you, Hortensia. Answer me! Is it true that you love him?"

"It is true," she answered steadily. "What is't to you?"

"Everything!" he answered hotly. "Everything! It is Heaven and Hell to me. Ten days ago, Hortensia, I asked you to marry me-"

"No more," she begged him, an arm thrown out to stay him.

"But there is more," he answered, advancing again. "This time I can make the offer more attractive. Marry me, and Caryll is not only free to depart, but no evidence shall be laid against him. I swear it! Refuse me, and he hangs as surely—as surely as you and I talk together here this moment."

Cold eyes scathed him with contempt. "God!" she cried. "What manner of monster are you, my lord? To speak so—to speak of marriage to me, and to speak of hanging a man who is son to that same father of yours who lies above stairs, not yet turned cold. Are you human at all?"

"Ay—and in nothing so human as in my love for you, Hortensia."

She put her hands to her face. "Give me patience!" she prayed. "The insult of it after what has passed! Let me go, sir; open that door, and let me go."

He stood regarding her a moment, with lowering brows. Then he turned, and went slowly to the door. "He dies, remember!" said he, and the words, the sinister tone and the sinister look that was stamped upon his face, shattered her spirit as at a blow.

"No, no!" she faltered, and advanced a step or two. "Oh, have pity!"

"When you show me pity," he answered.

She was beaten. "You—you swear to let him go—to see him safely out of England—if—if I consent?"

His eyes blazed. He came back swiftly, and she stood, a frozen thing, passively awaiting him; a frozen thing, she let him take her in his arms, yielding herself in horrific surrender.

He held her close a moment, the blood surging to his face, and glowing darkly through the swarthy skin. "Have I conquered, then?" he cried. "You'll marry me, Hortensia?"

"At that price," she answered piteously, "at that price."

"Shalt find me a gentle, loving husband, ever. I swear it before Heaven!" he vowed, the ardor of his passion softening his nature, as steel is softened in the fire.

"Then be it so," she said, and her tone was less cold, for she began to glow, as it were, with the ardor of the sacrifice that she was making—began to experience the exalted ecstasy of martyrdom. "Save him, and you shall find me ever a dutiful wife to you, my lord—a dutiful wife."

"And loving?" he demanded greedily.

"Even that. I promise it," she answered.

With a hoarse cry, he stooped to kiss her; then, with an oath, he checked, and flung her from him so violently that she hurtled to a chair and sank to it, overbalanced. "No," he roared, like a mad thing now. "Hell and damnation—no!"

A wild frenzy of jealousy had swept aside his tenderness. He was sick and faint with the passion of it of this proof of how deeply she must love that other man. He strove to control his violence. He snarled at her, in his endeavors to subdue the animal, the primitive creature that he was at heart. "If you can love him so much as that, he had better hang, I think." He laughed on a high, fierce note. "You have spoke his sentence, girl! D'ye think I'd take you so—at second hand? Oh, s'death! What d'ye deem me?"

He laughed again—in his throat now, a quivering; half-sobbing laugh of anger—and crossed to the door, her eyes following him, terrified; her mind understanding nothing of this savage. He turned the key, and flung wide the door with a violent gesture. "Bring him in!" he shouted.

They entered—Mr. Caryll with the footmen at his heels, a frown between his brows, his eyes glancing quickly and searchingly from Rotherby to Hortensia. After him came her ladyship, no less inquisitive of look. Rotherby dismissed the lackeys, and closed the door again. He flung out an arm to indicate Hortensia.

"This little fool," he said to Caryll, "would have married me to save your life."

Mr. Caryll raised his brows. The words relieved his fears. "I am glad, sir, that you perceive she would have been a fool to do so. You, I take it, have been fool enough to refuse the offer."

"Yes, you damned play-actor! Yes!" he thundered. "D'ye think I want another man's cast-offs?"

"That is an overstatement," said Mr. Caryll. "Mistress Winthrop is no cast-off of mine."

"Enough said!" snapped Rotherby. He had intended to say much, to do some mighty ranting. But before Mr. Caryll's cold half-bantering reduction of facts to their true values, he felt himself robbed of words. "You hang!" he ended shortly.

"Ye're sure of that?" questioned Mr. Caryll.

"I would I were as sure of Heaven."

"I think you may be—just about as sure," Mr. Caryll rejoined, entirely unperturbed, and he sauntered forward towards Hortensia. Rotherby and his mother watched him, exchanging glances.

Then Rotherby shrugged and sneered. "'Tis his bluster," said he. "He'll be a farceur to the end. I doubt he's half-witted."

Mr. Caryll never heeded him. He was bending beside Hortensia. He took her hand, and bore it to his lips. "Sweet," he murmured, "'twas a treason that you intended. Have you, then, no faith in me? Courage, sweetheart, they cannot hurt me."

She clutched his hands, and looked up into his eyes. "You but say that to comfort me!" she cried.

"Not so," he answered gravely. "I tell you no more than what is true. They think they hold me. They will cheat, and lie and swear falsely to the end that they may destroy me. But they shall have their pains for nothing."

"Ay—depend upon that," Rotherby mocked him. "Depend upon it—to the gallows."

Mr Caryll's curious eyes smiled upon his brother, but his lips were contemptuous. "I am of your own blood, Rotherby—your brother," he said again, "and once already out of that consideration I have spared your life—because I would not have a brother's blood upon my hands." He sighed, and continued: "I had hoped that you had enough humanity to do the same. I deplore that you should lack it; but I deplore it for your own sake, because, after all, you are my brother. Apart from that, it matters nothing to me."

"Will it matter nothing when you are proved a Jacobite spy?" cried her ladyship, enraged beyond endurance by this calm scorn of them. "Will it matter nothing when it is proved that you carried that letter, and would have carried that other—that you were empowered to treat in your exiled master's name? Will that matter nothing?"

He looked at her an instant, then, as if utterly disdaining to answer her, he turned again to Rotherby. "I were a fool and blind, did I not see to the bottom of this turbid little puddle upon which you think to float your argosies. You are selling me. You are to make a bargain with the government to forbear the confiscations your father has incurred out of consideration of the service you can render by disclosing this plot, and you would throw me in as

181

something tangible—in earnest of the others that may follow. Have I sounded the depths of your intent?"

"And if you have—what then?" demanded sullen Rotherby.

"This, my lord," answered Mr. Caryll, and he quoted: "'The man that once did sell the lion's skin while the beast lived, was killed with hunting him. Remember that!'"

They looked at him, impressed by the ringing voice in which he had spoken-a voice in which the ring was of mingled mockery and exultation. Then her ladyship shook off the impression, and laughed.

"With what d'ye threaten us?" she asked contemptuously.

"I—threaten, ma'am? Nay, I am incapable of threatening. I do not threaten. I have reasoned with you, exhorted you, shown you cause why, had you one spark of decency left, you would allow me to depart and shield me from the law you have invoked to ruin me. I have hoped for your own sakes that you would be moved so to do. But since you will not—" He paused and shrugged. "On your own heads be it."

"On our own heads be what?" demanded Rotherby.

But Mr. Caryll smiled, and shook his head. "Did you know all, it might indeed influence your decision; and I would not have that happen. You have chosen, have you not, Rotherby? You will sell me; you will hang me—me, your father's son. Poor Rotherby! From my soul I pity you!"

"Pity me? Death! You impudent rogue! Keep your pity for those that need it."

"That is why I offer it you, Rotherby," said Mr. Caryll, almost sadly. "In all my life, I have not met a man who stood more sorely in need of it, nor am I ever like to meet another."

There was a movement without, a tap at the door; and Humphries entered to announce Mr. Green's return, accompanied by Mr. Second Secretary Templeton, and without waiting for more, he ushered them into the room.

CHAPTER XXII

THE HUNTERS

To the amazement of them all, there entered a tall gentleman in a full-bottomed wig, with a long, pale face, a resolute mouth, and a pair of eyes that were keen, yet kindly. Close upon the heels of the second secretary came Mr. Green. Humphries withdrew, and closed the door.

Mr. Templeton made her ladyship a low bow.

"Madam," said he very gravely, "I offer your ladyship—and you, my lord—my profoundest condolence in the bereavement you have suffered, and my scarcely less profound excuses for this intrusion upon your grief."

Mr. Templeton may or may not have reflected that the grief upon which he deplored his intrusion was none so apparent.

"I had not ventured to do so," he continued, "but that your lordship seemed to invite my presence."

"Invited it, sir?" questioned Rotherby with deference. "I should scarcely have presumed so far as to invite it."

"Not directly, perhaps," returned the second secretary. His was a deep, rich voice, and he spoke with great deliberateness, as if considering well each word before allowing it utterance. "Not directly, perhaps; but in view of your message to Lord Carteret, his lordship has desired me to come in person to inquire into this matter for him, before proceeding farther. This fellow," indicating Green, "brought information from you that a Jacobite—an agent of James Stuart—is being detained here, and that your lordship has a communication to make to the secretary of state."

Rotherby bowed his assent. "All I desired that Mr. Green should do meanwhile," said he, "was to procure a warrant for this man's arrest. My revelations would have followed that. Has he the warrant?"

"Your lordship may not be aware," said Mr. Templeton, with an increased precision of diction, "that of late so many plots have been disclosed and have proved in the end to be no plots at all, that his lordship has resolved to proceed now with the extremest caution. For it is not held desirable by his majesty that publicity should be given to such matters until there can be no doubt that they are susceptible to proof. Talk of them is disturbing to the public quiet, and there is already disturbance enough, as it unfortunately happens. Therefore, it is deemed expedient that we should make quite sure of our ground before proceeding to arrests."

"But this plot is no sham plot," cried Rotherby, with the faintest show of heat, out of patience with the other's deliberateness. "It is a very real danger, as I can prove to his lordship."

"It is for the purpose of ascertaining that fact," resumed the second secretary, entirely unruffled, "for the purpose of ascertaining it before taking any steps that would seem to acknowledge it, that my Lord Carteret has desired me to wait upon you—that you may place me in possession of the circumstances that have come to your knowledge."

Rotherby's countenance betrayed his growing impatience. "Why, for that matter, it has come to my knowledge that a plot is being hatched by the friends of the Stuart, and that a rising is being prepared, the present moment being considered auspicious, while the people's confidence in the government is shaken by the late South Sea Company disaster."

Mr. Templeton wagged his head gently. "That, sir—if you will permit the observation—is the preface of all the disclosures that have lately been made to us. The consolation, sir, for his majesty's friends, has been that in no case did the subsequent matter make that preface good."

"It is in that particular, then, that my disclosures shall differ from those others," said Rotherby, in a tone that caused Mr. Templeton afterwards to describe him as "a damned hot fellow."

"You have evidence?"

"Documentary evidence. A letter from the Pretender himself amongst it."

A becoming gravity overspread Mr. Templeton's clear-cut face. "That would be indeed regrettable," said he. It was plain that whatever the second secretary might display when the plot was disclosed to him, he would display none of that satisfaction upon which Rotherby had counted. "To whom, sir, let me ask, is this letter indited?"

"To my late father," answered his lordship.

Mr. Templeton made an exclamation, whose significance was not quite clear.

"I have discovered it since his death," continued Rotherby. "I was but in time to wrest it from the hands of that spy of the Pretender's, who was in the act of destroying it when I caught him. My devotion to his majesty made my course clear, sir—and I desired Mr. Green to procure a warrant for this traitor's arrest."

"Sir," said Mr. Templeton, regarding him with an eye in which astonishment was blent with admiration, "this is very loyal in you—very loyal under the—ah—peculiar circumstances of the affair. I do not think that his majesty's government, considering to whom this letter was addressed, could have censured you even had you suppressed it. You have conducted yourself, my lord—if I may venture upon a criticism of your lordship's conduct—with a patriotism worthy of the best models of ancient Rome. And I am assured that his majesty's government will not be remiss in signifying appreciation of this very lofty loyalty of yours."

Lord Rotherby bowed low, in acknowledgment of the compliment. Her ladyship concealed a cynical smile under cover of her fan. Mr. Caryll—standing in the background beside Hortensia's chair—smiled, too, and poor Hortensia, detecting his smile, sought to take comfort in it.

"My son," interposed the countess, "is, I am sure, gratified to hear you so commend his conduct."

Mr. Templeton bowed to her with a great politeness. "I should be a stone, ma'am, did I not signify my—ah—appreciation of it."

"There is a little more to follow, sir," put in Mr. Caryll, in that quiet manner of his. "I think you will find it blunt the edge of his lordship's lofty loyalty—cause it to savor less like the patriotism of Rome, and more like that of Israel."

Mr. Templeton turned upon him a face of cold displeasure. He would have spoken, but that whilst he was seeking words of a becoming gravity, Rotherby forestalled him.

"Sir," he exclaimed, "what I did, I did though my ruin must have followed. I know what this traitor has in mind. He imagines I have a bargain to make. But you must see, sir, that in no sense is it so, for, having already surrendered the facts, it is too late now to attempt to sell them. I am ready to yield up the letters that I have found. No consideration could induce me to do other; and yet, sir, I venture to hope that in return, the government will be pleased to see that I have some claim upon my country's recognition for the signal service I am rendering her—and in rendering which I make a holocaust of my father's honor."

"Surely, surely, sir," murmured Mr. Templeton, but his countenance told of a lessening enthusiasm in his lordship's Roman patriotism. "Lord Carteret, I am sure, would never permit so much—ah—devotion to his majesty to go unrewarded."

"I only ask, sir—and I ask it for the sake of my father's name, which stands in unavoidable danger of being smirched—that no further shame be heaped upon it than that which must result from

185

the horror with which the discovery of this plot will inspire all right-thinking subjects."

Mr. Caryll smiled and nodded. He judged in a detached spirit—a mere spectator at a play—and he was forced to admit to himself that it was subtly done of his brother, and showed an astuteness in this thing, at least, of which he had never supposed him capable.

"There is, sir," Rotherby proceeded, "the matter of my father's dealings with the South Sea Company. He is no longer alive to defend himself from the accusations—from the impeachment which has been levelled against him by our enemy, the Duke of Wharton. Therefore, it might be possible to make it appear as if his dealings were—ah—not—ah—quite such as should befit an upright gentleman. There is that, and there is this greater matter against him. Between the two, I should never again be able to look my fellow-countrymen in the face. Yet this is the more important since the safety of the kingdom is involved; whilst the other is but a personal affair, and trivial by comparison.

"I will beg, sir, that out of consideration for my disclosing this dastardly conspiracy—which I cannot do without disclosing my father's misguided share in it—I will implore, sir, that out of that consideration, Lord Carteret will see fit to dispose that the South Sea Company affair is allowed to be forgotten. It has already been paid for by my father with his life."

Mr. Templeton looked at the young man before him with eyes of real commiseration. He was entirely duped, and in his heart he regretted that for a moment he could have doubted Rotherby's integrity of purpose.

"Sir," he said, "I offer you my sympathy—my profoundest sympathy; and you, my lady.

"As for this South Sea Company affair, well—I am empowered by Lord Carteret to treat only of the other matter, and to issue or not a warrant for the apprehension of the person you are detaining, after I have investigated the grounds upon which his arrest is urged. Nevertheless, sir, I think I can say—indeed, I think I can promise—that in consideration of your readiness to deliver up these letters, and provided their nature is as serious as you represent, and also in consideration of this, your most signal proof of loyalty, Lord Carteret will not wish to increase the load which already you have to bear."

"Oh, sir!" cried Rotherby in the deepest emotion, "I have no words in which to express my thanks."

"Nor I," put in Mr. Caryll, "words in which to express my

186

admiration. A most excellent performance, Rotherby. I had not credited you with so much ability."

Mr. Templeton frowned upon him again. "Ye betray a singular callousness, sir," said he.

"Nay, sir; not callousness. Merely the ease that springs from a tranquil conscience."

Her ladyship glanced across at him, and sneered audibly. "You hear the poisonous traitor, sir. He glories in a tranquil conscience, in spite of this murderous matter to which he stood committed."

Rotherby turned aside to take the letters from the desk. He thrust them into Mr. Templeton's hands. "Here, sir, is a letter from King James to my father, and here is a letter from my father to King James. From their contents, you will gather how far advanced are matters, what devilries are being hatched here in his majesty's dominions."

Mr. Templeton received them, and crossed to the window that he might examine them. His countenance lengthened. Rotherby took his stand beside his mother's chair, both observing Mr. Caryll, who, in his turn, was observing Mr. Templeton, a faint smile playing round the corners of his mouth. Once they saw him stoop and whisper something in Hortensia's ear, and they caught the upward glance of her eyes, half fear, half question.

Mr. Green, by the door, stood turning his hat in his hands, furtively watching everybody, whilst drawing no attention to himself—a matter in which much practice had made him perfect.

At last Templeton turned, folding the letters. "This is very grave, my lord," said he, "and my Lord Carteret will no doubt desire to express in person his gratitude and his deep sense of the service you have done him. I think you may confidently expect to find him as generous as you hope."

He pocketed the letters, and raised a hand to point at Mr. Caryll. "This man?" he inquired laconically.

"Is a spy of King James's. He is the messenger who bore my father that letter from the Pretender, and he would no doubt have carried back the answer had my father lived."

Mr. Templeton drew a paper from his pocket, and crossed to the desk. He sat down, and took up a quill. "You can prove this, of course?" he said, testing the point of his quill upon his thumb-nail.

"Abundantly," was the ready answer. "My mother can bear witness to the fact that 'twas he brought the Pretender's letter, and there is no lack of corroboration. Enough, I think, would be afforded by the assault made by this rogue upon Mr. Green, of which, no doubt, you are already informed, sir. His object—this proved object—was to possess himself of those papers that he might destroy them. I but caught him in time, as my servants can bear witness, as they can also bear witness to the circumstance that we were compelled to force an entrance here, and to use force to him to obtain the letters from him."

Mr. Templeton nodded. "'Tis a clear case, then," said he, and dipped his pen.

"And yet," put in Mr. Caryll, in an indolent, musing voice, "it might be made to look as clear another way."

Mr. Templeton scowled at him. "The opportunity shall be afforded you," said he. "Meanwhile—what is your name?"

Mr. Caryll looked whimsically at the secretary a moment; then flung his bomb. "I am Justin Caryll, Sixth Earl of Ostermore, and your very humble servant, Mr. Secretary."

The effect was ludicrous—from Mr. Caryll's point of view—and yet it was disappointing. Five pairs of dilating eyes confronted him, five gaping mouths. Then her ladyship broke into a laugh.

"The creature's mad—I've long suspected it." And she meant to be taken literally; his many whimsicalities were explained to her at last. He was, indeed, half-witted, as he now proved.

Mr. Templeton, recovering, smote the table angrily. He thought he had good reason to lose his self-control on this occasion, though it was a matter of pride with him that he could always preserve an unruffled calm under the most trying circumstances. "What is your name, sir?" he demanded again.

"You are hard of hearing, sir, I think. I am Lord Ostermore. Set down that name in the warrant if you are determined to be bubbled by that fellow there and made to look foolish afterwards with my Lord Carteret."

Mr. Templeton sat back in his chair, frowning; but more from utter bewilderment now than anger.

"Perhaps," said Mr. Caryll, "if I were to explain, it would help you to see the imposture that is being practiced upon you. As for the allegations that have been made against me—that I am a Jacobite spy and an agent of the Pretender's—" He shrugged, and waved an airy hand. "I scarce think there will remain the need for me to deny them when you have heard the rest."

Rotherby took a step forward, his face purple, his hands clenched. Her ladyship thrust out a bony claw, clutched at his sleeve, and drew him back and into the chair beside her. "Pho! Charles," she said; "give the fool rope, and he'll hang himself, never doubt it—the poor, witless creature."

Mr. Caryll sauntered over to the secretaire, and leaned an elbow on the top of it, facing all in the room.

"I admit, Mr. Secretary," said he, "that I had occasion to

188

assault Mr. Green, to the end that I might possess myself of the papers he was seeking in this desk."

"Why, then—" began Mr. Templeton.

"Patience, sir! I admit so much, but I admit no more. I do not, for instance, admit that the object—the object itself—of my search was such as has been represented."

"What then? What else?" growled Rotherby.

"Ay, sir—what else?" quoth Mr. Templeton.

"Sir," said Mr. Caryll, with a sorrowful shake of, the head, "I have already startled you, it seems, by one statement. I beg that you will prepare yourself to be startled by another." Then he abruptly dropped his languor. "I should think twice, sir," he advised, "before signing that warrant, were I in your place, to do so would be to render yourself the tool of those who are plotting my ruin, and ready to bear false witness that they may accomplish it. I refer," and he waved a hand towards the countess and his brother, "to the late Lord Ostermore's mistress and his natural son, there."

In their utter stupefaction at the unexpectedness and seeming wildness of the statement, neither mother nor son could find a word to say. No more could Mr. Templeton for a moment. Then, suddenly, wrathfully: "What are you saying, sir?" he roared.

"The truth, sir."

"The truth?" echoed the secretary.

"Ay, sir—the truth. Have ye never heard of it?"

Mr. Templeton sat back again. "I begin to think," said he, surveying through narrowing eyes the slender graceful figure before him, "that her ladyship is right that you are mad; unless—unless you are mad of the same madness that beset Ulysses. You remember?"

"Let us have done," cried Rotherby in a burst of anger, leaping to his feet. "Let us have done, I say! Are we to waste the day upon this Tom o' Bedlam? Write him down as Caryll—Justin Caryll—'tis the name he's known by; and let Green see to the rest."

Mr. Templeton made an impatient sound, and poised his pen.

"Ye are not to suppose, sir," Mr. Caryll stayed him, "that I cannot support my statements. I have by me proofs—irrefragable proofs of what I say."

"Proofs?" The word seemed to come from, every member of that little assembly—if we except Mr. Green, whose face was beginning to betray his uneasiness. He was not so ready as the others to believe, that Mr. Caryll was mad. For him, the situation asked some other explanation.

"Ay—proofs," said Mr. Caryll. He had drawn the case from his pocket again. From this he took the birth-certificate, and placed it before Mr. Templeton, "Will you glance at that, sir—to begin, with?—"

Mr. Templeton complied. His face became more and more grave. He looked at Mr. Caryll; then at Rotherby, who was scowling, and at her ladyship, who was breathing hard. His glance returned to Mr. Caryll.

"You are the person designated here?" he inquired.

"As I can abundantly prove," said Mr. Caryll. "I have no lack of friends in London who will bear witness to that much."

"Yet," said Mr. Templeton, frowning, perplexed, "this does not make you what you claim to be. Rather does it show you to be his late lordship's—"

"There's more to come," said Mr. Caryll, and placed another document before the secretary. It was an extract from the register of St. Etienne of Maligny, relating to his mother's death.

"Do you know, sir, in what year this lady went through a ceremony of marriage with my father—the late Lord Ostermore? It was in 1690, I think, as the lady will no doubt confirm."

"To what purpose, this?" quoth Mr. Templeton.

"The purpose will be presently apparent. Observe that date," said Mr. Caryll, and he pointed to the document in Mr. Templeton's hand.

Mr. Templeton read the date aloud—"1692"—and then the name of the deceased—"Antoinette de Beaulieu de Maligny. What of it?" he demanded.

"You will understand that when I show you the paper I took from this desk, the paper that I obtained as a consequence of my violence to Mr. Green. I think you will consider, sir, that if ever the end justified the means, it did so in this case. Here was something very different from the paltry matter of treason that is alleged against me."

And he passed the secretary a third paper.

Over Mr. Templeton's shoulder, Rotherby and his mother, who—drawn by the overpowering excitement that was mastering them—had approached in silence, were examining the document with wide-open, startled eyes, fearing by very instinct, without yet apprehending the true nature of the revelation that was to come.

"God!" shrieked her ladyship, who took in the meaning of this thing before Rotherby had begun to suspect it. "'Tis a forgery!"

"That were idle, when the original entry in the register is to be seen in, the Church of St. Antoine, madam," answered Mr. Caryll. "I rescued that document, together with some letters which my mother wrote my father when first he returned to England—and which are superfluous now—from a secret drawer in that desk, an hour ago."

"But what is it?" inquired Rotherby huskily. "What is it?"

"It is the certificate of the marriage of my father, the late Lord Ostermore, and my mother, Antoinette de Maligny, at the Church of St. Antoine in Paris, in the year 1689." He turned to Mr. Templeton. "You apprehend the matter, sir?" he demanded, and recapitulated. "In 1689 they were married; in 1692 she died; yet in 1690 his lordship went through a form of marriage with Mistress Sylvia Etheridge, there."

Mr. Templeton nodded very gravely, his eyes upon the document before him, that they might avoid meeting at that moment the eyes of the woman whom the world had always known as the Countess of Ostermore.

"Fortunate is it for me," said Mr. Caryll, "that I should have possessed myself of these proofs in time. Does it need more to show how urgent might be the need for my suppression—how little faith can be attached to an accusation levelled against me from such a quarter?"

"By God—" began Rotherby, but his mother clutched his wrist.

"Be still, fool!" she hissed in his ear. She had need to keep her wits about her, to think, to weigh each word that she might utter. An abyss had opened in her path; a false step, and she and her son were irrevocably lost—sent headlong to destruction. Rotherby, already reduced to the last stage of fear, was obedient as he had never been, and fell silent instantly.

Mr. Templeton folded the papers, rose, and proffered them to their owner. "Have you any means of proving that this was the document you sought?" he inquired.

"I can prove that it was the document he found." It was Hortensia who spoke; she had advanced to her lover's side, and she controlled her amazement to bear witness for him. "I was present in this room when he went through that desk, as all in the house know; and I can swear to his having found that paper in it."

Mr. Templeton bowed. "My lord," he said to Caryll, "your contentions appear clear. It is a matter in which I fear I can go no further; nor do I now think that the secretary of state would approve of my issuing a warrant upon such testimony as we have received. The matter is one for Lord Carteret himself."

"I shall do myself the honor of waiting upon his lordship within the hour," said the new Lord Ostermore. "As for the letter which it is alleged I brought from France—from the Pretender,"—he was smiling now, a regretful, deprecatory smile, "it is a fortunate circumstance that, being suspected by that very man Green, who stands yonder, I was subjected, upon my arrival in England, to a thorough search at Maidstone—a search, it goes without saying, that yielded nothing. I was angry at the time, at the indignity I was forced to endure. We little know what the future may hold. And to-day I am thankful to have that evidence to rebut this charge."

"Your lordship is indeed to be congratulated," Mr. Templeton agreed. "You are thus in a position to clear yourself of even a shadow of suspicion."

"You fool!" cried she who until that hour had been Countess of Ostermore, turning fiercely upon Mr. Templeton. "You fool!"

"Madam, this is not seemly," cried the second secretary, with awkward dignity.

"Seemly, idiot?" she stormed at him. "I swear, as I've a soul to be saved, that in spite of all this, I know that man to be a traitor and a Jacobite—that it was the letter from the king he sought, whatever he may pretend to have found."

Mr. Templeton looked at her in sorrow, for all that in her overwrought condition she insulted him. "Madam, you might swear and swear, and yet no one would believe you in the face of the facts that have come to light."

"Do you believe me?" she demanded angrily.

"My beliefs can matter nothing," he compromised, and made her a valedictory bow. "Your servant, ma'am," said he, from force of habit. He nodded to Rotherby, took up his hat and cane, and strode to the door, which Mr. Green had made haste to open for him. From the threshold he bowed to Mr. Caryll. "My lord," said he, "I shall go straight to Lord Carteret. He will stay for you till you come."

"I shall not keep his lordship waiting," answered Caryll, and bowed in his turn.

The second secretary went out. Mr. Green hesitated a moment, then abruptly followed him. The game was ended here; it was played and lost, he saw, and what should such as Mr. Green be doing on the losing side?

CHAPTER XXIII

THE LION

The game was played and lost. All realized it, and none so keenly as Hortensia, who found it in her gentle heart to pity the woman who had never shown her a kindness.

She set a hand upon her lover's arm. "What will you do, Justin?" she inquired in tones that seemed to plead for mercy for those others; for she had not paused to think—as another might have thought—that there was no mercy he could show them.

Rotherby and his mother stood hand in hand; it was the woman who had clutched at her son for comfort and support in this bitter hour of retribution, this hour of the recoil upon themselves of all the evil they had plotted.

Mr. Caryll considered them a moment, his face a mask, his mind entirely detached. They interested him profoundly. This subjugation of two natures that in themselves were arrogant and cruel was a process very engrossing to observe. He tried to conjecture what they felt, what thoughts they might be harboring. And it seemed to him that a sort of paralysis had fallen on their wits. They were stunned under the shock of the blow he had dealt them. Anon there would be railings and to spare—against him, against themselves, against the dead man above stairs, against Fate, and more besides. For the present there was this horrid, almost vacuous calm.

Presently the woman stirred. Instinct—the instinct of the stricken beast to creep to hiding—moved her, while reason was still bound in lethargy. She moved to step, drawing at her son's hand. "Come, Charles," she said, in a low, hoarse voice. "Come!"

The touch and the speech awakened him to life. "No!" he cried harshly, and shook his hand free of hers. "It ends not thus."

He looked almost as he would fling himself upon his brother, his figure erect now, defiant and menacing; his face ashen, his eyes wild. "It ends not thus!" he repeated, and his voice rang sinister.

"No," Mr. Caryll agreed quietly. "It ends not thus."

He looked sadly from son to mother. "It had not even begun thus, but that you would have it so. You would have it. I sought to move you to mercy. I reminded you, my brother, of the tie that bound us, and I would have turned you from fratricide, I would have saved you from the crime you meditated—for it was a crime."

"Fratricide!" exclaimed Rotherby, and laughed angrily. "Fratricide!" It was as if he threatened it.

But Mr. Caryll continued to regard him sorrowfully. From his soul he pitied him; pitied them both—not because of their condition, but because of the soullessness behind it all. To him it was truly tragic, tragic beyond anything that he had ever known.

"You said some fine things, sir, to Mr. Templeton of your regard for your father's memory," said Mr. Caryll. "You expressed some lofty sentiments of filial piety, which almost sounded true—which sounded true, indeed, to Mr. Templeton. It was out of interest for your father that you pleaded for the suppression of his dealings with the South Sea Company; not for a moment did you consider yourself or the profit you should make from such suppression."

"Why this?" demanded the mother fiercely. "Do you rally us? Do you turn the sword in the wound now that you have us at your mercy—now that we are fallen?"

"From what are you fallen?" Mr. Caryll inquired. "Ah, but let that pass. I do not rally, madam. Mockery is far indeed from my intention." He turned again to Rotherby. "Lord Ostermore was a father to you, which he never was to me—knew not that he was. The sentiments you so beautifully expressed to Mr. Templeton are the sentiments that actuate me now, though I shall make no attempt to express them. It is not that my heart stirs much where my Lord Ostermore is concerned. And yet, for the sake of the name that is mine now, I shall leave England as I came—Mr. Justin Caryll, neither more nor less.

"In the eyes of the world there is no slur upon my mother's name, because her history—her supposed history—was unknown. See that none ever falls on it, else shall you find me pitiless indeed. See that none ever falls on it, or I shall return and drive home the lesson that, like Antinous, you've learnt—that 'twixt the cup and lip much ill may grow'—and turn you, naked upon a contemptuous world. Needs more be said? You understand, I think."

Rotherby understood nothing. But his mother's keener wits began to perceive a glimmer of the truth. "Do you mean that—that we are to—to remain in the station that we believed our own?"

"What else?"

She stared at him. Here was a generosity so weak, it seemed to her, as almost to provoke her scorn. "You will leave your brother in possession of the title and what else there may be?"

"You think me generous, madam," said he. "Do not misapprehend me. I am not. I covet neither the title nor estates of Ostermore. Their possession would be a thorn in my flesh, a thorn of bitter memory. That is one reason why you should not think me generous, though it is not the reason why I cede them. I would have you understand me on this, perhaps the last time, that we may meet.

"Lord Ostermore, my father, married you, madam, in good faith."

She interrupted harshly. "What is't you say?" she almost screamed, quivering with rage at the very thought of what her dead lord had done.

"He married you in good faith," Mr. Caryll repeated quietly, impressively. "I will make it plain to you. He married you believing that the girl-wife he had left in France was dead. For fear it should come to his father's knowledge, he kept that marriage secret from all. He durst not own his marriage to his father."

"He was not—as you may have appreciated in the years you lived with him—a man of any profound feeling for others. For himself he had a prodigiously profound feeling, as you may also have gathered. That marriage in France was troublesome. He had come to look upon it as one of his youth's follies—as he, himself, described it to me in this house, little knowing to whom he spoke. When he received the false news of her death—for he did receive such news from the very cousin who crossed from France to avenge her, believing her dead himself—he rejoiced at his near escape from the consequences of his folly. Nor was he ever disabused of his error. For she had ceased to write to him by then. And so he married you, madam, in good faith. That is the argument I shall use with my Lord Carteret to make him understand that respect for my father's memory urges me to depart in silence—save for what I must have said to escape the impeachment with which you threatened me."

"Lord Carteret is a man of the world. He will understand the far-reaching disturbance that must result from the disclosure of the truth of this affair. He will pledge Mr. Templeton to silence, and the truth, madam, will never be disclosed. That, I think, is all, madam."

"By God, sir," cried Rotherby, "that's damned handsome of you!"

"You epitomize it beautifully," said Mr. Caryll, with a reversion to his habitual manner.

His mother, however, had no words at all. She advanced a step towards Mr. Caryll, put out her hands, and then—portent of portents!—two tears were seen to trickle down her cheeks, playing havoc, ploughing furrows in the paint that overlaid them.

Mr. Caryll stepped forward quickly. The sight of those tears, springing from that dried-up heart—withered by God alone knew what blight—washing their way down those poor bedaubed cheeks, moved him to a keener pity than anything he had ever looked upon.

195

He took her hands, and pressed them a moment, giving way for once to an impulse he could not master.

She would have kissed his own in the abasement and gratitude of the moment. But he restrained her.

"No more, your ladyship," said he, and by thus giving her once more the title she had worn, he seemed to reinstate her in the station from which in self-defence he had pulled her down. "Promise that you'll bear no witness against me should so much be needed, and I'll cry quits with you. Without your testimony, they cannot hurt me, even though they were disposed to do so, which is scarcely likely."

"Sir—sir—" she faltered brokenly. "Could you—could you suppose—"

"Indeed, no. So no more, ma'am. You do but harass yourself. Fare you well, my lady. If I may trespass for a few moments longer upon the hospitality of Stretton House, I'll be your debtor."

"The house—and all—is yours, sir," she reminded him.

"There's but one thing in it that I'll carry off with me," said he. He held the door for her.

She looked into his face a moment. "God keep you!" said she, with a surprising fervor in one not over-fluent at her prayers. "God reward you for showing this mercy to an old woman—who does not deserve so much."

"Fare you well, madam," he said again, bowing gravely. "And fare you well, Lord Ostermore," he added to her son.

His brother looked at him a moment; seemed on the point of speaking, and then—taking his cue, no doubt, from his mother's attitude—he held out his hand.

Mr. Caryll took it, shook it, and let it go. After all, he bethought him, the man was his brother. And if his bearing was not altogether cordial, it was, at least, a clement imitation of cordiality.

He closed the door upon them, and sighed supreme relief. He turned to face Hortensia, and a smile broke like sunshine upon his face, and dispelled the serious gloom of his expression. She sprang towards him.

"Come now, thou chattel, that I am resolved to carry with me from my father's house," said he.

She checked in her approach. "'Tis not in such words that I'll be wooed," said she.

"A fig for words!" he cried. "Art wooed and won. Confess it."

"You want nothing for self-esteem," she informed him gravely.

"One thing, Hortensia," he amended. "One thing I want—I lack—to esteem myself greater than any king that rules."

"I like that better," she laughed, and suddenly she was in

tears. "Oh, why do you mock, and make-believe that your heart is on your lips and nowhere else?" she asked him. "Is it your aim to be accounted trifling and shallow—you who can do such things as you have done but now? Oh, it was noble! You made me very proud."

"Proud?" he echoed. "Ah! Then it must be that you are resolved to take this impudent, fleering coxcomb for a husband," he said, rallying her with the words she had flung at him that night in the moonlit Croydon garden.

"How I was mistook in you!" quoth she.

He made philosophy. "'Tis ever those in whom we are mistook that are best worth knowing," he informed her. "The man or woman whom you can read at sight, is read and done with."

"Yet you were not mistook in me," said she.

"I was," he answered, "for I deemed you woman."

"What other have you found me?" she inquired.

He flung wide his arms, and bade her into them. "Here to my heart," he cried, "and in your ear I'll whisper it."